Chased by a killer, Rachel Winters; her dog, Bella; and Private Investigator Luke Reed must uncover a deep-rooted environmental conspiracy stretching across multiple state lines.

Don't miss the start of the series in the *Sierra Nevada Trail of Murder!*

"Jennifer Quashnick writes a fabulous first thriller. "

— *Tahoe Mountain News*

"'Trail of Murder' a provocative Sierra Nevada Tale of Fiction."

— *Tahoe World*

"Locals will dig into 'Sierra Nevada: Trail of Murder,' as will dog lovers and anybody who enjoys a solid whodunit tale. "

— *Tahoe Daily Tribune*

By Jennifer Quashnick:

Sierra Nevada
River of Lies

JENNIFER QUASHNICK

South Lake Tahoe, CA
www.mountaingirlmysteries.com

ISBN: 978-0-9906750-3-7

Library of Congress Control Number: 2015915433
Cover Design: Moya Sanders
Cover Photo: Moya Sanders
Copy Editor: Mary Cook

Orders, inquiries, and correspondence should be addressed to:

Mountaingirl Mysteries
PO Box 550145
South Lake Tahoe, CA 96155
mountaingirl@mountaingirlmysteries.com
www.mountaingirlmysteries.com

To the Great Outdoors.
I owe them my health, inspiration, and creativity.

The mountains are calling and I must go.

—John Muir

ACKNOWLEDGMENTS

I am deeply thankful to the following people, without whom I would not have been able to write this book:

My parents, Carol and Terry, whose love, encouragement, and support keeps me going. Additionally, my mother's first review is not only the "yes or no" button on the entire book, but it also leads to entertaining conversations.

My sister, Shelley Whittaker, who amazes me with all that she does for her family and friends. Someday soon we will have another "sisters' weekend"!

Moya Sanders, my friend, editor, and coconspirator. Not only would the book not be published without her help (and she gets credit for any successful marketing I do), but I'd also have a logo that looks like a duck.

My Aunt Linda, who continues to inspire me, not just in life, but also in outdoor adventures and interior design.

Diana Sanders, who once again read the first draft, flaws and all, and still wanted to read the actual ending…when I finally wrote it months later.

Kim Wyatt, owner of Bona Fide Books, who relentlessly supports and encourages local authors along with the million other things she does for Tahoe artists and communities.

Tamara Wallace, whose review gave me confidence the final book didn't reflect the number of late nights I spent working on it.

The talented and dedicated Tahoe Writers Works authors for their invaluable insights, feedback, and ample wine supply.

The wonderful, passionate people advocating for Lake Tahoe's protection. I am so lucky to know you and learn from you, and Lake Tahoe is lucky to have you.

And last, but not least, my sweet Bella. My companion, hiking partner, muse, comedian, psychologist (seriously, she won't let me be upset for very long), and one big bundle of happy energy.

AUTHOR'S NOTES

If you are looking for the amazing companionship a dog can provide, I urge you to do some research into breed characteristics with your lifestyle in mind. After that, if you decide to add a dog to your family, please first consider adoption/rescue. It won't be long before you find yourself asking exactly who rescued whom. Learn more at http://www.humanesociety.org/.

As for Bella's breed, Border collies are high-energy herding dogs; they are wonderful dogs but only with enough exercise, attention, and mental stimulation from their owners. We regularly hike, snowshoe, play games, do tricks, and have playdates with canine friends. Like me, when she doesn't get enough exercise and outdoor playtime, she's not a happy girl. For more information please visit http://www.bcrescue.org/bcwarning.html.

Prologue

Danielle's boy-cut hair ruffled in the breeze as she bounced down the trail in rhythm with the music streaming through her earbuds. Glancing at the sunlit granite peaks around her, she tripped but caught herself quickly. However, it was too smooth where she'd placed her foot, and as her shoe slid a few inches down a long, flat rock, she cursed her old pair of tennis shoes. She'd known the tread was almost worn off but figured a few more miles couldn't hurt.

"Damn shoes," she muttered, continuing along the trail. Danielle rounded a bend, giving her a full view of the almost mystical green and blue water of Lower Echo Lake and the small cabins that dotted the shoreline. Danielle gazed briefly and then focused her attention back on her footing. This section of the path had made her nervous on the way up. Three old hollow steel rods a few inches long protruded straight out of a large boulder along the trail. She had wondered why the rods had been left there, sticking out as they did. It seemed like a dangerous situation for anyone who happened to lose his or her balance in the wrong spot.

Startled by the movement in front of her, Danielle almost took a step back. It was the first person she'd seen on the trail that day. He was probably twenty, by her guess—not much different than her eighteen years—and he was pretty cute, at least what she could see of him. He wore a black ball cap over a mat of sandy blond hair, jean shorts, and a black T-shirt. As he came closer, he smiled.

1

"Hey, another person, how about that!" The stranger laughed.

"Hello," she said shyly as she reached over to her armband holder to pause her music. Although he seemed friendly enough, she didn't have time for idle chitchat. It's why she chose a path that wouldn't be heavily used on a weekday morning in the fall. Thanks to a sick professor who canceled her only Thursday class, and a well-timed holiday, Danielle had four consecutive sunny days in South Lake Tahoe, and she aimed to use them to explore the surrounding trails as much as possible. Once her classes began again next week in Reno, she'd be too busy to get up to the Tahoe Basin much until next summer. She watched as the man stopped at the sandy base of a small dip in the trail, waving for her to pass on by. She noticed his bright-yellow shoes and almost laughed aloud, but managed to suppress the urge and simply say, "Thank you," as she continued past him. Her eyes once again moved downward to focus on her footing. After stepping past the rock containing the worrisome protrusions, she looked up to thank the other hiker with a wave. He smiled, and she turned back around, her attention back on the path as she continued.

"Don't you know that hiking alone can be dangerous?" she heard him say behind her. His hands slammed into her back, pushing her forward. She fell, helpless to stop it.

~

The killer watched as blood oozed from where the steep pipe penetrated her forehead. It couldn't have gone any better, he thought. He took a few steps off the trail until he was standing right below the boulder with the steel pipes in it. Her face obscured against the granite, he noticed her sunglasses were held firmly against her eyes by the weight of her head. Under those dark lenses, which he dare not touch, he imagined her eyes wide open. He'd never killed anyone before, and he wondered what her last thought was. Pulling on latex gloves, he reached for the small device attached to her arm. She had touched it earlier, presumably pausing it to listen to him. Someone who accidently tripped would not have taken the time to stop her music during her fall, so he pressed the play button and music resumed. The faint sounds of heavy guitar

2

emanated from the small earbuds next to her dead body. The killer stepped over her sprawled form and began walking in the direction of the trailhead. When he saw a couple hiking in his direction in the distance, he quickly cut off from the trail and hid behind one of the small cabins on the shoreline until they passed. Once clear, he quickly made his way back to the main trailhead. His car wasn't parked at the regular lot that rested at the base of Lower Echo Lake. Rather, he continued on the Pacific Crest Trail another two miles toward Highway 50. His car waited for him in a small pullout used by hikers in the off-season. He turned the ignition, and the radio began blaring Aerosmith. As he drove away, a casual smile spread across his face.

Two weeks later

After two steep miles and a few precarious snow crossings along the trail, Bill and his female companion reached the small lake. Looking up, he was surprised to see cement-lined walls at the water's edge and a small structure nearby. The image didn't quite fit the landscape around it, which boasted rising mountains to the sides and amazing views of the June Lake area to the east. Although this did explain the historical purpose behind remnants of an old train-track-type tramway on the way up.

"Hmm, I didn't realize Agnew Lake was a reservoir. I thought it was natural," murmured Sonya from a few feet behind him. She was breathing hard, stopping several times on the way up so she could rest. She had joked about not being used to elevation, but she'd toughed it out and kept going.

"I guess many lakes are reservoirs," Bill responded, his last couple of words drowned out by the rumble of a motorcycle engine from the road over a thousand feet below. He doubted in a normal year there would be many bikers on the June Lake Loop in early November, but with the mild temperatures and lack of snow this fall, they'd seen a few on their drive in. Since there wasn't enough snow to open the slopes on Mammoth Mountain yet, at least people could get outside one way or another, he thought.

At fifty-one, Bill kept in shape through constant exercise,

making the two-mile hike up here fairly easy for him, but his partner struggled. He didn't get the impression she was a big hiker, yet he wasn't the one who had suggested they leave early for a short trek before heading to the lab. "Let's go check it out anyway," he said, readjusting his sunglasses.

"All right, professor," she agreed, following behind him. Bill had encouraged her to call him by his first name, but she occasionally lapsed into using the more professional title. Curious about the water temperature, he stopped to kneel down and stick his left hand into the lake.

"It's cold. I expected it to be warmer after such a hot summer," he uttered as he stood up, careful to keep his balance. It was warm, but certainly not enough to swim. "Well, want to keep going and find a lunch spot?" He glanced at his watch. "We've got the time. Going down will be much faster."

"I think I'm going to skip lunch," Sonya replied, her voice suddenly tinged with annoyance. Before he could look up, he felt a sharp sting in his neck, followed by the pain of something slamming into the back of his head. Quickly losing his balance, he fell into the lake. The cold water made it hard to breathe, but it also kept him alert as he fought against losing consciousness. He rose to the surface and looked up at her, his brain working to process her attack on him just seconds ago. Her image was blurry without the help of his glasses, which had fallen off. But he was certain she was standing on the edge, staring down at him. She tossed a rock into the water next to him.

"What? Why?" he yelled out as he tried to grip the slick cement wall that held the water in the reservoir. They didn't know each other that well, but they'd been on a few dates, and until today she seemed to be having a good time. She didn't respond.

"Please, Sonya, help me, for God's sake!" he called out frantically. The water was cold, and his mind seemed to be going numb.

"I'm sorry, Bill. I really am," she said, her image just an outline in bright sun. Her other hand held something. Although his vision was unclear, it looked like the outline of a large pen. "But I do have to thank you for making this so easy." Sonya raised her arm, the object gripped in her hand. "You'll be asleep soon, and by the time you are found, well, there will be nothing left to suggest anything other than an unfortunate accident."

Bill's mind was becoming foggy. The desire to sleep was overwhelming. He tried to fight it off. If he gave into it, he'd die. *Swim!* he told himself, but his arms and legs had grown limp. His body felt relaxed, his eyelids too heavy to hold open. Bill imagined himself resting under the warm down comforter on his bed, his cat, Buddy, warming his feet.

Chapter One

Rachel Winters looked out over the expansive view. The wide granite bed of Lake Aloha rested below her, now almost a collection of small puddles of water rather than a lake. It was much drier, however, than it should be in mid-November, she mused. In the distance, the clear blue skies overhead magnified the deep blue image of Lake Tahoe.

"Well, Bella, what do you think?" She reached down and rubbed the neck of her two-year-old Border collie and hiking companion. The pup looked up at the mention of her name. "Shall we hit the road?" Rachel asked. Not that she expected a reply, but she often talked to Bella. Frankly, she couldn't imagine why anyone wouldn't talk to a pet. Although she had, at times, wondered if a small human was trapped inside Bella's body, given how in tune the dog always seemed to be with her mood. Rachel leaned over to pick up her backpack, sweeping her long brunette braid away from her face. She took one last glance at the view from atop Pyramid Peak. "Absolutely beautiful." Rachel turned to descend, pondering again what drove her to come up here today as she slowly made her way down the expanse of large granite boulders that formed the peak.

When she woke up this morning, she expected another day of working and taking a short afternoon hike with Bella. But then she felt that mysterious anxiety take hold. It was a feeling that seemed to be coming more often lately. Rachel felt tense, frustrated, and depressed, and wasn't sure why. Although she'd had an argument with her boyfriend, Luke, a few days prior, she knew that wasn't the cause. In fact, she suspected her tense mood, or rather her reaction to it, might be causing an emotional distance that had recently developed in their relationship. The restless feeling had started to invade her senses months ago. Although she'd felt somewhat overwhelmed by work lately, it wasn't the first time, after ten years of dealing with the politics in Lake Tahoe. Yet this general emotional angst was new to her, and she didn't know how to deal with it. But she'd soon discovered that temporary relief came from pushing herself. Actually, Rachel thought as she began slowly walking down the eroding mountainside, it wasn't just pushing herself. She'd come to realize that she felt better only after doing something that gave her an adrenaline rush. Typically this involved some level of danger.

"Or rather stupidity," she said aloud, considering the hike they were currently doing. Almost ten years ago she'd promised herself she wouldn't attempt this route alone again. Now here she was, thirty-one years old and once again going it solo. The first part of the hike to Lake Sylvia, resting at the base of Pyramid Peak's southwestern edge, was easy. But then it required climbing almost two thousand feet up granite walls and scree. The ascent wasn't too bad; coming down the loose and slippery wall was outright dangerous. This went far beyond the other activities that would give her a small rush—flying down the mountain on her skis or long hikes exploring new territory. Her brain told her this was a bad way to deal with her restlessness, but her emotions craved the reprieve she felt afterward.

They soon arrived at the top of the largest vertical drop. Rachel looked down, her eyes scanning the area for the best path to descend. She took a deep breath and began her scramble, often having to use both her hands and feet. About a third of the way down, her foot lost its hold on a small granite rock surrounded by loose dirt; she slipped, facing outward as her tailbone slammed into the ground. Falling, she instinctively reached for anything to stop her. Finally, she caught hold of a solid rock ledge with both hands and held tight. Rachel remained there in place, assessing the damage—her tailbone ached for sure. She had a scratch or two on her cheek and a few scrapes on her leg, but otherwise nothing too bad. Bella had been following her path nearby, perfectly at ease with the steep descent. Rachel took a few deep breaths and then spoke to Bella.

"Sure, rub in how agile you are, my sweet girl," she chuckled. "But you also have two more legs than I do." Rachel stood up, brushed herself off, and continued. When they reached the lake at the bottom she looked back up at the wall they'd just come down. The frustrated, anxious feeling she'd had that morning—it was all gone. She smiled and scanned the area for a branch to throw into the lake for Bella.

~

Sonya smiled as she drove the stolen car north on Highway 395. She really had liked Bill. It was too bad he'd gotten in the way of their plans. She could have easily had an affair with him. Given his physique, that experience would likely have been immensely pleasurable. In fact, that same athletic build had made her efforts to weigh down his body more difficult, but ample supplies of granite around the reservoir helped. As for her feelings about killing him, it was certainly a shame. But they were racing the clock now, and external complications had to be resolved. He'd been one of them. Sonya pressed on the accelerator.

Chapter Two

Rachel sat quietly as the governing board discussed whether to approve zoning changes in South Lake Tahoe near the California-Nevada border. Her legs cramped after sitting through three hours of public comment and debate on a proposed resort project. The only break had been the few minutes she stood at the podium, expressing concerns with the project on behalf of her clients. Her lower back still ached from her fall the week before, making it both literally and figuratively painful to sit through the meeting. As an environmental scientist, Rachel's work involved focusing on science and how future development could help or damage the environment. She felt it was becoming more difficult to find projects that really helped Lake Tahoe.

"And here we go," her coworker Kristina whispered as a key project supporter took the podium and began talking. As often happened, the developers who wanted the project were given upward of thirty minutes to drone on about how great it was, while the public had been strictly limited to three minutes per person. It had become an ongoing joke among the public.

Rachel looked down to see what creative image Kristina sketched this time. She had once confessed to Rachel that doodling had become her way to cope with the long meetings. This time she'd framed her meeting notes with a unique twist of flowers and thorns.

"You should use colored pencils. Then you could frame those doodles and maybe earn some extra cash." Rachel whispered before looking back up toward the front of the boardroom. She had caught herself drawing in the margins once or twice, too, but she could only sketch one scene over and over. A mountain with trees, a river, and granite boulders. She had quickly conceded that an artist, she was not. However, in her own efforts to pass time at meetings, Rachel sometimes found herself penciling in the circles of printed letters.

A half page of filled-in *o's, d's, b's, p's*, and *q's* later, she stopped and looked up when she heard the executive assistant utter, "All in favor say, 'Aye.'" Several voices responded in unison. When he asked for an opposing vote, two voices responded, "Nay." The no votes belonged to the two board members who had asked clear questions about the impacts of the project on Lake Tahoe.

"It passes," the assistant called out into the microphone in front of him.

"All right, well, everyone, thank you for your vote," said the board's chairperson, a short fragile-looking woman with a surprisingly loud voice. The big smile on her face was almost obscured by the large thick-framed glasses she wore. The meeting adjourned, and Rachel stood up, anxious to feel blood coursing through her legs again. She had to grab the chair in front of her; her legs were half-asleep.

"Got something besides water in that bottle?" Kristina smirked. It was common at these meetings for people to carry aluminum water bottles.

"I wish," Rachel said as she smiled. "But then I'd definitely go past our three-minute allotment."

"Well, we did expect this," Kristina said, her tall frame towering over Rachel's five-foot-five height by a good six inches. She tucked her shoulder-length black hair into a crocheted beanie, and Rachel noticed a few strands of purple highlights sticking out the bottom of the hat.

"Yep, at least they didn't get the unanimous vote they've been pushing for," Rachel sighed.

"Should we go grab a beer?" Everett asked from behind Rachel.

Although he was sometimes hard to understand, she found his German accent appealing.

"Yes, please," Kristina replied. Rachel looked at her watch.

"*Vielen Dank*," she apologized to Everett. "Maybe next time? I have plans tonight," Rachel said, twisting her hair into a bun and securing it with a clip.

"Ah yes, with Mr. Lukas," he laughed. She'd given up explaining her boyfriend's name was just Luke. She'd also stopped trying to discourage Everett from giving her dramatic winks. He seemed to get a kick out of teasing her, so she decided to just go with it.

Rachel hadn't known him for very long, but Everett had impressed her from their first meeting. He had taken an environmental internship with the AmeriCorps program just a few months ago, although initially about half of his time was spent outside of the Basin, heading back and forth to Reno for a project funded by the University of Nevada, Reno. Even though he had a biology degree and years of experience from his native country, Rachel suspected Everett was still in his early twenties. Originally from Bochum, he'd come to California on a work visa for a year.

"Rachel, go have fun. We can talk tomorrow about what's next," Kristina announced as she stood next to Everett.

Rachel retrieved her bag and followed them out of the room. After the final good-bye for the day, she walked toward her Tacoma pickup, coated with dirt. As always, she promised herself she'd wash it tomorrow but knew better. She wouldn't. Even if there wasn't much snow in Lake Tahoe this year, she still drove over the mountain passes, where even the slightest melting of snow on the road splashed dirt on passing vehicles. Not much point in wasting water to wash it, only to have it get dirty again quickly. Luke, who obsessively washed his Subaru as if his life depended on a clean, shiny vehicle, thoroughly enjoyed getting on her case. Seated inside, she sent a quick text to him. "Mtng over. Project approved. I'll grab B & head over." She laughed, remembering when she'd started referring to Bella as "B" in text messages to friends.

Rachel set her phone down and started the ignition. A beep indicated a text reply. "Can't wait, Mountaingirl. Sorry about the project." Luke had started calling her Mountaingirl when they'd first met last summer after she'd witnessed a murder and sought his help as a private investigator. She smiled at the memory of Luke explaining he'd had to save "Mountaingirl" in his text program because the phone app wanted to keep separating it into two words. That was early on, before their relationship conflicts became more pronounced.

Rachel now felt relief at his lighthearted response. Last time they'd been together, they'd had a mild difference of opinion about what he called her "stubborn independence" and what she had labeled his old-fashioned, outdated idea that women needed to rely on men. Sure, last summer she'd needed his help, but at that time, gender had nothing to do with it—although it did matter when it came to the part where she fell for him.

She opened the front door to her small rustic cabin and was greeted, enthusiastically as always, by Bella. Rachel grabbed the end of the squeaky toy snake dangling out of the canine's mouth and began to play tug with one hand as she dropped her bag and keys from the other. A few moments later Rachel opened the back door, and Bella rushed outside. She checked her machine for messages; one was from her friend Taylor, confirming they were still going to Apple Hill that weekend. The other was from her mother, just "checking in," as she often did.

Rachel sent quick texts to them both, anxious to change out of her uncomfortable dressy slacks and blouse into jeans and a T-shirt. She let her hair down and brushed through it, tugged her shoes on, and stuck a few dog treats in her pocket. Rachel needed a positive night tonight. Not only because of the frustrating board meeting, but also because, in addition to the frequent periods of feeling anxious, her "IDD" had been setting in lately as well. She wasn't alone—after three years of drought, the impacts of climate change, and another too-dry fall season, locals began to feel what she'd started referring to as "intense drought depression." Many grew restless, if not outright crazy. Some would finally give in and ski or board the one strip of man-made snow at their local resort, dodging mountain obstacles like rocks, treetops, large swaths of bare dirt, and beginners who ignored the warning signs. During these difficult times, it required great effort not to drop everything, grab her ski gear and load up Bella, and drive a thousand miles to the Rockies at raging speeds, where she would remain indefinitely until sufficient snow fell in the Sierra Nevada. Even Bella lost a certain perkiness when the snow didn't fall.

"All right, girl, let's go!" she called out into her yard. A few minutes later Bella's black head was hanging out the side of the pickup's window as they drove away.

~

Luke realized he had just checked his reflection for the third time in less than ten minutes. He noticed the stubble on his face, and his dark-brown hair was due for a trim soon, but Rachel wouldn't mind. In fact, she said she liked his rugged look. He figured it went back to her inexplicable attraction to cowboys, which always boggled his mind because he was anything but western. He reached up to run his fingers through his hair, and the brief twinge of pain reminded him his shoulder muscles had not yet fully healed from the consequences of the gunshot wound last summer. Luke had to admit he had not been following the physical therapy routine he'd been given. He'd been too eager to get active again and had taken a few falls on his mountain bike over the last month. He knew the prescription painkillers he'd been taking just masked the symptoms of his injuries, but he wasn't good at taking downtime. Financially, he could handle it, but mentally, he couldn't stand the idea of having to take it easy and rest. That might be one reason he'd let Rachel believe he was handling everything fine.

"Damn," he whispered, reaching across with his other hand to rub the part of his shoulder that still often ached. He looked back into the mirror, critiquing his appearance. *My God, I'm acting like a nervous teen on his first date!* At thirty-three, Luke had certainly dated his share of women and left these small obsessions behind years ago. Or so he thought until a certain freckle-nosed, long-haired brunette walked into his office early last summer, afraid and angry at the world, doing her best not to show it. Dismissed by the local cops after the body of a murder victim she'd found had disappeared, Rachel sought his help when a sympathetic ear at the local police station had suggested she consider a certain private investigator. He smiled at the memory.

A beep sounded in the other room, disrupting the reverie that placed a firm smile on his lips. It was a text from Rachel. The meeting had gone as expected. Another board decision to allow another oversized resort in the Basin, even though it ran contrary to its own rules. Luke was not an environmentalist in the typical sense, but once he'd moved to Lake Tahoe, he never wanted to leave. Until he met Rachel, he'd taken the open forests for granted and, like most other people, assumed the land, at least what was owned by the federal or state government, would always stay open and undeveloped. He sent her a quick reply then glanced out back where his barbecue sat on a small square porch. He pulled the marinated pork ribs from the refrigerator, set plates on the dinner table, and once again felt like a shy teenager. Although he had just seen her a week ago, it felt like months had passed. Perhaps that was because lately it felt like something was coming between them. There had been fewer lighthearted moments and more awkward discussions. Plus, she had also been doing a few things lately that concerned him. He hadn't yet figured out what had changed—or why.

Chapter Three

The waves from the exterior explosion nearby reverberated through the old mine shaft, and more dirt fell from the walls. Carlton shifted and then stood completely still. Next to him, his young partner did the same. Both waited to see if anything else might fall, eyes focused on the dirty old tackle box tucked on the side of the small cave branching from the shaft. The blasts from the nearby open-pit mine operation caused vibrations far more extensive than they'd realized. A minute passed. Nothing else moved.

"Let's get out of here. Maybe next time you'll be smart enough to check the blasting schedule? They post it right on the highway." Carlton was frustrated. This wasn't the first time his new partner had failed to do something so basic. It was bad enough they had to come inside to check on the item for his boss, Sylvester. Even worse to do it when the whole damn place might cave in.

"Sorry, sir, I'll . . . um . . . make sure to check next time," his companion stuttered, clearly anxious to leave.

"Yes, you will. Now, let's move," Carlton said, stepping in front of the nervous kid. He glanced down at his cohort's bright-colored shoes—today's pair a blur of neon orange—then shook his head, turned, and strode toward the entrance to the mine, ducking as he went out. The ceiling was perhaps six feet high; Carlton was six feet three inches tall—another reason he did not like having to come here. He passed a rust-covered "No Trespassing" sign as he exited

15

and walked over the half-fallen chicken-wire fence entangled by various desert bushes.

"Let's head to town, let Sylvester know what's going on." He called out. Carlton's associate followed in silence as they trekked back to their white pickup and remained quiet all the way to Virginia City. They found an open spot along the crowded, tourist-laden main street and, after parking, made their way down the wooden-planked walkway, passing numerous shops and old-time photo booths along the way. As usual, they had been forced to park several blocks down from the Bucket of Blood Saloon, where Sylvester was waiting.

~

"Everything go as expected?" Sylvester asked. A black hat covered his crew cut. His red face and deep wrinkles suggested years of hard drinking, and his overweight stature, a failure to exercise. Sylvester, or, as most acquaintances referred to him, "Silver"—the nickname being a mystery Carlton was left to wonder about—looked at them cautiously, waiting.

"Yes," Carlton said, pulling a wooden chair out from the small table. When he sat down, his thighs hung over the sides of the small chair. Although he had a few extra pounds, it was more that he had a big frame. This discomfort happened a lot in Virginia City; everything was built when people were smaller. He wondered if there would ever be full upgrades, although the tourists didn't seem to mind much.

"Very good to hear. How about our other problems? Have they all been resolved?" Sylvester's teeth clinked against his glass as he took a deep swallow of whiskey.

"Not quite. A couple of them are still in the wind, but we're getting close to finding them." Carlton waited as his hefty boss slowly shook his head before responding.

"If it's not one thing, it's another. First, that goddamn mining company moves in—of all places. Then those academics start sniffing around. I can't afford any more setbacks." Sylvester sighed. Carlton did not reply, knowing there would be more.

"You've got two weeks. If you can't fix this, I'll find someone else who can."

Carlton was already irritated, and the threat just aggravated him more. He'd been heavily involved in one of Sylvester's projects for over a year. It wasn't his fault Storey County approved the open-pit mine that now infuriated Sylvester, nor was it his doing when some graduate students decided to take a field trip just as they were making progress on their plans up north.

"It will be done, I assure you." Carlton stood up, slammed his chair against the small table, and walked out. He thought his partner was following him, but he didn't care enough to look back. Around him, the noise of slot machines and voices followed him until he emerged out front on the historic walkway, strolling along the strips of old cement and uneven wooden planks.

Chapter Four

"What happened to your face?" Luke asked, gently running his hand down her cheek. Rachel hadn't told him about her climb to Pyramid Peak last week. Not that she had gone out of her way not to, but when it hadn't come up, she just failed to mention it. He already worried when she'd hike alone, and they'd had a fairly heated argument after a recent news report regarding a girl who had a fatal accident on the Pacific Crest Trail near Lower Echo Lake. Rachel hadn't seen Luke since and had forgotten that a faint outline of her bruise remained. But put on the spot, she wasn't a good liar.

"Oh, I slipped on one of my hikes last week. Nothing major," she responded, eyes inadvertently glancing down toward her leg where the scratches were almost gone. She heard Luke sigh and looked up to see an irritated expression on his face. Rachel waited. He didn't speak right away, instead appearing to carefully consider his next words.

They were sitting on Luke's soft leather sofa. It was comfortable, but often too warm in the summer and too cold on several recent fall evenings when she still had shorts on. Rachel had been filling him in on the days leading up to the board meeting. He sat next to her, Bella's head resting on his lap, as if the dog were carefully following their conversation. He let his hand drop from her face.

"I won't say it. You know how I feel." He leaned back and ran his fingers through his hair. A moment later he continued, his voice calm. "Where was the hike?"

"Pyramid Peak. You know, out there past Lake Aloha," she said, smiling, although an awkward tension penetrated the air.

"Sounds like a difficult hike," he uttered. She reached for his hand and took it lightly.

"How about you come with me next time?" It wasn't that she hadn't asked him before. He said he'd been busy at work, plus his shoulder still bothered him and he was afraid to do any steep hikes or climbs. It had been surprising to her, because she had joined him on several bike rides this fall and he didn't seem to be holding back. She watched as Luke paused, seemed to make an internal decision, and then looked her in the eye, smiling. Bella shifted, resting her nose on top of their clasped hands. This was followed by the puppy stare, moving from Luke and then back to Rachel.

"Yes, I'd love that. Just don't give me too hard a time when you have to wait up for me." He grinned and squeezed her hand. A loud sound from outside distracted her.

"They're burning," Rachel said, noticing smoke rising above Luke's porch.

"What?" Luke asked, looking up as he nudged Bella's head to the side.

"I can get it." She jumped up and rushed across his dining room toward the back door.

"It's fine, I can—" she heard him call out, but Rachel was already sliding the glass door open.

"Looks like the fat dripped down and caused some flames," Rachel stated while opening the lid to the grill. As she turned the heat level down, she felt Luke standing next to her.

"I can handle it," he said, reaching for the tongs nearby. She sensed slight irritation in his tone and suspected she'd reacted too hastily.

"Sorry, I'm so used to doing my own . . ." Rachel trailed off. They had been dating for just a few months; her tendency to jump in and take over had already caused a few issues between them. She turned away from the heat and smoke with an apologetic smile.

"It's fine. I just wanted to cook *for you* this time," he replied and then shifted to face her with a slightly distracted look. Rachel reached up and ran her hand through his shaggy brown hair before lightly caressing the back of his neck. She pulled him close until his lips met hers, as she'd wanted to do since the moment she arrived. She heard the tongs drop to the ground when the kiss grew deeper. A moment later she felt his arms around her, his body pressing against her. Just as she began to fantasize about turning off the barbecue and leading him into his bedroom, the phone in his kitchen started to ring. It blared out four more times before it went quiet. They enjoyed a few seconds of silence before it began again.

"You'd better go check it," she whispered, stepping back.

"Let it go to voice mail." Luke reached to push a strand of loose hair behind her ear. The ring persisted.

"It could be an emergency," Rachel replied. Few people called him on his home number. Luke sighed, stepped back, and walked into the kitchen, reluctantly answering it on the fourth ring. Rachel remained standing on the porch, looking out over the open land behind his small home. Several hundred yards away, sun poured through the open forest where the 2007 Angora Fire had burned. Immediately behind his house a small patch of dense pine trees still stood, spared only by shifting winds. His raised voice caught her attention, and she turned to look at him.

"My sister? Are you sure?" His voice indicated annoyance. And concern.

He'd once told Rachel about how he'd lost touch with his younger sister about fifteen years ago, after she chose to take his father's side on a matter that still hurt Luke's heart to this day. Luke had been raised in a wealthy family; however, the dysfunctional and sometimes criminal way his family and their social acquaintances treated each other had driven him away the minute he turned eighteen. Although he tried to keep in touch with his younger sister, she had disconnected him from her life. This phone call can't be good, she thought. He listened, reaching for a nearby piece of paper and pen.

"Okay, okay. What's the number?" She watched as he scribbled something down. A moment later he hung the phone up and stared at the counter. Rachel walked inside.

"What's going on?" she asked, gently touching his shoulder. Her action seemed to bring him out of deep thought.

"Apparently my sister is missing." He paused.

"Your sister? What?"

"From somewhere off I-80 between Reno and Truckee. Her husband was driving, and there was an accident; their car ended up in the river. They recovered his body but can't find her." He pulled a stool out from beneath his countertop and sat down. Sensing their dinner plans had just ended, Rachel quickly turned to walk back outside.

"I'll get the barbecue," she said, still absorbing the unexpected news. When she came back in, he was sitting with his elbows resting on the table in front of him, hands rubbing his cheeks. Retrieving the stool next to him, she inquired, "How did they know she was in the car?"

"There were suitcases containing both male and female clothes, and they found her name on documents in the glove box. The car was tipped on its side in the Truckee River. It looks like her husband drowned because the driver's side was submerged. He must have lost consciousness or couldn't get himself out in time."

"But no sign of her?" she asked. "When did this happen? How did they track her to you?"

"I don't know all of the details yet, but the person who called said she's a friend of theirs. She was following them back from Reno but had gone front of them after they had stopped for gas. She knew I was her brother and looked me up." He sighed and looked across the room, where Bella noisily chewed on a squeaky toy.

Rachel stood up and went to retrieve the loud item so she and Luke could hear each other better. She exchanged it for a different toy that Bella had already relieved of the plastic objects. Bella bit down intently, likely hoping that new squeakers had been inserted. "Fifteen years of silence and then she pops up a hundred miles away?"

"I know." Luke looked down.

"What's the phone number they gave you?"

"The highway patrol. The locals are involved now, too. This friend of hers said they'd like me to come up there and help with

21

the search." He sounded surprised.

"Do they know you and Kimmy have been out of touch all these years?" The room had grown oddly silent.

"Don't know. But what am I supposed to do? I mean, she's my sister." Rachel felt Bella's wet nose nudging her knee. Without the noise, Bella was likely angling for a ball to retrieve instead.

"Then I guess you have to go," she sighed, reaching for his hand. "Can I help?"

Luke returned her caress, backed up the stool, and stood. "I don't know. This just doesn't seem real." He started walking toward the patio.

"I'll clean up. If you feel you should be up there, then you need to get going," Rachel encouraged. She kept in touch with her brothers, for the most part. She couldn't imagine not seeing them for so many years, let alone getting a call like this.

"Okay, uh, thanks. I guess I should make that call," he muttered, distracted. He reached for his phone and then stopped. Luke's gaze settled on hers, and he pulled her into a tight embrace.

Ten minutes later he backed his car out of the driveway. Rachel placed the partially cooked ribs into a container to bring them back to her house, hooked Bella's leash, and walked out, locking the front door behind her. Something nagged at her, but she couldn't quite place it.

"Well, Bella, guess we'll go home and finish these up on our barbecue."

~

Dr. Jillian Reynolds had just cut the man's chest open to begin her autopsy when one of her interns stuck his head through the door.

"Jill, Ms. Rachel Winters is on the phone," he announced.

"Tell her I'll call her back in a few minutes." Her gaze remained focused on the figure of the presumably drowned man lying on the steel table. She prepared the body to allow her a moment's break, stepped outside of the morgue, and removed her gown, gloves, and face mask. Anxious for fresh air, Jill exited the small changing room so swiftly that her short ponytail bounced back and forth, tickling her ears. She picked up the phone as soon as she reached her desk. Although they'd only met a few months ago when Jill was the assigned medical examiner on a case Rachel became entangled with, Jill knew something was wrong for her new friend to call her at work.

"Hey, Rachel. Everything okay?"

"I'm not sure. I'm so sorry to bother you, but I could use your instinct on something." Rachel's voice sounded odd.

"Sure, what's up? I have about ten minutes until I have to return to work on a drowning victim. Oops, I can't believe I just said that." She chastised herself. Although she figured it was fine; it's not like Rachel would know the victim or tell anyone the information. The phone call went silent for a moment. As she waited, Jill took a sip of her cold coffee and glanced at the picture of her kids perched on her desk in front of her. The oldest had just turned twelve. She couldn't believe how time flew. Her thoughts were interrupted by Rachel's strained voice.

"Any chance that victim came from a car crash in the Truckee River off I-80?" At Rachel's question, Jill half choked on the stale liquid.

"I can't share that information yet. I'm sorry."

"Got it." Rachel's tone of voice revealed that she understood. Jill's failure to say no indicated the answer was yes, but her job did not allow her to discuss it.

"What's going on?"

"Luke's brother-in-law just drowned after his car drove off the highway into the Truckee. His *wife* is still missing." Jill coughed and reached for the bottle of water on the corner of her desk.

"Rachel, my friend, if you and Luke didn't have bad luck, you'd have no luck at all," she commented once the water had cleared her throat. Jill looked at her watch, knowing she would be on the phone for the entire ten-minute break she'd allowed herself.

~

It had been so easy. Luke Reed had believed her story. *Typical man*, Sonya thought. Just as easy as telling Bill that she'd set up the appointment with that laboratory near Mammoth Lakes to "save him the trouble" of doing so himself. Instructors could be far too trusting of their students. Sonya ended the call before looking around at the general commotion throughout the highway patrol station. She had the impression that officers in Truckee, California, probably didn't see such action very often. Sonya sipped her coffee, nodding as an older female officer walked toward her.

"How are you doing, Ms. Blake?"

"Please call me Sonya. I'm fine. Any word on my friend Kimmy?" she asked, feigning anxiety. The officer shook her head.

"Nothing yet. But it's dark. Given we're looking in a river that drops well below the highway downstream, and with the rain falling from these thunderstorms that just popped up out of nowhere—it's going to be tough. But we have search dogs on the way." When she paused, Sonya shifted in her seat and twirled her red hair around her finger as many women did when nervous. The older woman patted her shoulder reassuringly. "We also have officers on the way from nearby stations, and more locals are showing up, too. Don't give up hope."

Sonya nodded, a tear leaking from the corner of her eye.

"Poor Eddie. I can't believe he's dead. If Kimmy—"

"Never give up hope," the officer cut in as Sonya retrieved a tissue from her pocket and dabbed at her tears. Sonya had hope all right. Things had fallen in place so far, and now the infamous brother would soon arrive.

Chapter Five

Carlton wanted to be careful with this one. The stakes were high, and time was short. He watched from inside his darkened vehicle as the couple settled in for the night. Too bad Mr. and Mrs. Martinez would have to pay for their son's misfortune. But two fatal accidents were already pushing it. He needed their son out of the way, and this was the best way to do it. He had watched all of them for weeks now. The kid visited his parents often, making the excursion to Winnemucca from Reno at least three times per month. It had quickly become obvious he was close to his family, and that had sparked an idea.

Carlton had planned it down to the minute. Dusk was settling upon the quiet neighborhood suburb in Winnemucca, and it would be completely dark soon. He smoothed out his grey uniform as he casually walked to their front door, reminding himself not to mess with the wig he was wearing. Like the fake beard, the headpiece itched but remained secure. He'd been pleased that his long hair had tucked up well enough to be unnoticeable. Knocking with one hand, Carlton held a clipboard in the other. The door opened, and a handsome Hispanic man, just an inch shorter than him, stood inside with a pleasant smile on his face.

"Can I help you, son?"

The man's accent reminded Carlton of Cesar Millan, the "Dog Whisperer." His ex-wife had been an obsessive fan of the man's TV show to the point that she drove their friends away by criticizing how they all treated their pets.

"Yes, sir. I'm with the natural gas company. We've received a report of a leak in the area. We are going around the neighborhood checking lines."

"I haven't smelled anything odd," the man said, the smile beginning to leave his face.

"That's good. But we'd really like to confirm." The man didn't budge as he looked Carlton up and down.

"Which company, did you say?"

"Honey, what's keeping you?" A female voice, presumably from the kid's mother, called from behind the man, momentarily distracting him. That's all Carlton needed. He pulled out his gun and aimed it.

"Do what I say and no one gets hurt," he lied as he pushed his way through the entryway.

Twenty minutes later he stepped back into the dark night and walked carefully to his car. He stowed the stolen items from the home on the backseat, removed the props he'd used to distort his image, and drove away, making one phone call before he began to search for a new car to drive back to Reno.

"It's me. One more down, one to go," he said.

"How did you do this one?" his partner asked, sounding far too eager.

"The student's fine. He just may be returning home for an extended stay in order to help his mother out. His father has just passed away, and she's not doing so well."

A large exhale preceded the kid's next words. "It would have been much easier to just take him out directly."

"Boy, you've got a lot to learn." Carlton admonished. "Now, how are you doing with your task?" he asked impatiently.

"Working on it."

"I'll expect a report by the time I'm back," Carlton said before abruptly ending the call.

~

Luke drove north on the winding two-lane highway as it skirted Emerald Bay. Although frustrated by the lack of snow in the Tahoe

Basin, having the highway open and clear tonight was a relief. As he drove, Luke thought about the last time he'd seen his sister, Kimmy. She'd been lying in her hospital bed, a pale skeletal image.

"Kimmy, I don't understand why you are doing this. You're killing yourself," Luke said, *pointing to the heart monitor as it registered a fluttering heartbeat. She didn't respond right away, although her eyes were wide open, staring at the TV behind him. "Is that it? Do you want to die?"*

"You'd never understand," she spat at him. Shocked by the reaction, he took a step back, stuttering to respond. His sister leaned forward and continued before he could figure out what to say. "You think you're better than this family? You left us behind to go running off to college." She paused and took a breath. "Dad's barely spending any time at home anymore. Mom blames him for running you off. It's miserable there!" The heart monitor began to race, and Kimmy leaned back against her pillows. Luke waited a moment before speaking in the calmest voice he could muster, not wanting her to get any more worked up than she was.

"I'm sorry, but like I said before, you can come live with me. You're eighteen now, and—"

"Really? Just like that? Not all of us can just pick up and run, Luke. Someone needs to keep this family together," she said. The beeping on her monitor increased again. Luke feared she'd have a heart attack and die right there, in front of him.

"Look, I'm sorry. But after what they did to Trenton and his family, I couldn't forgive them. And I didn't want to be a lawyer. Now please, stay calm. You're—"

"Don't tell me to calm down!" she yelled and then began to cough. He handed her a glass of water from the nearby table. She seemed to consider it for a moment and then grabbed it from him. After she had taken a few sips, she continued, her voice now quiet. "Luke, we all do things for our family we may not like."

"But we shouldn't have to give up our entire lives to be something we don't want to be," Luke said, struggling to keep his voice reasonable, although he felt he was fighting a losing battle. "I wish Mom and Dad would have supported our own choices, like many parents do. But, sis, back to the bigger issue of why you are here—in a hospital. What does starving yourself have to do with keeping them happy? They are worried about you, too." He watched in surprise as she began to laugh.

"It's all about beauty and who you know, Luke. Think the truly powerful men want overweight women? You should have figured this all out a long time ago. And just so you know, you aren't getting a dime."

"I don't want any money from them. Or you. But I love you, and I don't want you to kill yourself. Especially to please Mom and Dad, or some guy so shallow that he wants a stick-figure Stepford wife." Luke stepped toward her and reached for her too-thin hand. *"Please, maybe just come and stay with me for a few weeks. See how you feel."* She tugged her hand back as if his touch had scorched her.

"Go away. I don't ever want to see you again." Kimmy turned her gaze back toward the television screen. Luke stood for a moment, unsure of what to do or say. *"Leave,"* she demanded.

"Okay, I will. For now. I'll check in later," he said, turning to go.

"Don't bother."

Those were the last words he'd ever heard her speak. Luke had tried returning to the hospital room, but she had instructed the staff not to let him in. For years he called, always getting her voice mail. He wrote letters. She only rarely responded, sending a few short notes that succinctly reiterated her request that he leave her alone. After five years, he stopped trying. Now he might have the chance to see her again. His foot pushed down on the pedal, and he quickly passed through the small rural communities sprinkled along Tahoe's west shore.

~

"Given your potential tie with the victim, I definitely should step carefully on this one," Jill asserted after Rachel gave her the rundown on Luke's call from his sister's friend.

"So, it's not just a typical drowning?" Rachel asked, although she knew Jill was right, and she didn't want to get her friend into any trouble. Last summer, Jill had assisted a South Lake Tahoe police detective, Ted Benson, when he needed help identifying two murder victims. She'd also kept a lid on the names in order to provide Rachel and Luke more time to figure out why a killer was hunting them down.

"You know I can't tell you those details," Jill whispered.

"I know. It's just, well, it's odd," Rachel acknowledged. As if on key, a large sigh drifted from the napping dog at her feet. She often wondered what Bella dreamt about. The canine would frequently "run" in her sleep—not unusual for dogs. But she'd also intermittently moan or loudly whimper.

"I agree," Jill replied. "I'd better get back to work, but a departing thought—I *could* provide any interesting observations I might find to an *officer*, if requested." Rachel knew Jill was suggesting she ask Ted for help.

"Why, thank you for the advice, my friend," Rachel chuckled conspiratorially. "I'll keep you updated if I find anything out on my end." Rachel hung up and called Ted's work number, although she expected he'd be off duty by now. Unless there was an emergency, Ted often left around five p.m., catching a good bike ride or hike before dinner. At forty-two, he was more than ten years her senior, but Ted looked barely a day over thirty due to a healthy lifestyle, thick blond hair, and a smooth yet tanned, wrinkle-free face most women his age would give an appendage for. His cell phone went to voice mail, and Rachel left him a message, first apologizing for asking for a favor, and then requesting said favor.

~

Ted never liked the time change in the fall. It was only seven p.m. and already dark. He still hadn't become used to switching his porch light on before he left. Still cooling down from a good bike ride up Powerline Trail, he adjusted his headlamp downward toward his front door lock as he searched an over-filled key ring. As he entered his home, he heard his cell phone alerting him that he had a voice mail. Switching his living room light on, he set his helmet down, shut the door behind him, and then played it back. Rachel's voice blared through the speaker. After listening to the entire message, Ted placed a call.

"Jill, it's Ted," he said.

"Teddy, hey," she responded with the nickname she had used for years. They'd known each other long before they worked together on the murders that forced Rachel and Luke on the run a few months before. "I'm guessing Rachel called you?"

"Yep. I must say I had no idea Luke had a sister."

"Me either. Word is he hasn't seen her in fifteen years."

"Oh, I see." He paused. "So, what's the story?" Ted hoped this would amount to nothing. Things were just getting back to normal at the station. A few months back he had to arrest one of his fellow officers for leaking information to the man now incarcerated for sending a killer after Rachel and Luke last summer, among other things. Jill ran through what she had learned from Rachel and relayed a few basics about her examination of the drowning victim.

"I did find something a bit peculiar . . . ," Jill said with hesitation in her voice. "Sure you want to know what?"

"Might as well tell me, especially if Luke's heading up there tonight," Ted sighed. They'd become friends, although they didn't discuss the details of their family histories. But they often met up for occasional trail rides, Luke sharing Ted's interest in mountain biking as well as the law. Luke had also done a few investigative favors for the station; Ted figured it was his turn to help out Luke now.

"All right, but I did give you an out," she laughed. "It's clear this victim drowned—no doubt about that. But there is some bruising on his wrists; it looks premortem."

"In what way?" Ted had to admit he was intrigued.

"My first guess is that it looks like the kind of bruising handcuffs would leave, if someone had been pulling on them extremely hard. But the bruises circle his wrists almost entirely. If someone were dragged in cuffs, or yanked on them repeatedly, you'd expect bruises on just one or two sides of the wrist. Like if you pull up on the face of your watch, you feel the pressure on the other side of your arm." Ted hadn't needed the extra description, but he knew Jill's job often required her to explain things in more general terms.

"And this guy was found in a car that had driven off the road and what—maybe rolled once or twice before hitting the water?" Ted surmised, an idea already forming.

"Yes, but according to the list of his belongings, there were no handcuffs found at the scene, or anything odd to suggest something other than an unfortunate car accident," Jill said, letting the last few words hang in the air.

"His wife is missing, but her stuff was in the car?"

"That's what Rachel said."

"This doesn't sound like it bodes well for Luke's sister," Ted sighed. "I'll call Truckee PD and see what I can find out. If they are willing to share. I don't exactly have jurisdiction there." Ted paused and then asked, "How did you end up on this? Wouldn't Truckee or Reno departments be handling it?"

"Normally, yes. It's a long story. I'll explain later." Before Ted could inquire more, she continued. "I'd better get back to work, but please let me know if you find out anything."

"Will do. And Jill—tell the kids I'll see them this weekend."

"Thanks again for booking that horseback ride. They're going to have a blast." Jill's ex-husband was, in Ted's mind, a complete loser who'd taken advantage of Jill and then abandoned his kids to move in with his new girlfriend. Ted did his best to help out, trying to schedule activities and hangouts with them. It also gave Jill a reprieve to enjoy some solo time.

"Looking forward to it myself," Ted said. Only a half-truth. He had a great time with her kids, but he wasn't looking forward to spending the afternoon bouncing around in a hard saddle. Chances are he'll be sitting on ice packs afterward.

Chapter Six

"They still haven't found her," Luke said as soon as Rachel answered the phone. She could hear the anxiety in his voice. It was close to midnight. He'd texted her almost two hours ago to let her know he'd arrived in Truckee, and she'd since been anxiously awaiting any news. When the phone finally rang, she'd jumped.

"I'm so sorry. Have they located . . . anything?" Rachel questioned tentatively.

"Nothing new. They've got quite a crew out, but it's pouring up here. They're hoping once they get the car up on the road they can learn more."

"How about your sister's friend? Have you been able to talk to her?" Rachel reached out to rub Bella, who was sprawled on her back next to her.

"Not yet. They said she was tired, so they suggested she find a room for the night and return in the morning." She could hear faint conversations in the background of the station.

"Maybe you should do the same?" She knew he wouldn't but suggested it anyway.

"I couldn't sleep if I tried. It's Kimmy, Rachel . . ." Sadness crept into his voice. He'd told her about how his younger sister had developed an intense eating disorder, eventually ending up in the hospital with heart problems caused by her anorexia. But she'd chosen to stay in the fray of her family, stuck in a world where physical appearances were too often valued above all else. Although he'd moved on with his life, he always spoke of her—and only to Rachel as far as she was aware—with a hint of regret.

"I understand. Have your parents been contacted?" She knew the last time he'd spoken to them had been days before his last conversation with his sister.

"Someone mentioned calling them but said they were unavailable, or some BS like that. I didn't want to hear more. They're probably on a vacation and don't want to be bothered," he said with disdain in his tone.

"Sorry. Well, just—be careful. And keep me posted if you learn anything."

"Okay." She could hear someone speaking to him. "Gotta go. I'll call tomorrow." Luke abruptly hung up.

"Bye," she murmured into an empty phone line as she reached for Bella's toy and saw the pup's bushy tail initiate its back-and-forth motion.

~

Carlton stared at his digital clock, hand clenching a glass of red wine. He was just preparing to grab his keys and go searching for his new, younger partner when his phone finally rang.

"Yes?" he snapped.

"Reporting in, sir," the young man responded, a nervous tremor in his voice.

"And?"

"I managed to get into the right databases. Our last problem will be resolved come tomorrow morning."

"Why not tonight?"

"Because such a notification would be expected during business hours, *sir*. It's after midnight." Carlton didn't like his associates's condescending tone but knew the explanation made sense.

"All right. I'll see you tomorrow. Ten a.m." Carlton finished his wine in one large gulp and stood up. For the first time since they'd learned about the students, he felt like he would be able to truly follow through on his promise to Sylvester.

Chapter Seven

Rachel stared at the body. It was David Payton, lying on the forest floor, motionless. Nearby rested the remnants of a fallen Jeffrey pine, its horizontal trunk almost four feet high. Birds chirped in the distance, and the breeze hushed through the trees. Everything was moving in some way, including the blood drop that oozed from the bullet hole in his forehead. Bella brushed against her leg, distracting her for a moment. Rachel looked down at the pup. Something moved in her peripheral vision. It was David Payton. He was glaring at her, his dead-white face colored only by the deep red hue of the blood. Backing up, she tripped over a pinecone and landed on her backside. As pain beat up her spine, the image changed, and it wasn't David anymore. It was Matt, with the same expression he'd worn when he'd attacked her all of those years ago. He winked. The image changed again, the eyes blue and partially shaded by a ball cap. Luke looked in her direction, but his stare was blank. Empty.

A loud sound burst from nearby. Was it a phone? Rachel looked around, and resting on the transparent image of a downed tree about five feet away was a clock with large red digital numbers. The noise penetrated again, and Rachel finally awoke from her dreamy state enough to realize the alarm was going off. Bella stirred, tucking her nose against Rachel's arm, tail wagging at the other end of the bed. That canine greeting always helped to quickly diminish the terror from these occasional nightmares.

Rachel crawled out of bed and noted the clock read 6:00 a.m. a moment before slapping the snooze button. The dreams involving the events of last summer had been coming less often, but they still left her feeling shaky when she first woke up. As if mornings weren't already distasteful enough. She'd been lucky to recall last night, at around one a.m. when she decided to attempt sleep, that she had to attend a meeting in North Shore—an hour's drive—at 8:30 this morning. She despised early mornings, although she willingly made exceptions for long hikes and good powder days on the slopes. Now she had an hour to wake up her brain before she had to begin her drive.

As she let Bella outside, Rachel checked her cell phone for any texts from Luke—nothing. She looked at the machine connected to her home phone, wondering if he could have called without her waking up. There were no messages and no missed calls. Had he found his sister? Or perhaps her body? She still hadn't heard from Luke when she took Bella for a quick morning walk in the forest out back, nor over an hour later when she watched as the Placer County Planning Commission officially began its meeting.

~

The phone rang at exactly 9:06 a.m. Everett noticed the time, having been worried about answering a call on his cell phone after just arriving at his office in South Lake Tahoe. It took the college administrator who had called just one minute to tell him his funding had been discontinued and his position would end that day. He couldn't believe it. These AmeriCorps positions were supposed to run at least eleven months. That was the term he'd agreed to when he'd left a good-paying job back home to live on very low wages. But he'd wanted the experience.

"I'm so sorry, Mr. Veerdeen, but I was just informed this morning," the pleasant, sympathetic female voice said.

Everett was speechless. He finally recovered enough to speak. "*Danke* . . . I mean, thank you for letting me know right away," he said, his plans falling apart in an instant. "What now?" he pleaded.

"Well, with your position unfunded, you may want to check on how this may affect your work visa." Everett hadn't even thought of that, and his heart sank further.

~

Ted's phone rang just as he took the first sip of the tea he'd just heated. The young officer recently assigned to be his new partner—Nolan Ramos—still hadn't arrived. Ted wasn't surprised; Nolan was a slacker with a bad attitude. Ted assumed he'd made detective as a result of family connections around the area, not based on his limited skills. Ted missed his last partner, Leona, who had been fired when it was discovered she was managing an illegal grow house a few miles out of town. It was a tough situation; her son had cancer, the bills were piling up, and her husband had been laid off. As far as Ted was concerned, she was a good cop who'd been faced with impossible circumstances and made a bad decision.

"Yeah?" he answered casually.

"Officer Benson?" a scratchy female voice asked.

"Yes, and who is this?"

"Officer Boice from the Truckee PD. I'm sorry I wasn't able to return your call last night."

"Oh, yes, I appreciate you getting back to me. I know it's out of our jurisdiction, but your car accident victim and his wife may have a connection to someone in my area." Ted held his breath, hoping she wouldn't tell him he needed to use official channels for the information. She didn't speak right away.

"So far as we are aware, this was nothing more than an unfortunate car accident. We are doing our best to locate the wife, but it doesn't look promising," the officer sighed. "Crews have been out searching all night. We've found nothing."

"I'm sorry to hear that," Ted replied. He figured either they didn't know about Jill's suspicion regarding the bruises, or they weren't going to say anything. "Well, I appreciate your call. Would it be too much to ask you to let me know if you find her, or hear any news?"

"Well . . . ," she stuttered a bit and then continued, "how are they connected to your area?" Her voice held the undertone of suspicion.

"They may be related to an officer who used to work here," Ted responded.

"Would that be someone named Luke Reed, by chance?"

"Yes it would." Ted smiled at the officer's quick ability to connect the dots.

"He's been here, imposing himself into our searches." It was obvious she wasn't a big fan of Luke's intrusion.

"That sounds like Luke," he chuckled.

"Speak of the devil, he's here now." Her voice grew distant, as if she were moving the phone away, and then she spoke into the receiver once more. "I'll call if anything develops, Officer Benson."

"Thank you," Ted replied, a dial tone already on the other end of the line.

Chapter Eight

"They want to allow *what*?" Rachel whispered to Kristina as they listened to a county staffer begin a presentation about an upcoming development project. She couldn't believe it. Over a hundred new homes on an unbuilt forested mountaintop above North Lake Tahoe. It was inconceivable that any agency would start allowing new buildings up there.

"Despicable," Kristina responded, not at all concerned with keeping others from hearing her. At almost six feet tall, her friend and coworker seemed to exude a kind of special presence that allowed her to make opinionated comments without others around her complaining.

"What ever happened to Tahoe being a national treasure?" Rachel sagged in the uncomfortable chair, gazing on the map being presented to the planning commissioners. "It just never ends," she sighed. Kristina began to say something, but the vibration of Rachel's cell phone in her coat pocket distracted her. She looked at the screen and nudged Kristina's arm, holding the display out for her to read it.

"How could they end Everett's position? He has eight months left!" This time, at least, Kristina kept her voice low. Rachel reread the text, wondering the same thing. She sent a short message to let him know she'd call him as soon as possible. She also noticed it was after ten a.m. and she still hadn't received an update from Luke.

~

Carlton sat on the bench, looking straight ahead as he tossed bits of stale bread to a group of nearby Canada geese. His partner was late—no surprise there. It was almost 10:15 a.m. when a figure approached and sat down about a foot away. Carlton noticed another pair of bright Vans shoes. This time, they were yellow. Last time, orange. Carlton had already instructed him to wear indistinct outfits, given the delicate nature of their operations. Clearly, the kid hadn't listened.

"Nice of you to join me," Carlton said sarcastically. His partner paused before speaking.

"The AmeriCorps student has been notified. I've got a call in to find out how quickly they can revoke his visa. Mr. Veerdeen should have other more important things to occupy his time now." The younger man sniffed and then coughed. This was yet another unpleasant habit Carlton was forced to overlook—frequent and unusual congestion. But Sylvester was very clear about keeping the kid involved, although Carlton silently questioned the decision. Even though the boy had the ability to carry through some activities that required a rather firm and unsympathetic approach, he lacked in the strategizing department.

"Good. How's our old buddy, Fred, doing these days?"

"I hear he's in and out of awareness but still refuses round-the-clock supervision. It shouldn't be long now, though." Another snort, followed by a loud clearing of his throat.

Carlton stood up, more than happy to conclude their meeting. "We don't have much time left, you know." He paused and then mumbled, "Keep me updated," as he slowly walked away, tossing another crumb to the goose standing nearby. "And get yourself a damn pair of brown shoes."

~

Old Red Fred. That's what those kids were calling him. Lord knows why—he wasn't a commie. Not Fred. Hell, he wasn't really much of a Republican, either, although he certainly wouldn't call himself a Democrat now that a bona fide "African American" was president. *Goddamn liberals, always having to be different and rock the boat.* He heard a creak in the other room. Or was it in the garage?

39

"Nathaniel? Irena?" he asked and then wondered from where those questions originated. *Who were they, and why had their names crossed his mind?* Fred looked around the room as he sat up in his old leather chair. There were several portraits of various people, some older, some younger. The third one he examined brought recognition. His granddaughter, Irena.

"Sir, did you call me?" A short, rotund man entered the room. Fred gazed at him, surprised. The man appeared to be in his fifties, mostly bald, the small exception being a horizontal strip of hair that wrapped around the back of his head from ear to ear. *Who was this man?*

"Why are you in my house? Get out before I call the police!" Fred yelled, placing his hands on the arms of his chair to push himself up from the rigid seat.

"Sir, my name is Sam. Your family hired me to help you out. You are experiencing some memory loss . . ."

"According to whom?"

"Those papers right there will explain it," the man said. Then as he turned, Fred heard him say, "Again." Fred looked at the stack the man had pointed at. He began reading. Several medical files documented a decline in his memory, and notable "fluctuations" in his behavior, for the last year or so. As he read the third report, distant recollections returned. He had read these papers before. Many times. Fred looked up, but the room was empty. He noticed a new glass of liquid had been set on the nearby coffee table. Sam must have put it there. Fred leaned over to pick it up, smelling the sweet odor of the best Kentucky whiskey in the world. The first sip went down smooth. His enjoyment was short-lived as a strong floral scent invaded his senses. He looked around for the source. There was a small tea light set up in some kind of liquid candle contraption on a nearby table.

"What is that?" he asked loudly, pinching his nose. He saw the small man come back to the opening that separated the rooms.

"Sir?"

"What is that horrible scent?" He pointed toward the candle.

"Sorry, sir. This is from your granddaughter, Irena. She gave it to you last Christmas. I think it's some kind of rose blend." Fred didn't respond; he couldn't even picture the girl. *How can I forget something so basic as a gift from my own granddaughter?*

Chapter Nine

As she drove away from the restaurant where she'd met with Everett and Kristina, Rachel noticed the clock display in her dashboard read 2:34 p.m. Bad enough that one of the smartest and friendliest people she'd worked with just lost his job and could be facing a quick deportation out of the country, but there was also no call or text from Luke. *You can think about that later,* she reminded herself. Right now, after discussing the AmeriCorps situation, let alone the haste to which Everett had been told he may have to go back to Germany, they'd decided to do some digging. Rachel wasn't sure anything like this had ever happened in the program—she wanted to spend some time learning more. She owed it to Everett to try. Rachel recalled the first time they'd met. She had been sitting in her office on a phone call when she noticed Bella's form moving oddly on the floor next to her. She'd looked down to see the dog twisting and turning, legs frantically pawing in the air. She'd tossed the phone and jumped to the side of Bella, trying to calm her down. But the pawing continued, and the dog didn't seem to react to her voice or her hands. Rachel retrieved the dropped device, calling the first person she expected to be home this time of day—Kristina. But it was a male voice that answered. She soon learned Kristina had gone to the store. Upon hearing the reason for Rachel's call, Everett—this man she hadn't yet met—had dropped everything and driven straight to her house.

It turned out Bella had a seizure, a rare side effect of a medicine she'd just been prescribed for stomach irritation. It hadn't lasted long after she'd called Kristina's house, but she was happy to have Everett drive her to the vet anyway, allowing her to hold the pup in her arms. Now, she'd do her best to help Everett. It had also occurred to her as she drove home that focusing on something new might help alleviate some of the odd restlessness that had continued to plague her emotions lately.

After greeting Bella, Rachel let her outside into the backyard and then sat in front of her computer. She'd agreed to call some of the people associated with the non-local projects Everett had been involved in, while Kristina contacted nearby South Shore people. Rachel looked at the rigid and clear handwritten notes from Everett. He'd made a list of four names. Three were associated with the University of Nevada, Reno, where he'd been asked to assist with identifying some "small water bugs," as he often called them when speaking in more public forums—not only to help explain what they were in more general terms, but Everett also had trouble correctly pronouncing their scientific term, "macroinvertebrates," due to his heavy German accent. He'd also included the letters "CDFW—Susanville" next to the last name. Rachel knew this was the California Department of Fish and Wildlife. She typed in the first name from UNR—Professor William Scottsfield. Expecting various links to his department to show up in her Google search list, she was surprised when an article from the *Reno Gazette-Journal* was included at the top of the list. The link took her to a story from one week ago, titled "Local professor still missing." Just as she began to read, a cold nose interrupted, nudging her arm.

"I know, sweet girl. I just got home and I'm on the computer already." She ran her hands up and down the canine's silky black coat, continuing the rhythmic pattern as she returned her gaze back to the screen. Rachel sent the article to the printer and then selected a few more links, which displayed the expected information from various UNR pages.

Rachel typed in the next name—Danielle Watson. This time, links to local South Shore articles came up. Apparently, the young student was the unfortunate hiker that had tripped and sustained fatal injuries while hiking the Echo Lakes trail recently. Very few details were included.

"That's odd . . . ," Rachel said aloud. After printing several iterations of the story documenting the accident, she moved on to the third name—Raymond Martinez. This time, there were no newspaper articles. Instead, generic yellow-and-white page listings included a name and contact information for the male student on the list. She dialed the one and only phone number but gave up after it rang ten times. A thought occurred to her. "Maybe he's at the lab where he does his research. Probably the same one managed by Professor Scottsfield," she said, again feeling no discontent for speaking to what some would consider an empty room. To Rachel, Bella was her audience. At least that's what she told herself. Rachel dialed the number listed for the lab Professor Scottsfield had managed at UNR.

Five minutes later she'd learned from another student that Raymond had abruptly dropped out of the graduate program, citing a family emergency. The student had cleared out all of his items sometime overnight, leaving a short note stuck to the lab's notice board. Next, Rachel called the California Department of Fish and Wildlife in Susanville.

"Mr. Holden has been temporarily reassigned to another office," said the scratchy female voice that had answered the main department line. Rachel found this didn't surprise her; a certain pattern was taking shape.

"Oh, was this recent? I'm supposed to talk to him about—"

"Earlier this week," the woman cut in. She didn't sound upset with Rachel, just annoyed in general. "As if we aren't already understaffed here," she sighed.

"I'm sorry to hear it," Rachel voiced and paused, pencil in hand. "My apologies for bothering you, but would it be possible to get in touch with him at his new location? A phone number, or e-mail perhaps?"

"Well, I can give you a number, but I've been told he's out doing extensive fieldwork. He could be unavailable for days. You aren't the first person who's called to ask for him. I've left about three messages since Friday . . ." Rachel listened as the woman quickly recited ten digits, thanked her, then hung up and immediately dialed the new number. It went straight to voice mail. Rachel left a message about Everett and asked Mr. Holden to return her call as soon as possible. After hanging up, she looked at the clock: 3:42 p.m. No word from Luke.

"Bella, how about a short hike up the old grade?" The paved section of the original Highway 50 wasn't the most intriguing hike, but it was a good way to work off anxiety and allow Bella to visit with other dogs encountered on the old highway. The view from Echo Summit at its crest was also worth the climb. Bella's bushy tail began ferociously wagging as the pup jumped up.

On their way back down the popular local trail, Rachel finally received a text from Luke, telling her he was home and asking if she could come by his place tonight. Half-annoyed that it had taken him all day to be in touch, yet anxious to find out what was going on, she picked up her pace after texting back, "Yes."

Chapter Ten

The sky had turned almost completely dark by the time Rachel parked in front of Luke's house. She had left Bella home, sensing that the dog's comedic acts might not be appropriate. A new passenger car—she couldn't tell the model in the faint light—was parked next to Luke's light-green Subaru. It looked like a rental. She hoped the extra car indicated good news. She knocked on the front door as she announced herself.

"Hey, it's me." Rachel waited a moment and reached for the handle. It turned just as she touched it, and the door opened. The porch light was dim, but there was enough illumination to reveal the tired look on Luke's face. He hadn't changed his clothes since she'd seen him the night before. She moved in to hug him, and he stepped back.

"Wait, let me first tell you—"

"Hello?" a woman's voice called out from the other room. *Is that Kimmy?* Rachel wondered.

"Did you find her? Your sister?" Rachel reached for his hand. He let her take it and closed the door behind her as she stepped in.

"No," Luke replied abruptly. Before she could turn to look at him, a woman appeared in the hallway. With long, fiery red hair, a slim shape, and a good six inches of height on Rachel, the woman was beautiful. The only things that marred her image were the dark circles under her eyes. Although a brief twinge of jealousy ran through her, it was quickly followed by a strong sense of unease she couldn't explain.

"This is Sonya, the friend of Kimmy's who called," he said, waving his free hand toward the woman. She smiled and approached Rachel.

"Rachel, hello. I've heard quite a bit about you. Sorry if my presence caught you off guard. I just didn't know where to go, and Luke wanted to know more about Kimmy, so . . ."

"Hello, Sonya," she said, letting go of Luke's warm palm and stretching her hand out. The woman complied, her grip firm. Rachel quickly shifted her attention back to Luke. "Did you find her?" The question slipped out before Rachel considered the situation. A friend of hers was here, not Kimmy. Luke wanted to know more about Kimmy . . . obviously he couldn't find out directly from his sister. Which meant they hadn't found her, or something worse.

"No, but they're still looking. I debated staying, but Sonya was beat, and they weren't too thrilled to have me around, so it seemed best to return home. It's less than two hours away if they find any— Kimmy," Luke said, moving toward the kitchen. She hadn't seen him look so defeated, ever. Even when he was lying on the hard ground in Wyoming, a fresh bullet hole in his chest.

"How did this all come about? Where's your sister been all this time?" she inquired of Luke, placing herself on one of the stools below his kitchen countertop. Sonya sat next to her and immediately interjected.

"She's been happy. She married Eddie several years ago, rest his soul . . ."

"Is that who they found in the car?" Rachel asked.

Sonya nodded. "The three of us were on our way home from a conference in Reno. I was driving my own car. They'd stopped in Verdi to get gas, and I'd gone on. Eddie drives faster than me, so I figured they'd catch up in ten minutes or so. I waited in Truckee for a good half hour. They weren't answering their phones. Finally, I drove back toward Verdi. That's when I saw those skid marks, and . . . ," she stuttered, a tear falling down one cheek. "I knew it wasn't good."

Rachel waited a moment, but Sonya didn't continue. "Have her parents been reached yet? This shouldn't all fall on Luke's shoulders." A small mumble from Luke suggested his discontent with the subject.

Sonya looked at Rachel, then to Luke, then back at Rachel. "You didn't know?"

At this, Luke perked up. "Know what?" He looked at Sonya expectantly.

"Your dad was arrested and convicted about two years ago on fraud and embezzlement charges. Your mom didn't take it well and began drinking. She's spent the last six months in an alcohol rehab facility. She even refused to speak to your sister." The room went silent. Rachel internally counted eleven ticks of a nearby clock before Luke commented.

"I had no idea," he sighed.

"It broke Kimmy's heart. Especially watching your mom get worse and worse. At least she finally got her to admit herself into treatment."

~

Kristina left a message for Rachel. She was anxious to share what she'd discovered. After several calls with local agency staffers and related volunteers, it was clear no one had any idea why Everett's position had been cut. One of the managers stated the order came from "higher up," as he'd called it, but that no more information had been provided. She asked about the local projects, and the responses were generally similar to what Everett had already explained—a few educational programs regarding local aquatic systems. But 40 percent of his funding came from UNR, and he had been assisting a professor and several graduate students with a new research project. The kicker was—no one knew much about his task, other than that it involved identifying and cataloguing the small insects in lakes and streams. She'd called Everett to ask for more details. His usual cheerful voice instead sounded anxious when he picked up the phone.

"Everett, can you tell me more about your project with UNR?" Kristina was talking fast, but she was too excited to slow down.

"Oh, uh, yes. Basically, they had a project where they were

looking at old abandoned mines and some of the streams near them. They wanted to compare the different invert communities—sorry, macroinvertebrates—"

"Got it. I know enough to understand you mean the small water bugs, like the water boatmen, mosquito larvae—those kind of creepy-crawlies."

"Yes," he said. "Generally speaking."

"Do you know where the samples came from?" Kristina held the phone tight to her ear.

"Not the details. The labels were just letters and numbers. I think there were several different locations."

"All right. That makes sense. Keeps objectivity and all. But you gave Rachel a list of people you've been working with on that?"

"Yes, although I have been waiting for another set of samples. But they have not come. They have been late before. I did not think much of it," he said, his voice trailing off. Kristina paused, deciding she would follow up with Rachel on her plan to contact his UNR associates.

"Everett, ya doing okay?" she asked sympathetically.

"I am hanging in there . . . as you Americans say."

"We are behind you. Call if you hear anything on your end. I'll touch base with Rachel and let you know if we learn anymore." She heard his voice crack as he began to respond.

"Thank you."

Chapter Eleven

It was after ten p.m. when Rachel finally returned home, an anxious Bella waiting for her at the door. She shut it behind her and fell to her knees, rubbing the dog's back and laughing as Bella deposited a toy in her lap. She finally let go of some of the tension she'd been holding in since she had walked into Luke's house.

"I love your greetings!" she laughed. The dog dropped down, her two front legs on the floor—yet another one of her comedy moves. Bella loved to have her lower back scratched as she propped her butt into the air. It was how she'd greeted Rachel the first time they'd met. "Oh, girl, I needed this." The atmosphere at Luke's had been sad and oddly strained. He was heartbroken at the idea he might have come so close to seeing his sister, only to lose her. He was also exhausted after being up for over twenty-four hours straight, so she suggested he get some sleep and they'd talk in the morning. Luke had agreed, and she helped prepare the guest room for Sonya. The woman seemed friendly enough, but there was something off about her. At first Rachel thought maybe she really was just jealous; the woman was gorgeous. Things with Luke had been strained; she herself had been on an emotional roller coaster of sorts. But that just didn't seem to be it. Rachel couldn't pin it down. Just a feeling, perhaps.

After a few more rubs for Bella, Rachel stood up and noticed the blinking light on her machine. She hit play, and Kristina's voice boomed into the room. Knowing her coworker was a night owl, she knew it was safe to call her back. It took less than five minutes for them to swap the information they'd gathered.

"Something is not right." Rachel sighed, taking a sip from her water bottle. She never drank from open glasses due to the "Bella bomb"—her name for Bella's swishing tail.

"I agree."

"Kris, maybe we should head up to Reno tomorrow. See what we can learn about this project. You game?"

"I have a conference call at three, but worst case I could call from my cell. Although if we got there at eight, and then—" She was cut off by Rachel choking; after a moment, Rachel cleared her throat and responded.

"A.M.?" Rachel didn't function well in the morning. It took a good two hours to wake up enough to be able to verbally communicate. She didn't understand perky morning people, especially those like Kristina that could stay up until midnight and wake up at six, rearing to go.

"Sure, we could leave around six thirty," Kristina stated.

"How about we leave at eight? I mean, really . . . how many students would likely be in the lab so early in the morning? A lot of classes are scheduled for eight or nine."

"I'm kidding. You know I love giving you a hard time," Kristina laughed. "Okay, meet at the Y at eight?" The intersection of State Route 89 and Highway 50 in South Lake Tahoe was a good middle-ground meeting point for them.

"Sounds good," Rachel said and then added, "Kris, you scared me for a moment there."

~

Luke opened his eyes. Although groggy, he felt well rested, if he didn't count the throbbing shoulder pain he'd been waking up with far too often. His clock, now partially bathed in sunlight, read 7:29 a.m. He glanced at the bed next to him, hoping Rachel would be there, accompanied by Bella at their feet. But all he saw were knotted-up sheets. When the smell of coffee invaded his senses, he recalled his houseguest. Normally he prepared coffee grinds the night before and set a timer, but last night he'd been so exhausted he'd gone straight to bed, leaving Rachel to help Sonya. If only he could have fallen asleep right away.

Instead, Luke had tossed and turned, his mind racing with questions. How could his sister have literally been just hours away after all of these years? It sounded like she was happily married and considering going back to college. Why hadn't she tried to look him up? With the Internet, it wouldn't be difficult to find out he was in South Lake Tahoe. But should he have kept trying as well—continued to spend countless hours struggling to locate her? These thoughts had tormented him for hours until he finally fell into a restless sleep.

Now, with hope that the new day and some rest would bring a fresh perspective, Luke got up and walked into the bathroom to shower, thankful it was connected to his room. He swallowed a pain pill, stepped into the shower, and let the hot water clear his senses. Twenty minutes later he emerged from his bedroom to find Sonya standing in front of the stove, the smell of eggs and bacon emanating through the air. Her hair was wet; she must have figured out how to operate the sensitive shower controls in the guest bathroom.

"Good morning." She smiled, although it was slightly strained. He nodded.

"Any news?" he asked.

"I called. They haven't found anything."

"Damn." He collapsed onto a stool. A moment later she placed a full plate in front of him.

"Eat."

"Thanks," he replied, picking up a fork while eyeing an empty mug nearby.

"I gauged from the large bags of coffee beans, this high-powered grinder, and your rather impressive coffeemaker that you're a coffee drinker," she said, holding up a full decanter of thick dark liquid.

"You'd be right," he uttered as she poured. "Does Kimmy drink coffee?" he wondered aloud.

"Not often. She said it upset her stomach." She sipped a glass of juice. It was likely the only other flavored beverage she could find.

"That doesn't surprise me. She sure tore up her insides when we were kids, barely eating and all," he said. "I don't suppose that's great on the GI system." He forked a piece of bacon. "So, can you tell me more about her interest in college? Did she have a major in mind?" Sonya smiled, appearing to relax.

"Geology. She is fascinated with it." Luke paused, surprised by this.

"Really? The 'neat rocks' or 'world geology' kind of major?"

"I'd say both."

"How about you? Weren't you in Reno for the same conference?" The caffeine was starting to awaken his brain cells.

"I think it's cool stuff, but I was going more because she asked me. It's not really my thing," Sonya sighed. "She figured Eddie might spend more time on the slots and in the saunas than join her, so I just assumed she was interested in the company."

"Was he a big gambler?"

"I think there might have been more going on with that than she'd tell me. If and when she wants me to know something, she'll eventually open up." Luke noticed she never referred to his sister in past tense. That provided him some comfort.

~

Ted set his mug of tea down so hard on his kitchen countertop that he looked for cracks underneath. Although Jill had officially reported her autopsy findings, including the bruising around the man's wrists, the locals were still focusing most of their resources on the search for the wife—Luke's sister. Ted understood their decision, knowing he'd likely do the same thing. But he was also the kind of person who needed to understand the *how and why* of things. It's the reason he became an officer and focused his career on earning his detective's badge.

Adding to his anxiety, Rachel e-mailed him late last night, explaining her visit to Luke's and the unexpected houseguest. Ted decided it might be a good idea to meet this Sonya—get a feel for her. Although his first impression of Rachel last summer had not been a flattering one, he'd since learned to trust her instincts. He called Luke's cell and received a tired "Yeah?"

"Luke, glad to hear you are back home. Rachel has kept me

updated on your, er, situation."

"Oh, yes. Can you believe it? My sister? I just . . . I can't imagine this would happen and that she might be gone already," he said gravely.

"There's always hope, my friend. You know that as well as I do." Ted paused, taking another sip of tea. "How about I stop by and see if I can help in some way?" He knew Rachel would likely be gone most of the day. She'd mentioned heading to Reno with a coworker.

"Uh, sure."

"All right. I'll be there in a little while." After a responsive grunt from Luke—clearly he was still working on his first cup of coffee—Ted disconnected the call.

Chapter Twelve

"Let's just park on this side street and walk over to the lab. Probably easier." Rachel pointed toward a dead-end street near the railroad tracks lining the eastern side of the college. Parking on campus was hard to come by this time of day. Kristina nodded. They'd driven Kristina's car to Reno since it used less gas. Rachel left Bella at her neighbor's house, the dog more than happy for the playdate with the Labradoodle next door.

"Where should we start?" Kristina inquired, turning off the engine.

"Everett mentioned that he had visited this one lab a few times for his project. I checked out the campus map online, and it's on this side. It should be just up and over that hill." She waved.

"I'll follow your lead." Kristina smiled and removed the knit cap she'd been wearing. After the cooler Tahoe morning, the Reno air felt extra warm. Rachel removed her coat before ascending the small hillside. Kristina trotted up behind her.

"Do trains actually use these tracks?"

"Not sure anymore," Rachel said, crossing the track and walking down the other side of the hill. She was almost at the bottom when she stepped on a small area of loose gravel. Her foot slid, and she lost her balance. In an odd kind of slow motion, she fell and landed right on the bruised tailbone she'd earned on her not-so-smart hiking expedition last week. With the breath knocked out of her, she didn't have the chance to speak before Kristina was at her side.

"You okay?"

"Holy . . ." Rachel exhaled. "Yes, I think so." She sat for a moment, waiting for the initial pain to subside. As she stood up and brushed off the dust, she chimed, "Well, if I wasn't fully awake before, I am now."

"You, uh, seem to be hurting quite a bit from that tiny little slip," Kristina teased. "Going soft on me?" Rachel debated and then decided to confess.

"You know the hike I did up Pyramid last week?"

"You mean the *climb*?" Kristina had already expressed her concern about what she referred to as Rachel's recent "reckless behavior." Rachel nodded.

"I may have left out the part where I had a little incident. But I'm fine. Just a couple of bruises where I landed today. Again." Rachel began walking, anxious to get moving and change the subject. She knew if Kristina pushed her hard enough, she'd probably pour out the full extent of her recent emotional roller coaster. She still hadn't figured out what was driving her, and it scared her. But she was also embarrassed.

"It's *your* ass," Kristina said, smiling after a brief pause. "Literally and figuratively," she added and began walking. Relieved Kristina wasn't pushing the issue, Rachel chuckled and followed her. As they approached the first building on the campus, Kristina pointed to one of the larger doors. "Is that where we go in?"

"I think so. Let's go find out," Rachel replied, picking up her step while doing her best to ignore the continued soreness from the fall. She hadn't been to the University of Nevada, Reno, in years, and memories of her time in graduate school were returning. Kristina opened the door, and they walked inside. Before browsing the directory of offices and labs, Kristina reached into her purse and removed her reading glasses.

"Kind of small print," she mumbled. Kristina made no secret of her dislike for her new glasses, recently prescribed by her optometrist. She'd called Rachel after her last appointment, ranting about how thirty-six was too young to need reading glasses.

"There," Rachel said as she pointed. "Scottsfield. Room 628.

How about we check it out and see if there are any students around? If it's like when I attended, his office probably branches off the laboratory he is in charge of."

"A lot of good these did," Kristina whispered as she jerked her glasses off, dropped them into a purple case, and tossed it into the bag at her side.

Taped to the front of his office door were several letters and notes, expressing either hope, sympathy, or a combination of both for the professor's unexplained disappearance. While reading through the sentimental messages Rachel heard the approaching sound of footsteps. She turned to see a tall, skinny student, perhaps in his early twenties, staring at them awkwardly. Rachel smiled.

"Hello. We're here from South Shore and were hoping to talk to some of the professor's students—"

"If you're reporters, forget it." The student appeared slightly nervous, but his response included a hint of assertiveness.

"We aren't. We work with Everett Veerdeen," Kristina said, putting her hand out. The kid, clearly skeptical, made no move to shake her hand. She let it drop.

"Not sure who that is." He remained tentative. Rachel suspected he had encountered a few eager journalists in these halls.

"He is, well, *was* an AmeriCorps member helping the professor on a project related to macroinvertebrates." She let the statement hang for a moment.

No response. Blank stare.

"Heavy German accent . . . about my height, always smiling." Rachel hoped this would spur recognition. Then again, this could be just a student walking by who was curious about the onlookers.

"Oh, the bug kid. Speaks a bit formally and all?" he asked, his tone lightening.

"Yep, the one and only," Kristina confirmed.

"I know him. Well, I've seen him a couple of times. He was always bent over a microscope, though. I didn't talk to him much."

"That's okay. We were hoping to learn more about the source of the project he was working on." Rachel removed her sweater, unable to tolerate the heated hallway any longer. "His position was abruptly cut, and we're trying to find out why. Is there someone we could talk to who might know more about it?"

"Why not just ask the kid, if you work with him?" A logical question, Rachel knew.

"We did. But he didn't know the details. Although he was given samples to ID, he wasn't provided the backstory." She watched his reaction, hopeful. The kid looked over his shoulder and then back to Rachel.

"There's one or two girls who have been in the lab a lot. They might know something. I don't think they are here yet, though."

"We can wait," Kristina said. Rachel saw that beads of sweat were forming on her friend's forehead.

"Uh . . . sure. There are some chairs around that corner." He gestured down the hall.

"Thanks." Before the student could walk away, Rachel added, "Has anyone learned any more about what happened to Professor Scottsfield?"

"Not that I've heard." Contrary to what he said, his abruptly tense posture suggested otherwise. "No rumors, even?" Kristina prodded.

"Well, I did hear a couple of students talking about a research lab down by Mammoth, wondering if something happened down there."

"What kind of lab?" Kristina encouraged. Before he could reply, his eyes squinted and he began to sneeze repeatedly. As he pulled a Kleenex out of his pocket, Rachel spoke.

"There's a well-known aquatics research laboratory down that way, off Highway 395. It's a bit past the Mammoth area. I'd bet that's the one." Rachel noticed the student perk up.

"Yeah, sounds like a pretty cool place," he beamed in between sneezes.

"You okay? Can I get you some water?" Kristina wiped her glistening forehead as she glanced down the hall at a nearby water fountain.

"Yeah," the student replied, wiping his nose. "Allergies. You don't by chance have a cat in your purse there, or something?"

"Not today," Kristina replied quickly. "I bring the stroller when I want to take my cat for walks." It was Kristina's dry sarcasm at work. She delivered it with a perfectly serious expression, but it appeared not everyone appreciated Kristina's sense of humor. "Sorry, bad joke." She stepped back.

"So, what do you think this lab has to do with his disappearance?" Rachel interjected into the awkward silence. Apparently recovered, the young man responded.

"Word was Dr. Scottsfield had a collection of bug samples to run down for identification. The samples are missing, so there has been some speculation that maybe he drove down and had a car accident or something."

"Has anyone looked?" Rachel was intrigued.

"I would expect the cops did, don't you think?" He nervously shifted the backpack hanging off one shoulder as he glanced at his watch. "Look, I need to get to class." He began to step away. Rachel tried asking one more question.

"Anyone else MIA that might have been working with him?"

There was a slight hesitation before he responded. "One of the girls in his lab had an accident just before Halloween. Like, it was bad. She died. But she was just up hiking in Tahoe."

"I think I read an article about that. Up on the Echo Lakes trail?" Rachel prodded.

"Sounds familiar, I guess," he shrugged. "I really need to go. Last time I was late, the professor made a huge deal of it," he said, moving to rush past them.

"Got it. Thanks," Rachel said as he scurried down the hall. She received a dismissive wave in return.

"Well, now what?" Kristina chimed.

"I guess we grab some chairs and wait. And . . . I think I'll give Ted a call to see if he can find out whether there have been any accidents on 395 that could be related." Rachel felt bad asking Ted for yet another favor, but she didn't want to alert Luke to their actions. They were simply following up on a work-related matter, really. He had his hands full with his sister's situation. No need to bother him with it.

They waited for almost an hour before the other lab students arrived. Although they didn't have any new information related to their instructor's disappearance, they were familiar with the project

Everett had been tasked to assist with. Rachel stewed over the new information as they crossed the railroad tracks on their way back to the car.

"Sounds like the professor had planned to ask Everett to go through a set of macroinvertebrate samples for a preliminary classification of what the water bugs were. Then they'd likely have them professionally evaluated—presumably by experts at the aquatic research lab—to confirm the results."

"Yep," Kristina said. Her foot caught on the track, but she corrected herself before falling. "Why would they go through that trouble of having him work on it if they were going to contract with the lab to do it anyway?"

"My guess is it was meant to be a learning exercise for Everett. Maybe that's why he hadn't yet seen the newest set of samples or been told the full scope of the project." When they reached the paved road, Kristina stopped and looked at Rachel.

"This is all a bit weird, don't you think? That girl on the trail, okay, that was an accident. But the professor is MIA, Everett is let go, and this other kid just drops out of the program? All of them happen to be working on the project involving these bug samples, which they say the lab never received," Kristina speculated.

"Agreed."

"So, now what?"

"Good question," Rachel mused as they reached the car. "I suppose it makes some sense that Everett's work here would be discontinued given everyone involved seems to have disappeared, transferred, or quit. Maybe it really is just one huge coincidence; perhaps they couldn't find enough new funding to support his position. Although I've still never heard of such a thing. Or the idea his visa could potentially be revoked so quickly." Rachel unwrapped her sweater from her waist.

"You don't believe it's just a coincidence, either, I gather?"

"I'd be shocked."

"Well, what can we do, then?" Kristina asked as she reached for the door handle.

"Not sure. But let's see if that guy from Susanville calls me back. I'm curious about this mining project those girls mentioned."

"Any word from our friendly neighborhood cop?"

Rachel glanced at her phone as she sat in the passenger seat. "No, not yet." As she pulled the door shut and reached for the seat belt, unexpected movement in the side-view mirror caught her attention. "What the . . . ?" she stuttered as someone in a hooded grey sweatshirt stepped up next to the car. She heard Kristina mumble something at the same time she noticed the gun pointed at her from directly outside her window.

~

The phone rang, and the SUV's speaker system blared an annoying chime Ted hadn't yet figured out how to turn off. He glanced at the display. Unknown number. Another telemarketer—not worth answering. However, he did see he had a voice mail, although his screen didn't identify who had left it; he'd only learn that once he dialed in. Being less than a minute from Luke's place, he decided to check it later.

As Ted stepped onto the front porch, the delicious scent of fresh bacon and eggs caught his attention. His stomach growled. He hadn't eaten real bacon and eggs in a long time—the rich flavors were almost forgotten after years on a healthier, mostly green diet. Almost. His mouth began to water. Ted knocked, and a moment later Luke opened the door.

"Come on in." Luke skirted back, and Ted followed him inside. A tall red-haired woman stood in the kitchen. Her skin had the dark tint of someone who either sunbathed too frequently or abused tanning booths. She smiled as she opened the cabinet and removed a third plate.

"Nice to meet you. Ted, is it? Please, there's plenty."

For a woman whose best friend is missing, she seems awfully cheerful, Ted thought.

"Thanks, but I'll just have some OJ." He nodded toward a container of orange juice on the counter. "So, Sonya, sounds like you've had quite the experience?"

"Don't interrogate her," Luke snapped.

"I'm not. I simply want to hear what's been going on and see if I can help," Ted said, keeping his tone light. "If you, or Sonya, prefer not to discuss it, then okay—"

"I don't mind," Sonya cut in as she poured the thick liquid into a glass. Luke didn't reply. Ted noticed he had returned to staring blankly at his plate while moving food around with his fork. Rachel had mentioned he was torn up over his sister, but Ted didn't realize just how much until now. He felt he needed to help keep an eye on the situation. Luke was a great detective, but when someone was this emotionally involved, things could be overlooked. Ted returned his focus to Sonya as she began telling him her story.

When she was done recounting the fatal accident west of Reno, Ted nodded and reached for the carton of juice to refill his glass. The room grew silent for a moment, the only sound the sizzling of the greasy meat on the stove.

"I'm going to call the Truckee cops again," Luke said abruptly. He stood up and retrieved his house phone. Ted watched Luke pace across the room, occasionally speaking but not loud enough to decipher all of his responses. Luke returned, set the phone down, and looked at Sonya, then Ted.

"They still haven't found anything," he sighed. "Officer Boice didn't sound too hopeful."

"Surely they wouldn't stop looking so soon!" Sonya exclaimed.

"She said they are still searching, but I just got the sense they don't expect to find anything. Or they expect to find a body downstream," he mumbled.

"You never know. There are a lot of possibilities—" Ted said.

"Let's go back and keep looking. Maybe you'll recognize something of hers that they overlooked," Luke cut in, gazing questioningly at Sonya.

"Have they found any items other than her luggage and purse in the car?" Ted asked as he shifted on the stool. It was about as uncomfortable as any seat could be. Then again, he hadn't anticipated sitting here for this long, listening to the woman's scattered recounting of what happened. Ted still couldn't help but wonder how she remained so calm. Unaffected, even. Being speculative in nature, and armed with the knowledge from Jill about the bruises on the man's wrists, Ted's instincts told him there was more to this story.

"No," Luke replied. "Well, they said they found a sweater a few hundred yards down the river. We haven't seen it, but Sonya said it sounds like one of Kimmy's, at least from the description."

"That's easily explained by the shifting in the accident." Ted took another sip from his glass. "I'm sure the luggage bounced around, flew open."

"Is there something you can do, Mr. Benson? Luke mentioned you were a detective, although I know it isn't your jurisdiction." Sonya appeared earnest, but her voice didn't match. Ted slid off the stool, anxious to wake up his tingling legs.

"I'll see if I can poke around some," he promised. "Thanks for the OJ." Ted turned to Luke, nodding to indicate he wanted to speak with him privately. After a moment's pause, Luke seemed to understand.

"Hey, let me walk you out," he said as he stood with Ted.

Once they'd stepped on the small porch, Ted eyed the door. Luke slowly closed it.

"Do you know something you aren't saying?" Luke asked nervously.

"Do you?" Ted replied, more curtly than he'd intended. Luke looked startled.

"Why would you ask that?"

"It's just . . . something isn't right here. I can't put my finger on it." Ted lowered his voice. "Do you believe this woman?"

"I suppose. I haven't seen a reason not to."

"Okay, just . . . be careful. I'll see what I can find out, if anything. And I don't think it would be a good idea for you to head back up there. Let the search teams do their jobs. It's what they are trained for."

"I know," Luke sighed. "I know . . ."

"Have you spoken with Rachel today?" Ted changed the subject.

"No. I really haven't had the chance yet."

"Well, maybe see if she's up for a hike or something this afternoon. Get yourself out of the house." Ted began to walk toward his SUV. "I'll be in touch. And—keep your eyes open." On his way out, he scrawled down the license plate number for the rental car. *Can't hurt*, he thought.

Chapter Thirteen

The sun's glare on the barrel of the gun almost blinded her, and Rachel quickly shifted her gaze to the side. She tried to see his face.

"What do you want?" she managed to ask, silently telling herself to remain calm. The window was closed, not that it would matter if he pulled the trigger. There was no response; the silence was unnerving. Finally, the guy—at least, he looked like a male with his tall, wide outline—motioned with his weapon. The gesture implied he wanted them to get out of the car. Kristina was frozen next to her. Rachel did her best to speak without moving her lips.

"When I open this door, slam on the accelerator," she whispered. Was that calm, rational voice really her own?

"But—"

"Please." Assuming Kristina's silence meant consent, Rachel kept her eyes locked on the hand holding the gun while she raised both of hers into the air. "Okay. Just don't shoot. Whatever you want, you can take it."

Another beckoning movement with the gun.

"I'm going to reach my right hand down to open the door . . ." She moved her slowly. Although wanting to appear afraid, the trembling of her hand took no acting. Her left hand still raised, she slowly grasped the door handle with her right. At the same time, she quietly moved her leg, bringing her foot closer to the door. It clicked to open, and Rachel quickly turned her hips to the side to face outward, leaning back across the console. She kicked sideways, and the door whipped open as she yelled out, "Go!"

The force of the car door swinging open was diminished as the car lunged forward. Holding it open with all the leg strength she had, Rachel was relieved when it smacked hard against the attacker's gun-wielding hand. A shot rang out. Rachel didn't see, or feel, any bullet holes. The vehicle continued moving forward quickly. As she caught her breath, she yelled out, "You okay?"

"Yes, you?" Kristina responded as she swiftly turned the car onto the main street.

"I think so." Rachel took a deep breath, her body slightly trembling. She turned to look back as they weaved around the corner and saw the man running in the other direction. Rachel did a double take—she could swear he was wearing bright-orange shoes.

"Was that a carjacking? What the hell?" Kristina asked. Rachel noticed tears in her eyes.

"I don't think so. The guy approached on the passenger side, for starters. But it just didn't feel that way. I had the sense if we got out of the car, he intended to do something to *us*, not to the car." The adrenaline rush that had carried Rachel through the last few moments began to wane. The car's interior went silent for a moment as they put several blocks between the attacker and themselves.

"He could have shot us. What if your *sense* had been wrong?" Kristina's exasperated voice erupted. The frustrated tone caught Rachel off guard, and she paused before responding.

"I just . . . I reacted on instinct. It didn't feel like a car—"

"How would you know, Rachel? You ever been carjacked?" Kristina yelled.

"No, but—"

"Look, I haven't said much, but this time, you could have hurt someone besides yourself." Kristina pulled into the parking lot of an old diner, parked, and then turned toward her passenger. "Okay, learning to shoot, I get it after last summer. Self-defense courses— same deal. But you've been taking some big chances lately, and we're all worried about you." Rachel opened her mouth to respond, but she didn't know what to say. She had asked herself some of the same questions; she just hadn't realized anyone else had noticed.

"I'm sorry," Rachel finally managed.

Kristina shifted her gaze forward and spoke. "I don't know if it's about Luke. Or he just hasn't noticed. Maybe you can keep him in the dark because he hasn't known you that long. But those of us who have can see something is going on with you. We're worried." The car rocked as a large U-Haul truck drove past them. "Okay, just . . . if you want to talk to me, I'm here. But either way, maybe it's worth seeing a professional."

"I'll think about it," Rachel mumbled. The anxious yet excited feeling she'd experienced minutes ago was now completely gone. Kristina put the car back into gear, checked her mirror, and pulled back onto the street.

"It's a start," she finally said. "Now, you're the navigator." She lightly smacked the wheel. "Where should we go?"

"We report it, I guess," Rachel sighed. Focused once again on their situation, she dreaded filing another report with the police. Rachel's previous experiences didn't go very well. Her cell phone startled her, but relief swept over her when she saw it was Ted calling her back.

"Hey, Rachel," Ted said cheerfully.

"It is so great to hear your voice right now," she blurted out.

"Uh . . . what?" He sounded surprised.

"We just had a gun pulled on us." She heard a muffled sound. Was he laughing?

"My God. How do you get into these messes? What happened?"

"Are you amused by this? Really?" she quipped. Then she slowly began to join in. Kristina glanced her way with a strange look. It took only a few seconds for her to follow their lead.

"I hope you two feel better now," Ted eventually interjected.

"We do. Thanks." Rachel smiled and then explained what had happened.

After listening, asking only a couple of questions, Ted told her where the police station was in Reno. "Probably just the wrong place at the wrong time. What are the odds of anything else? Then again, knowing you . . ."

"Gee, I appreciate the vote of confidence." Rachel smirked.

"Just sayin'," he chuckled. "Now, what did you call for earlier?"

After quickly giving Kristina directions to the police station, Rachel explained their interest in the missing professor and finding out if there were any car accidents or odd incidents between Reno and the Mammoth Lakes area. "One of the students thought he drove a smaller tan car, but she wasn't certain which model. So . . . got any friends down there?" she asked, biting her lip.

"Not necessarily, but I don't see the harm in asking about car accidents. It's public information anyway." He sighed. "Isn't this the kind of favor your *private investigator* boyfriend could be doing for you? I think the distraction would be good for him."

"I'm not so sure. Telling him about Everett's project is one thing. Explaining that our little incident involved a gun—that's another. He's already stressed out."

"Got it. But just for the record, I still think you should let him know what you are up to."

"Suggestion noted," she replied.

"Uh-huh," he said. "And yes, I'm amused. So long as you don't actually get hurt." She could hear the beginning of a small laugh as he ended the call.

~

He wasn't exactly a close buddy with Luke, but Ted knew him well enough to know that Luke would not like what Rachel was getting involved in. Or at least the part where she wasn't telling him about the potential carjacking. But it wasn't Ted's relationship, so not his concern, he told himself. Ted sat at his small kitchen table, his laptop open searching the Internet to for highway patrol stations in the Mammoth Lakes area. After a few calls, he'd learned that no accidents involving an unidentified single driver had occurred within the last two weeks. Ted moved his chair back, staring out his kitchen window and wondering what other avenues he could pursue. Another idea occurred to him. He typed in a new search. Several tow companies for the area populated his browser; he began calling each, asking about unclaimed vehicles. By the fourth company he was losing hope fast. As he'd done three times, he again explained who he was and what he was seeking.

"Yeah, I might have what yer lookin' for out there," the man replied with a scratchy voice. Ted sat up, interested and so surprised at the possible lead that he knocked his steaming mug off the table. The man coughed and continued. "About a week ago, we did a tow from a hot springs lot. Not the easiest place to get in and out of, I'll tell you."

"Hot springs?" Ted asked, grabbing a hand towel. He'd heard about several hot springs east of Mammoth Lakes, including complaints about the Bureau of Land Management blocking roads to some of the lesser-known—and therefore typically locals-only—hot springs. But that was a long time ago.

"Hot Creek." The guy responded as if this were all the information Ted should need.

"I'm sorry, I'm not familiar . . ."

"Hot Creek Hot Springs. It's a developed area off the old fish hatchery road. Very popular with the skiers. You can Google it, I'm sure." Another small cough. "We were told this vehicle—a tan Mazda—had been sitting in the lot for several days. Cops had us tow it. There was no registration, and the VIN number had been scratched or somethin'. Looks like someone dumped it."

"Do you still have it?" Ted asked anxiously, wiping away the last drops of liquid from his floor.

"Yep, collecting dust out in our lot as we speak."

"Mind if I come check it out?" Ted wasn't looking to spend his entire day on the road, but at the same time, he was intrigued.

"Sure. Heck, we'd love it if ya hauled it off for us, too."

"Can't promise that, but I can get there in about three hours or so. That work?"

"I'll be here," the man responded.

Ted thanked him and dialed Rachel back to share the news.

"So maybe he did try to take the samples to the lab . . . ," she responded.

"What lab?" Ted asked.

~

"Sir, we may have a slight problem," his partner said when Carlton answered the phone.

"Now what?" He was only half-listening.

"Some ladies were sniffing around the lab at UNR." At this news, Carlton gave his full attention.

"Are you kidding?"

"Sir, I don't kid."

Smartass, Carlton thought.

He continued. "One of our friends gave me a call. He'd overheard them asking around. I drove over, and they were still there, chatting up some girls. When they were done, I followed them out to their car. I tried to stop them, but . . . well, they got away." Now this was news that made Carlton nervous.

"How did you 'try to stop them'?" He was certain he wasn't going to like the answer. Although he'd come through on occasion, his young cohort didn't think things through all of the time. At least when decisions had to be made on the fly.

"I had my gun and ordered them to get out of the car, but . . ."

"Enough. Did you get anything? Names? License plate?" Carlton worked hard to keep his voice calm.

"Plate number."

"Okay. Give it to me, and I'll see what I can find out." He wrote the number down and hung up without another word. *That dumbass kid pulled a gun out in bright daylight, next to a popular campus.* Taking the girl out on that hiking trail a few weeks back was questionable, but he'd been lucky. Now this. *How stupid is he?*

~

Luke noticed it was almost two p.m. How did the day go so fast already? Sitting on the edge of his bed, he glanced up at a picture of Rachel and Bella. He knew he hadn't been handling this situation well in terms of keeping in touch with her. It was at that moment the irony of his actions—or perhaps hypocrisy, if he was going to be honest with himself—hit him. He'd been upset when Rachel had shut him out during some of her recent stressful situations, not always keeping him up to speed when he felt he could have helped. And yet he was doing the same thing to her now. Not telling her the full extent of his shoulder pain, well, that was temporary; he figured he'd be fine soon. But this deal with his sister, and her friend— thank God Rachel wasn't the overly jealous type, or this could be far worse. Then again, he wouldn't mind if she did feel that way sometimes. But maybe that was just his ego talking.

"I'm going out for a walk. Want to join me?" Sonya's voice rang out from the other room.

"No thanks. I need to check in with a few people," he called out, deciding it was time to end his pity party and do something. Anything.

"All right."

The front door closed a few minutes later, and he stood up, stretching his arms over his head. The dull ache in his shoulder instantly grew. Luke hadn't been active enough the last few days. That was probably part of the problem. After opening his laptop, Luke retrieved the prescription bottle from his shaving kit and swallowed another Vicodin. His computer beeped, alerting him the operating system was loaded and ready for use.

Luke was anxious to learn more about his sister's interests. Sonya mentioned they were returning from a conference at UNR when the accident happened. He typed in the UNR website and searched for events; no recent conferences related to geology were listed. Luke checked the calendar from the previous week. Nothing. He thought Sonya said it was at the college, but maybe he misunderstood and it wasn't at UNR, just nearby. Or was it at Truckee Meadows Community College? He'd ask her later before spending more time trying to find it.

He searched for information on Kimmy's husband, the now deceased Edward Nunez. The usual links to Facebook and various people-finder websites popped up. A listing for an Edward Nunez, thirty-seven years old, in Berkeley, California, appeared to be the most likely match. The wife was, indeed, listed as Kim Nunez, thirty-one years old. Sonya had shown him a picture of Kimmy on her cell phone, although she said it was several years old. Luke was anxious to see something more recent. He'd tried looking off and on over the years but never had Kimmy's married name. He'd tried many of the same channels he used for work but oddly never found anything. Luke clicked to open Eddie's Facebook page and cursed when it didn't allow the public to see posts or pictures. He tried Kim Nunez. No Facebook, just more people-finding website links.

On a hunch, he typed in Sonya Blake. There was a picture-less generic Facebook page that indicated it was "born" in 2012. But otherwise, there were no social media sites under her name, either.

"Well, not everyone has a Facebook page," he said aloud. He'd ask Sonya a few questions when she got back. Luke closed the laptop and glanced at the picture of Rachel. Her hair was pulled back into a braid—her typical hairdo for hiking. She once referred to it as her "antitangle" strategy. Maybe she'd be interested in meeting up for dinner. And Ted was right. Luke needed a break. He also missed her and was excited at the prospect of some alone time with her. He dialed her number, but it went straight to voice mail.

"Damn," he swore under his breath before leaving a message. Luke stood up and walked out of the room.

Chapter Fourteen

The sun was already hugging the jagged ridgeline along the tall mountains that stretched along the west side of Highway 395. Ted had not been down this way in years; he'd forgotten how breathtaking it could be. The towering mountains were different here than near Tahoe. Although many peaks lacked the pine trees that covered other mountaintops in the Sierra Nevada, they were beautiful in their own way. He passed the turnoff for the June Lake Loop—another place he hadn't seen in years. Perhaps he should take the loop on his way home. In fact, Ted began to wonder if he'd been spending too much time working. Traveling just to see other places, even a few hours away, had become almost foreign to him. How long was it since he had taken a real vacation? Pondering this question and caught up in the scenery, Ted almost missed the turnoff for Minaret Road—the main route heading to Mammoth Lakes. Now would be a good time to turn on his GPS system.

As he entered town he was directed to the tow company's lot. After Ted pulled into the half-paved parking lot and opened his door, he was surprised to see a man with grey hair covered by a dirty cap standing just a few feet away. Smoke rose from the cigarette in his left hand.

"You Ted?" he asked in a friendly tone.

"Yes, got here as fast as I could," he replied.

"I'm Steve. It's over here." The man turned and walked past

several cars toward the corner of a small lot. Ted noticed the Mazda was in good shape, probably less than ten years old. It wasn't the kind of vehicle someone would dump, unless it had been used for something illegal, maybe. "It was unlocked, but there were no keys found."

"Mind if I take some time to search through it?" Ted asked. Steve paused and Ted retrieved his badge. After a quick glance, the man nodded.

"Be my guest. I just got another call, so I'll be in the office tracking down one of my guys."

Ted nodded, reaching for the driver's side door as Steve sauntered away. He stopped, first retrieving a pair of latex gloves from his pocket. After all, someone had tried to obliterate the VIN number. When he opened the door, he checked around, looking for a label that would contain identifying information. He located remnants of what was likely a sticker, but it was gone.

When Ted sat in the driver's seat, one of the first anomalies he noted was the closeness of the seat to the steering wheel. He didn't know what the professor looked like, but this seemed awfully close for an average American male, unless the man was thin or short. Ted leaned over and opened the glove box. Other than some fast-food napkins and old salt and pepper packets, it contained nothing of importance. In fact, there were no papers, no maps, or any other identifiers. Rachel had mentioned something about samples, but there were no boxes, bottles, or vials.

"Curious," he whispered, looking around. Ted noticed a small lever displaying the image of a trunk lid and pulled. He heard a clicking sound and climbed out of the car to check the trunk. It was empty, with the exception of a spare tire and a few scattered tools. Ted leaned in, feeling around for anything odd. There was nothing out of the ordinary. He walked back to the front and peered around the lower part of the windshield. There it was—the VIN number plate, or what was left of it. If he were officially on the case, he could have the local CSIs check it out. Ted had learned a lot about what the crime scene investigators could and could not recover from evidence. But he wasn't on the case. Yet, according to Rachel, a missing-person report had been filed by a concerned coworker at the college. Ted removed his cell phone from his pocket and dialed the Reno police department. After a few transfers, he was eventually connected to the officer in charge of the missing-person report. Ted explained who he was and what he'd found.

"I think it's your professor's car."

"How, exactly, did a South Lake Tahoe police officer come to locate this car in Mammoth Lakes?" The abruptness in the man's tone surprised Ted.

"Long story, and I'm happy to explain and file any reports you need. But I think it's worth getting this car back to Reno and taking a look at it."

"I'll decide what's worth it," the officer snapped.

This guy sounds like a real winner, Ted thought. "Of course, officer."

"Give me your information, and I'll let you know what we decide to do." Working hard to remain pleasant, in lieu of a sarcastic response that would no doubt earn him an enemy he didn't need, Ted provided his name and number, saying he'd appreciate the follow-up. The man grunted and hung up.

"What an ass," he whispered under his breath. Ted stepped out of the car and walked toward the office. He told the owner what he'd found and relayed his call to Reno. "I'd like to check out these hot springs. Can you give me directions?"

"Good idea. Always relaxing after a lot of driving." The man winked. Ted didn't correct his misunderstanding. Although, Ted surmised, maybe it would feel good to take a quick dip. Problem was he had no swimsuit or other clothes. The decision to drive down here had been spontaneous. Even if there was no one else around, he was not one to go in his birthday suit.

"Sounds good to me," Ted replied as the man scrawled directions on a sheet of paper. After thanking him once more, Ted walked toward his SUV and glanced at his watch. It was already after four p.m. He knew the lab was nearby but wasn't sure exactly where. Chances were they'd be closed soon. Maybe it would be worth getting a room for the night so he didn't have to drive back to Tahoe so late. He didn't have to work tomorrow—why not enjoy some downtime? Ted contemplated this as he followed the rough "map" to the hot springs and was surprised to see about half a dozen vehicles parked in the small lot next to a building that appeared to contain restrooms. The road was high above the river that the hot springs flowed into it.

Ted parked and walked along a well-traveled paved path as it approached the steep riverbanks, peering over to see the waters below. About ten people bobbed in the swirling currents. This was not the typical safe constructed hot spring "tub" like the one he was familiar with at Grover Hot Springs near Markleeville. Here, there were several warning signs posted about the changes in water temperature and other hazards. If the professor came here to relax after dropping off the samples, maybe he had drowned or had experienced some other kind of innocent accident no one had yet discovered. Although that was one possibility, Ted still intended to check with the lab Rachel had mentioned to see if he ever made contact or left samples that had been misplaced. It was a long shot, but sometimes things got overlooked. This, of course, confirmed his decision to spend the night in town. He'd head out to this "bug lab" in the morning. The sound of laughing below him brought Ted out of his reverie.

That does look quite relaxing. He glanced down at the soothing waters below, where steam rose in small patches. The water shouldn't hurt the shorts he was wearing. It would just be a soggy ride into Mammoth later, but he could deal. He continued down the path, a large grin emerging on his face.

~

Rachel had offered to drive Kristina's car back to South Lake Tahoe. Her friend was still shaken from the encounter with the gunman. *Who am I kidding? So am I,* she thought to herself. But maybe due to her recent experiences with being shot at, she was able to delay her own reaction to it for a while. Odd, she felt . . . calm. Before Rachel could analyze that realization any further, her phone beeped.

"Can you see who called?" she asked, pulling her phone from the pocket of her light coat and handing it to Kristina.

"Luke."

"Oh."

"Want me to play it, or, hmm, might I overhear sex talk that would give me nightmares?" Kristina laughed, and this time it wasn't nervous.

"Ha ha. You wish. Heck, I wish, given how things have been going lately," she smirked. "Yes, go ahead and play it for me on speaker."

Rachel was relieved to hear that he sounded more like himself than last night. It was a short message—asking if she was up for dinner out.

"You going to mention what happened today?" Kristina wondered.

"At some point. Guess I'll feel that one out." Rachel was still distracted, catching herself checking the rearview mirror a few times too many, half-expecting to see a car speeding up behind them. Maybe the incident had brought back more feelings from the previous summer than she'd considered. On the other hand, Luke's message, and the more regular sound of his voice, brought back some feelings she'd like to relive.

"Men! I am still surprised you would end up with someone so different. A mountain biker? *And* a snowboarder, no less!" Kristina teased.

"I'm working on it. I might have him convinced to try skis this winter . . . if we get any snow." She sighed, playing along.

"That would up the sexy factor for you, I bet."

"Always. Although frankly I don't need much help in that department. One look at the man and I melt anyhow," Rachel laughed.

"I don't need details."

"Don't worry, I won't share them. You might steal him away." Rachel reached forward and turned the knob to blow cooler air. "But honestly, one or two sticks, wheels or boots, I don't care as long as he wants to be outside."

"I agree. So, is he still on your case about hiking alone?"

"A little. I remind him he goes biking alone, and that has generally ended the discussion." She smiled.

"Sounds like a wise man," Kristina replied. Before she set Rachel's phone down, it rang. She glimpsed the display. "It's Ted."

"Oh, answer it!" Rachel said excitedly and Kristina touched the screen.

"Hey, Ted, did you find anything?" Rachel immediately asked. She was probably blowing out Kristina's eardrums, but she couldn't help yelling into the speakerphone. Kristina's car did not have a Bluetooth option.

"I think I found the professor's car." Ted launched into a rundown of his afternoon. "Not sure why it was out at the hot springs, though. I asked some locals there about overnight stays, and they said it was technically only open during sunlight hours, but enforcement could be a bit lax."

"Are you heading back now?" Kristina asked as she changed the phone into her other hand, holding it above the console so they could both hear better.

"Actually, no. I'm taking a night off and staying here in Mammoth Lakes. Found a nice little bed-and-breakfast, and I—"

"Who are you, and what have you done with Ted Benson?" Rachel joked.

"Rachel, you haven't known me that long, my young friend. I just might surprise you." He laughed. "Actually, I plan to head over to that lab tomorrow and see if I can find out something."

"Awesome. Oh, ask them if they've done any IDs for the professor in the past. It's possible he collected seasonal samples and may have sent previous sets, depending on the study."

"Good suggestion. Will do."

They both thanked him then ended the call. "I think that man is underpaid for the good work he does," Rachel said.

"It also sounds like he needs to loosen up a little, from what you've told me," Kristina responded. "In fact, I'd be happy to help him do just that if I could join him in those hot springs . . ." Kristina grinned. "He's pretty hot."

"That's right, you *have* met him." Rachel had forgotten they'd been introduced at a recent birthday party for a mutual friend. She recalled they were the only ones eating veggie burgers, which had been left off the grill. "And yes, I noticed. But I'll never admit that in public. Seriously, though, he's like a big brother."

"To *you*."

"Ask him out," Rachel suggested.

"I just might. So, speaking of sexy men, are you going to meet up with Luke tonight?"

"Nice segue," Rachel chuckled. "I guess I'll call him when I'm back and see what's what."

~

Carlton stared at the e-mail he'd just received. It listed the owner of the green car his partner had failed to stop.

"Kristina Smith," he read aloud. The official address on file with California was a post office box in South Lake Tahoe. "It's still easy enough to find you," he mumbled. Carlton decided he'd look into the situation himself. No room for screwups. If he were lucky, Sylvester would never know.

"Actually, if I'm lucky, these girls won't follow up," he said under his breath. He decided to check out the owner of the vehicle first and keep an eye on her—he could worry about the passenger later if he had to. Perhaps it was a one-time deal. Maybe just a hopeful student looking for a position in the graduate department and his young partner overreacted. They'd been very careful to tie up loose ends in a variety of ways so that nothing would appear too obvious. For now, it was best to lay low. He hadn't realized he was staring at the screen until his cell phone alerted him to a new text. Sonya had sent him a short note proclaiming that everything was "on track." Carlton smiled.

Chapter Fifteen

After parting ways at the South Lake Tahoe "Y," Rachel had promptly driven home and walked next door to retrieve Bella. Her neighbor was quite the talker and this time kept Rachel on the porch for over ten minutes as she recounted how Bella and Citrus, her Labradoodle, had run in circles in the yard playing chase. Rachel had once inquired about where the name Citrus had come from. The response had been a long story involving an abandoned dog, a picnic, a squirrel, and a fruit salad. Managing to eventually extricate herself from the conversation, Rachel returned home and called Luke back, suggesting they meet at Lake Tahoe Pizza Company.

An hour later, she was sitting across from him in a small booth. He looked better, more alert than last time she'd seen him. His brown hair was mussed chaotically, but it was a sexy look for him. He recounted his earlier conversation with Ted and the intermittent discussions with Sonya about his sister.

"I was hoping to ask her more, but she hadn't come back from her walk yet. I was more anxious to see you, so I left a note." He smiled, reaching for her hand. She leaned toward him across the table.

"Thank you for inviting me. I was worried about you. Still am," she said quietly.

"I'll be fine. I guess the shock is beginning to wear off. I know they are still searching for Kimmy, but think it might be time to start accepting that her body washed away, and it was just a horrible accident." He looked down at the tall glass of beer in front of him. Per Ted's request, Rachel hadn't mentioned the information from Jill about the handcuff-type bruising. Ted suspected Luke would take the information and raise hell to get answers. Now there were *two* things she wasn't telling Luke. Perhaps Rachel had, on occasion, been too fast to judge others who made decisions to hold things back because here she was doing the same thing "for his own good," or so she told herself.

"Well, don't give up hope. But if the worst case comes true, at least you've had the chance to learn where she's been. And that she's been happily married. That's something." It was a poor consolation, Rachel thought to herself, but he still smiled.

"True."

Their pizza arrived, and Rachel sat back in her seat. As Luke reached for the first slice, he asked, "So, can you distract me? How did the meeting go yesterday? What have you been up to today?" Rachel took a sip of wine, transferred a slice of pizza to her plate, and doused it with red pepper flakes. She noticed Luke smirk and almost laughed.

She talked about the planning commission meeting and then briefly referred to the news about Everett before mentioning what she called a "quick trip" with Kristina to see if they could learn why his position was cut so abruptly. Rachel explained the missing professor, the odd circumstances of the two students, and the mystery of the lab samples, but carefully omitted the less pleasant parts of their visit.

"A lot of coincidences, I agree." He paused and then looked straight at her. "You've been busy."

"So have you," Rachel countered. She looked at him as she tipped her glass of wine. Their eyes met in an intense and knowing glare. She set the glass down. They both remained silent. Rachel saw Luke's gaze move to her lips. She knew that look and welcomed it.

"Take the rest to go?" he asked in haste.

"Yes," she replied, almost before he'd finished his question. Five minutes later they'd paid their bill and exited into the parking lot. He walked with her to her pickup. She opened the door, placed the to-go box inside, and turned around to say something. She was pleasantly surprised when Luke quickly closed the distance between them, pushed her up against her pickup, and crushed his lips onto hers. She sighed, reaching up and running her hands through his hair. Her fingers gently glided down to his neck and then pulled his head toward her, deepening the kiss. Rachel felt the light touch of his palm on her back, lightly stroking up and down with a subtle pressure that drew her hips closer to his. His kiss was so intense, his tongue gentle and yet demanding, she wasn't sure she could take this much longer. She gently pushed her hand against his chest. Luke moved back, his mouth pausing barely an inch away from hers. They were both breathing hard.

"We should take this somewhere else," she whispered.

"I think so."

"Follow me to my place?"

He nodded and pulled her against him for one more kiss. Finally, they parted. Rachel jumped into her truck so fast she almost tore the seat cover. This is what they'd been missing lately. This intensity. She hadn't been sure why, but now she didn't care. All that mattered was getting home and feeling his bare skin against hers as soon as possible.

~

Sonya was annoyed. She'd returned to Luke's place to find a short note about meeting up with Rachel for dinner. The scrawled message indicated she was welcome to any food in his house. Typical. His sister was still missing, likely dead, but all he was concerned with was getting laid. Well, it did give her a chance to browse without interruption. She had to wonder what kind of person was so trusting of someone he'd just met. He believed every word she'd said. Not that she was complaining; it was exactly what she'd hoped for.

"So, Mr. Luke Reed, time to find out a bit more about you," she said as she gently pushed his bedroom door open. The first thing she noticed was a laptop positioned on a small desk across the room. He actually left it there out in the open, almost begging anyone to go through his files. *What an idiot.* She walked over to it and moved her fingers across the touchpad. The screen lit and the page asked for a password.

"Really?!" she exclaimed. She turned and looked around his room. It was mostly bare, decorated only with a few nice paintings and carved bears, as if he were transitioning from having decent taste in the arts to becoming another uncultured mountain man. At least, that's how she viewed all people who would live in small towns in the woods like this. Sonya opened the drawers in the desk below his laptop. Nothing interesting was inside—just the usual paper, notepads, and pencils. She looked through his drawers, checking underneath the clothes and careful to put them back as she'd found them. Nothing unusual was hidden there, either. As she checked his nightstand drawer, the picture of Rachel posed with a black-and-white dog caught her eye. It was sitting next to a small lamp on the nightstand.

"Gold digger," she said, imagining no other reason such a woman would be interested in Luke Reed. She resisted the urge to slam the picture down, but left it untouched and in place. Carefully she closed the drawer and looked around again. Sonya noticed the bathroom door was ajar. Maybe he hid his documents in there. Who knew what went on in the minds of men? She went through all of the drawers in the vanity, finding nothing, with one exception. A prescription bottle for Vicodin was tucked into a drawer. The label showed it had just been filled two weeks ago, and the bottle was already half-empty.

"Now this bit of information could come in handy," she said aloud before placing the bottle back where she'd found it. For now, she had to focus on her primary task. Perhaps he kept his important documents at his office, not at home. She turned the light off, stepped out of the room, and placed the door in the slightly ajar position he'd left it in.

Chapter Sixteen

Rachel lay on her side next to Luke, her fingertips stroking light circles on his chest. He reached for her hand and held it.

"I've missed you. Not sure where you or I went, but . . . I missed you," he said, gently placing her palm against his lips.

"Me too."

"And I missed *that*, too," he laughed.

"Agreed." They both heard a slight nudging sound at the bedroom door. "I think someone else needs some attention now."

"I'll let her in," he said, and Rachel watched as he slid from beneath the sheets. He was an avid mountain biker. It did well for him, she thought. He opened the door, and Bella burst in, jumping up on the foot of the bed. Luke slid back under the sheets and asked, "What's that grin about?"

"Just enjoying the scenery." Bella quickly intruded, standing between them and savagely wagging her tail. Luke appeared to be considering a response but paused as Bella demonstrated one of her more charming moves. Her back legs still standing, she dropped the front of her body onto the bed, her two front paws splayed out in front of her, nose resting on top. It was immediately followed by "the stare."

"I know I left you home twice today, but you spent a lot of time with Citrus, girl. You can't complain," Rachel playfully reminded Bella as she rubbed her neck.

"I thought you just ran down to UNR and back," Luke remarked, his fingers scratching the underside of Bella's chin.

"We had to wait to file the report, and—"

"What report?" Luke inquired. *Oh no, she'd slipped.* The cat would be out of the bag soon enough. Rachel paused, deciding it was best to tell him the whole story from start to finish. Afterward, she waited for his reply.

"First, I'm glad you are both okay. But second, what the hell, Rachel? Why wouldn't you tell me about something like that? And what were you thinking with that door maneuver? Is your life worth her car?" As his voice elevated, Bella's tail slowed and then stopped.

"Calm down. I didn't want to worry you. You've had enough on your mind—"

"Really? That's your excuse?" At his clipped reply, Bella stood, moved backward, jumped off of the bed, and left the room.

"I was going to tell you. I just didn't think I needed to call you up right away."

"But throughout dinner, you carried on and on and never mentioned this. Why?"

"Maybe *this* is why!" Her temper flared. "Would you feel the need to call me up right away and tell me if something happened to you? Lord knows you get into some precarious positions in your job."

"But . . . that's different," he rebutted, reaching down next to the bed for his shirt.

"How so?" she demanded.

"One, I'm trained. Two, I'm stronger," he said, pausing. "You keep doing these things on your own without thinking or running it by me first."

"Luke, I'll concede the training bit. But I didn't go to Reno expecting anything dangerous. We intended to question students, period. But as for getting upset with me for, what, having a mind of my own? Being independent? I can't believe we're back to this conversation again!" She reached for the robe near her side of the bed.

"It's just. Well, I worry about you," he said, softening his voice.

"I worry about you, too. But do I tell you to change your job?

84

Not take chances? No. Because I respect that's who you are. I just wish you could do the same for me." She looked away. The room went silent. "I'm sorry for not telling you sooner, but I won't apologize for failing to run my decisions by you first."

"Okay, I hear you. But I can't stop being who I am, either. I'm trying here. You aren't like anyone I've ever met before," he conceded.

"Neither are you," she responded, her voice lightening. She looked over at him and he leaned in and placed a soft kiss on her lips.

"I'm going to keep trying. Just want you to know that," he said.

"I will, too." She leaned back and looked at him. "I know I can be stubborn. But I appreciate that you call me on it. I honestly do, even if I don't necessarily agree."

"Can I get that in writing?" he said with a grin. She punched him with a pillow. "Well, I'd better get back and check on my houseguest and see if there's any news." The last few words came out as a whisper. She nodded.

"Good night, Rachel." He kissed her again, his lips lingering on hers for a few extra moments before reluctantly leaving.

~

As usual, Ted was awake before sunrise. He had already taken a long walk on the streets of Mammoth Lakes and finished his breakfast by nine. After calling the lab to make sure someone would be in, he checked out of his room and drove straight there. It was an easy route; he'd checked where it was last night after his dip in the hot springs. He knocked, and a young woman in her late teens or early twenties opened the door.

"Officer Benson?" she asked as she removed a band from her hair. Ted noticed the contrast in color, from full-on black hair on top to bleached light-blond below a straight horizontal line about ear height. The style reminded him of his cousin's teenage daughter.

"Yes. I take it you don't get many drop-ins?" He smiled. She shook her head.

"No, but come on in." She gestured inside, opening the door. As Ted stepped into the building, his senses were hit with a strong alcohol odor, not the pleasant drinking kind. He winced.

"Sorry, it's probably the ethanol. We use it to preserve the inverts . . . I mean the insects we collect from streams and wetlands, stuff like that."

"Got it." He glanced around the office, observing microscopes, sample bottles, and marked-up whiteboards. There were several tall cabinets in the back of the room.

"So, what can we help you with?" She sat in a worn leather chair, haphazardly patched with duct tape, and turned toward a desk stacked high with papers and a laptop. "You mentioned a professor from Reno?" Ted glimpsed a lab stool nearby and sat down. It was no more comfortable than Luke's kitchen stool. He tried to hide his discomfort.

"Thanks. It's a long story, but are you familiar with a Professor Scottsfield from UNR?" He watched, resigned as she shook her head.

"No, but I'm not the only one running samples here. Um . . ." She leaned over, shifting around some of the papers on her desk. "Let me check the recent logs."

"My friend mentioned that it's possible your lab may have run some samples on a seasonal basis?"

"Good point. I'll look further back," she responded enthusiastically. She didn't turn around but called out as she continued fingering through papers on the desk, "Cecil, can you come in here for a minute?" Her sudden loudness caught Ted off guard.

"Coming," a male voice echoed from across the room. Ted hadn't even realized anyone else was there. A short, slightly overweight man appeared, standing beside one of the tall cabinets in the back. His grey hair suggested he was likely several years older than the woman, but his face appeared extremely youthful.

"Do you know a Professor Scottsfield? From Reno?" she asked the man. He looked briefly at Ted and then back at her.

"Might. What's the deal?"

"Hi, I'm Officer Benson from South Lake Tahoe; I'm trying to help a friend locate this professor that went missing a few weeks ago." He held his hand out. The lab technician responded by holding up two gloved hands. Ted nodded, returning his own to his pockets. "I understand he may have dropped some insect samples by here, either very recently or perhaps in the past year?"

"You know, this sounds vaguely familiar," Cecil said. "Let me check something." He walked back to his space behind the cabinet, and Ted heard him typing—if you could call one letter at a time typing—although Ted was certainly not one to judge. He would never win any speed contests in that department. The technician reemerged.

"Yes, about six months ago, he brought samples by the lab. I think he talked about getting in touch for us to run another set this fall. But now that you mention it, I haven't heard from him."

"Can you tell me anything about the project these samples were related to? It could help us figure out where he is." Cecil looked at his coworker, both shrugging in unison.

"Sure, don't see why not. Come on back." He waved at Ted as he turned. A moment later Ted had relocated from the uncomfortable stool to a lopsided folding chair. After sitting down, he noticed a magnet haphazardly attached to the back of the cabinet that read "Cecil's Desk."

Ted watched the man's slow pecking continue. He had removed the gloves, and Ted noticed two fingers wrapped together, as if he had broken a bone. *That could explain the slow typing,* he thought.

"It looks like the samples were related to a Superfund site." He read from the screen and then typed in another few letters.

"I've heard that term, but remind me again what that is?" Ted asked, retrieving his small notebook and pen.

"It's a federal program that pays for environmental cleanup of hazardous materials. For example, there are places where there were large chemical spills decades ago, where the soil may still be contaminated. There's not always someone to pay for cleanup. Like, maybe the responsible party is long out of business, or they didn't discover it until decades later. So they have this Superfund program that can cover the costs." Cecil turned toward Ted. "Unfortunately, there are far more places with hazardous conditions than there are dollars to pay for the cleanup or people to hold accountable."

Ted nodded as he hurriedly took notes and then asked, "Where is the project located that he was involved in?"

"It appears to be somewhere near Susanville, up north of Reno. Do you know where that is?"

"Yes, I'm familiar with the area. Is there anything more you can tell me about the project?"

"I've got a contact for the CDFW office up there, and we were tasked with confirming the IDs of the macroinvertebrates." He opened the desk drawer, retrieved a stack of business cards, and began shuffling through them.

"Okay, do you just report on the identifications then? Or are you asked to do any other analysis?"

"Just the IDs." Cecil appeared to find the card he was seeking. He continued. "I think they have students go through them first, then bring them to us to confirm their work is correct before they use the results in any official capacity." He leaned back, and his chair almost fell over. He recovered quickly, grabbing his desk to pull himself forward. "Dang chair," he murmured, his face slightly flushed.

"The study stuff makes sense," Ted inserted, suppressing a chuckle. "Can you provide me with that contact name? Also, would it be possible to get a copy of the results of the previous samples you ID'd several months ago?"

"I can give you the name and number for this—er—Mr. Holden up in Susanville, but UNR contracted with us for the results, so you'll need to get that info from UNR. Sorry," he sighed, reaching for a nearby sticky-note pad.

"I understand. I do appreciate the information you've provided. It might be what we need to find out where this man is, or what happened to him." Ted stood, eager to be out of the chair. "Is there anyone else I can talk to who might have dealt with him?"

"I can check around, but it looks like the tech who did the IDs on the last samples moved back east a few months ago. I can get in touch with him and ask him to contact you, if that would help?" Cecil stood. His head was about chest height to Ted, making him feel awkward standing next to the man in the small space. Ted heard the sound of a printer shooting out paper.

"Yes, please," Ted said, watching as Cecil turned and reached somewhere behind his desk, returning with printed documents in hand.

"I hope this is helpful. Sorry I can't tell you anything more."

"Thank you." Noticing the man hadn't put the gloves back on, Ted put his hand out again. Cecil awkwardly complied with a very light up-and-down shake. Ted pulled a business card from his wallet. "I appreciate you asking your ex-coworker to give me a call, too."

A few minutes later Ted was back in his SUV calling Rachel to share what he'd learned.

~

Kristina invited Everett to stop by her house around eleven a.m. As usual, he arrived exactly on time. The dark circles under his eyes suggested he hadn't slept well since receiving the news about his AmeriCorps position.

"How ya doin'?'" she asked sympathetically, waving him inside toward her small sofa. Her cat, Nemo, immediately emerged from behind the couch and jumped onto his lap. Not at all surprised, Everett absently reached up and began stroking the orange-and-white striped fur of the tabby—exactly what the cat expected, Kristina thought to herself. It was a well-choreographed setup for all human visitors.

"I'm still hanging in there." An attempt at a smile followed.

"Rachel just called. It's a long story, but first, we think that we've located Professor Scottsfield's car." Everett sat up so quickly that he startled Nemo. The cat stood, waited, and then nestled back down on his lap.

"Is he okay?"

"It was only his car. Our officer friend found it down in the Mammoth Lakes area." Everett seemed to digest this for a moment, glancing at the floor and then back at Kristina.

"Isn't that near the aquatic research lab?" he asked. She nodded. "I don't understand. You found his car, but not him? Where did he go?"

"Don't know. However, we wondered what you could tell us about a Superfund site connected to your work? Does that ring any bells?" Kristina noticed he looked confused, so she rephrased. "Do you recall any Superfund sites, perhaps up by Susanville?" She watched as he appeared lost in thought for a moment, eyes focused on the cat's slowly swishing tail.

"That sounds familiar. Would an old mining site be a Superfund project?" Everett inquired. He appeared more energetic than when he'd first arrived.

"Around the West, that's fairly common. Old mining operations from decades, in fact centuries, ago are still spewing toxic chemicals into the environment." Kristina took a sip from the coffee mug she'd just filled and asked, "Want something to drink?"

"A glass of water would be nice," he said. "Thank you." She stood up and walked into the kitchen.

"Were you helping with any projects like that?"

"Now that you said the name, I do think the professor planned to have me help with one. In fact, I remember he had to correct me on the program name. I kept saying *super fun*. Professor Scottsfield once laughed and said it could be called that for researchers who loved the work, but that most people probably wouldn't agree." He paused as Kristina handed him a cold glass. "He said they were collecting samples from a project and running tests on the water, sediment, and the bodies of the macroinvertebrates. He wanted to have someone identify the invertebrates and asked if I'd be interested. They had found some anomalies in their previous sample, and he talked about trying to locate the files for a nearby Superfund site. But I believe it was a project that had already been completed years ago. I do not know what they were looking for. Why would this matter?"

"We don't know. But . . . something seems weird. The professor goes missing. The man he was working with in Susanville was transferred to a remote area, out of contact. Another student quits out of the blue, and the most recent samples they collected disappeared." Kristina took another long sip. "Your position is cut, and no one knows why. Oh, and it's probably unrelated, but one of the undergraduate students had an accident about six weeks ago. She was hiking and fell—she died." At this, Everett sagged.

"Danielle. I met her once. I heard about her accident. Very sad. She seemed nice," he reminisced. Kristina nodded, letting a moment pass.

"Yes, it is," she agreed and then pushed her sleeves up her arms before asking the next question. "Everett, did you ever receive any files related to this Superfund project?"

"Not yet. Professor Scottsfield e-mailed me—maybe over a month ago—and said he would contact me when they had new samples ready. I never heard from him after that."

"Okay. Is there anyone you met who might be able to get you more information?"

"I cannot think of any people right now," he replied. He continued to massage Nemo's back as he gulped down more water. The silence was broken by a sound not unlike an engine roaring to life. Nemo had started to purr.

"If you can think of someone . . . the aquatic research lab said they could provide files from past samples they examined on this project only if the university requested it."

"You think his research has something to do with my position? And the professor's disappearance?"

Kristina nodded, waiting for his reaction.

"Kris, this does not sound good. I mean . . . it does not sound safe."

"Well, any time we get involved in a project we risk upsetting people." Kristina recalled the fear she felt when she'd first seen the man with the gun approaching their car in Reno. She raised her coffee mug, hoping Everett didn't notice the slight tremble in her hand. After a moment, she continued. "This is just another project. But what they did to you—it's not right."

He did not agree nor disagree but just nodded slightly and then spoke. "And Rachel is helping you?"

"Yes. Honestly, I think she likes the distraction. We were both upset by that last commissioners' meeting, plus this big new resort proposed in North Shore. We both need something else to focus on for a while. And I suspect—although she hasn't said much—that things with Luke have been a bit rocky lately."

"Ah, Mr. Lukas." He smiled. "That is unfortunate. Rachel is a good woman."

It was still amusing to Kristina how Everett seemed to treat them both as if they were many years apart, yet Rachel was less than five years older than him, and Kristina just a few more. She suppressed a smile and asked, "Well, what do you think? Might you know anyone who could request the files?"

"I will, as you say, give it some thought." Everett set his glass down and then carefully picked up the loud bundle of fur on his legs. The cat sagged like a limp rag as he moved the creature from lap to sofa.

"Thank you for coming by." Kristina stood, knowing not to take umbrage at Everett's abrupt decision to leave. He was not one to linger.

"I am very thankful you and Rachel are so concerned. But I do not want you to get into any trouble doing this for me, either."

"We won't." She had decided there was no reason to think the gun incident in Reno was related to Everett's situation, so she held the information back. Less than ten minutes after he left her phone rang. *That was fast*, she thought as she noticed Everett's number on the caller ID.

"I called a student I met at the university who was learning entomology—I mean, how to identify the bugs." He paused.

Kristina guessed he was used to having to explain his profession.

"He knows one of the girls at the lab. I think he has a crush on her," he speculated. "He said he would call her and see if she can send him the previous reports."

Kristina stood up from her computer. "Everett, this is great! How soon will he let you know?"

"He is trying to contact her now. I will call you back when I hear from him."

After the call ended, Kristina sent Rachel a text, letting her know they might have a way to learn more about this mysterious project.

~

Carlton was parked about a block down the street, watching the woman's house. When he had spotted the boy arriving earlier, he called his partner with a description. They both agreed the visitor was probably the AmeriCorps student from Germany. Given a few calls had been made to expedite the kid's return to his homeland, Carlton had hoped he'd be busy packing, preparing for the long flight. Yet they had been warned the visa could not likely be revoked so quickly. Regardless, the idea that the same woman who was poking around at UNR was now having this guy over to her place was not a good sign. Thankfully, Carlton had taken the extra precaution of having a work associate—who happened to also be a skilled hacker—begin tracking her phone calls the night before. Carlton had also done some online digging to learn the basics about the woman.

Ten minutes after arriving, the young man left the house and walked back to his car. Carlton waited several minutes longer, but the woman did not follow him. He placed a call to check whether she'd made or received any phone calls. Apparently she had contacted a number in Vermont earlier in the morning. It was likely a family call, Carlton figured; he'd learned she was originally from Vermont. Next, she'd called the German. Her most recent call traced back to a local number for a Rachel Winters. Carlton decided it would be prudent to keep an eye on both of the women as well as the European kid. Frustrated, he dialed his partner again.

"I need you to keep an eye on someone up in South Shore," he commanded when his partner answered.

"Let me guess. One of those girls from the car?" Carlton was surprised. Normally his partner didn't make connections that quickly. It often seemed as if his brain needed a moment to boot up before he could think.

"Yes. I'll be focusing on the driver, named Kristina Smith. I want you to find out what you can about a Rachel Winters. I suspect she was the passenger."

"That bitch who slammed me with the door? I'd love to have a follow-up visit with that one," he muttered. Carlton sensed too much enthusiasm about this task and grew wary.

"No contact, just a visual. That's the order. Can you handle that?" He waited, wondering if this assignment would be a mistake. But Sylvester had been very clear about how to "train" his new partner. Carlton was doing his best to be patient, but it had been difficult not to just shoot the kid a few times to shut him up. He heard a sigh and then a mumbled response.

"Yes, I can handle that."

"Good. Now find out what you can about her, and get up here. I expect a report within two hours. That should give you enough time to locate her basic specs and drive up. Remember—just watch."

"Got it." The reply sounded sarcastic, but Carlton let it slide.

Chapter Seventeen

"I think they are giving up," Sonya said to Luke after talking to a police officer in Truckee. A tear slipped down her cheek as she set the phone down. She hoped Luke would notice. He was sitting at his small kitchen table, tapping on his laptop. He paused, taking a sip of what she counted as his third cup of coffee. If anyone could justify the fancy coffeemaker in his kitchen, this man could.

"It's only been what—seventy-two hours?" he said, exasperation in his voice. "They wouldn't do that; it's too fast."

"They claim they've covered everything they can. Although they didn't say it, I feel like they are winding things down . . ." Her voice trailing off, Sonya sat on one of the stools. She nervously tapped her spoon against an empty bowl of cereal.

"I've never heard of a search being called off that quickly. I don't see it." He swallowed more coffee.

"Like I said, just a sense I have from how they are talking. Maybe they aren't officially calling it off, but they certainly aren't expecting to find her."

Luke didn't respond. He was looking out his kitchen window into the distance. Annoyed with the silence, Sonya stood and placed her dishes in the sink. She had managed not to give away her frustration when earlier this morning he'd apologized for returning so late the night before. She'd responded that it was fine; the last thing she wanted to do was interfere with his personal life, and he seemed to accept her feigned sincerity. Now, ironically, she hoped he'd leave again, whether to spend time with Rachel or do something else. Anything but go to his office—because that's what she intended to do the first chance she had.

"I . . . can't just sit here and wait for news," he finally said.

"Maybe it would help to talk to Rachel? Or your friend Ted?" she suggested.

"I'm debating about driving back up to Truckee," he admitted, finally looking at her.

Sonya was pleased the wet streak on her cheek hadn't yet dried.

Luke continued. "But I'm being selfish. Here you've known her for years, yet I haven't seen her since we were kids. How are you handling all of this?"

"I don't know. I can't imagine she's gone. I also feel, well, guilty." She planted the seed carefully. Luke's expression grew curious. She had overheard his cop friend warning him to be careful, presumably about her. So she'd decided it might be best to come up with a story to explain any reservations people might have about her.

"Why?" he asked.

Perfect, she thought. "There's, well, something I haven't told you. I just—I feel awful. You've been so kind through this and I—" She stopped speaking and looked down at the floor in front of her.

"What is it?" he queried, scooting his chair around a few inches to face her.

"I'm so sorry . . . I had an affair with Eddie," she confessed, meeting his gaze and hastily continuing, speaking quickly as anxious people often do. "It was a few months ago, and it just kind of happened one night. I couldn't look Kimmy in the eye for two weeks. I told her I had a horrible flu so I could take some time away from her. I had planned to lay it all out to her once we were in Reno while Eddie was busy gambling. But there just wasn't a good time. And now—" She visibly sagged, running her hand through her hair, fresh tears streaming down both cheeks. "Not only have I lost one of my best friends, but I never got a chance to tell her how sorry I was. I mean, I don't think she knew. She suspected he was sleeping around, although she never thought it was with me. Hell, I still don't know what I was thinking. I'm a horrible friend." She paused and then added, "I can't imagine what you think of me."

"Wow, I . . . look, we all make mistakes. Clearly you cared for her," Luke responded quietly, appearing at a loss for words.

This couldn't be going any better, she decided. "I, uh, need a moment," Sonya choked out before she quickly slipped off the stool and hastily walked to the guest bathroom.

~

Luke hadn't known what to say to Sonya about her affair with his sister's husband. Rachel and Ted had both warned him something was off about the woman; they had been right. *How could she sleep with her best friend's husband?* he wondered. But the look of anguish on her face, and the tears. Her sorrow appeared real, and she'd been visibly distressed about Kimmy since they'd first met. Luke wasn't sure how to process this new information. Briefly, the thought had occurred to him that this kind of twisted betrayal was so typical in the circles he'd grown up in and he'd been glad to get away. Not that he hadn't seen his friends and acquaintances make bad decisions, either, but something about Sonya's betrayal seemed elevated. On the other hand, maybe this is why she'd occasionally seemed reserved. Luke decided it was best to give her some alone time. Perhaps he could swing by the station and check in with Ted. He briefly contemplated calling first, but decided it might be a good idea to just get out of the house and let the woman be by herself. Plus, he could use the distance to consider how he felt about her revelation. He stood, closed his laptop, and tucked it under his arm as he walked toward the front hallway.

"Sonya, please, take all the time you need. I'm glad you told me about this. Honestly, I'm not quite sure what to say," he said loudly so she could hear him through the bathroom door. "You obviously cared about her. Just—that's important, all right?" He paused. No response. "I'm going to run over to the police station, see if Ted has learned anything." He waited. Finally, he heard a muffled "okay" from the other side of the door. Luke grabbed his keys and walked out.

~

Rachel couldn't believe it. Everett's friend had been able to request the files from the lab. The turnaround was abnormally quick, although she suspected Ted's visit had been why. Excited, she sat in front of her computer and opened the e-mail Everett had just forwarded. Glancing at the papers nearby reminded her that she had actual paid work to get done as well. However, with her concern for Everett, combined with the curiosity about this project and the appearance that it had something to do with his position being cut, well, it was too much to pass up. That was one of the reasons she loved her job—not only did she get to focus on what she cared about, but her tasks frequently involved sifting through various reports, data analyses, documents, and other materials in order to piece together information. Or uncover new data. She'd once told Luke it was her own kind of investigating. Waiting for the files to open, Rachel considered it was probably time to upgrade her computer. A moist nose pressed gently against her wrist, and Bella slipped her muzzle under Rachel's hand in an effort to "steer it" to rub the dog's head. An old dragon toy, now touting about two of the original seven squeakers, hung out of her mouth. Her tail began wagging when Rachel made eye contact, and the breeze it generated caused some papers in a nearby pile to stir.

"Bella, we just played hide-and-seek for what—half an hour? Can you give me some time before putting on the pressure?"

Rachel intended to break around noon and enjoy a short hike with Bella. Not comfortable taking more than a few hours away with everything going on, she planned to make her way up to a small overlook of Lake Tahoe that was along the Tahoe Rim Trail. It would be a nice break from the tension of the past few days. She hadn't slept well after the argument with Luke, although she believed they were both trying to get used to each other and were just experiencing various bumps in the road. It had started to cross her mind that not telling him about her recent exploits and her strange bouts of restlessness could be contributing to the problems growing between them. They certainly didn't lack in the physical department, and there was a clear emotional connection. On the other hand, there were some issues that just kept reemerging. She wasn't about to give up on him, though. She had never been so attracted to anyone before and had never wanted to know someone so completely—mind, body, and soul. He also challenged her. While frustrating at times, she believed it also brought them closer. She needed that—needed someone who would call her out on something questionable, or debate an issue, rather than simply agreeing with everything. She stared down into hopeful puppy eyes and then back at her computer. The attachments had finished downloading. She clicked to open them.

"Okay, five minutes, then I look these over," she said, taking hold of the toy in Bella's mouth. When she returned, the files were completely opened. Rachel noticed that only one report came from the lab near Mammoth; the others appeared to be results from a laboratory in Oregon. Apparently Everett's friend had sent all of the related files, not just the bug IDs. The first file opened to reveal a short summary followed by multiple data tables. She skimmed the text, noting that the laboratory had measured high concentrations of "Hg"—the scientific abbreviation for the toxic metal mercury— in sediment samples taken from a riverbed in Northern California. The second file noted elevated amounts in water samples. The list from the bug lab included several biological summaries of the macroinvertebrate species. There were annotated notes in all of the files, and she looked back at the first one. Someone had added a side comment: "Compare to CASF-DSM results: 2012."

"What . . . ?" she mused aloud. Rachel opened her Internet browser and typed in the abbreviated name. The search engine found nothing with those specific letters. She spent the next hour digging through the various files, trying to piece together a picture of the situation. She was abruptly pulled from her reverie by loud barking from the other room.

"Quiet!" she yelled out. Usually that one command was enough to distract the dog from whatever other canine or person she was seeing out of the front window in the living room. Several people in the neighborhood walked their dogs regularly on the street out front. But when Bella continued, Rachel went to investigate. The pup was on the sofa, peering through the large window at an angle, as she had done before when her attention followed something down the street. By the time Rachel stood next to her, the barking had ceased. All Rachel observed was a car that was driving the other direction several houses away. Bella whimpered and scooted off the couch. *That was odd.* Unless, perhaps, there were several muzzles hanging out the windows of the car.

"You good?" she asked the pup. She knew Bella didn't understand. Well, not everything she said, but sometimes she wondered if the dog understood human speech but pretended not to for Rachel's sake. When she turned around, Bella was standing behind her expectantly.

"Ten more minutes, then we'll go." She rubbed Bella's head. As the pup followed her back into her home office, Rachel's phone rang.

~

He had located the house easily enough and parked a couple of houses down before initiating a quick call to check in with Carlton. Roughly five minutes later he noticed the dog in the window, although the reflection of the glass made it difficult to see what kind of dog it was. All he could tell was it was dark. Maybe black. He had a fondness for them—unlike people, most of whom he could care less about. Curious to see the canine closer, he drove forward. Another twenty feet wouldn't be so suspicious as to give him away to the owner. The dog began barking ferociously. The truck parked in the driveway suggested she was home, and he decided it safest to pull away before she could be alerted even more to his presence. He eased his car into gear and drove on by, doing his best not to look toward the house. He would have to come back around on another street and find a better spot to observe from. One thing he could not do was fail to follow Carlton's orders. He knew he had used up most of his chances with both Carlton and Sylvester. He also hoped for the chance to pay this woman back for what she'd done to him in Reno. His wrist still throbbed from the impact of the car door. A few hundred feet to the north he drove past a house with dark-red trim. It reminded him of the blood oozing from the girl's head on the trail. He smiled.

Chapter Eighteen

Sonya waited for at least ten minutes after Luke drove away before opening the kitchen drawer where she'd discovered his extra set of keys the night before. One of the keys had to be for his office. After grabbing her own set, she dashed out of the house and slid into her car. With him heading to the police station—almost in the opposite direction of his office—Sonya felt it was the perfect opportunity to see what she could find. She turned north from the large intersection of Highways 50 and 89, noticing the tall mountain Luke had referred to as "Mount Tallac" in the distance. The barest patch of snow filled in "The Cross," as locals called it. Luke had been told it was in reference to old Washoe Indian lore. Or something like that. She could care less.

Having already mapped out directions to his office, she easily made the left turn off the highway and soon drove by it. After parking down the street, she casually strolled back. There were just a few homes, and, of those that might have a view of the yard behind his office, it appeared all were vacant except for one. On average, she'd heard over half the homes in Tahoe were second homes and therefore often empty. The lone house that appeared to be lived in full-time had no garage and no cars parked out front. She surmised the occupants were likely at work this time of day.

Sonya continued her casual walk, looking around at each house or vacant lot as she passed by. *Just another tourist walking through the neighborhood,* she thought to herself. She stepped over a small wooden fence and walked across a bare dirt yard to the back of Luke's office, stepping up onto the porch. Sonya assessed her location; her actions to put on a pair of slender gloves would likely be hidden to anyone behind her. It was the fifth key that worked in the deadbolt; she quickly slipped inside.

The daylight made it unnecessary to turn on any additional illumination. This was good. Given the sun's position, anyone driving by would likely see his or her own car reflected in the large front window. She looked around at a surprisingly elegant office. Most of the furniture was either leather or glass. His desk was a deep dark-colored mahogany. There was a space between a stapler and wireless keyboard where he clearly placed his laptop. Small tables rested on either side of two chairs that were obviously situated for him to face clients. Each end table was bare, with the exception of a heavy statue of a wolf atop one table and a lamp on the other. Aiming to complete a quick visual search of his entire office, she looked to the other side, viewing a small kitchen area and a door. She opened it, and as expected there was a small bathroom. Otherwise, there were no other rooms.

Sonya walked back to his desk, observing several locked file cabinets on the side. *That was good.* Although people often kept important files on their computers, or in distant "iClouds," someone who had this much paper to file probably kept both electronic and hard copies of important documents. Glimpsing at Luke's spare key ring, it appeared none of them matched the smaller size of the cabinets' locks.

Swearing under her breath Sonya looked around, concentrating. Luke was a man. Men forget things. Chances were he had a spare key somewhere in this office. It had to be well hidden, but a place he could also access it without too much difficulty. She checked behind the half-dozen paintings and large posters hanging on the walls, finding no special envelopes or keys taped to the back.

Several small pictures rested on a shelf behind his desk. One included an image of Luke, Rachel, and a black dog with speckled white paws, posing with the large deep blue image of Lake Tahoe in the background. She checked the back. Nothing. Perhaps he'd tucked it inside. She removed the frame. It was empty. The next image displayed two men dressed in standard mountain biking gear, their helmets and bright glasses catching the glare of the camera's flash.

"Hmm, maybe that's the winner," she whispered. But that one also held nothing. On the next shelf up a colorful sunset picture boasted pink- and blue-colored clouds. The dark outline of pine trees framed the sides of the otherwise spectacular image. It was either a professional photo in an unprofessional frame or something that had been given to him. She didn't see Luke as the kind of guy who'd take such a picture and frame it himself. She reached for it just as she heard the sound of a motor out front. Her view partially blocked and her body shielded by a large bookcase, she peered around to look out the front window. Luke's Subaru had just pulled into the small parking area.

Cursing, Sonya glanced down at the back of the photo, eyes immediately drawn to a small curve on one of the edges. She made a quick decision, picked up the wolf statue, and waited behind the front door. It opened, and Luke clamored inside. He was looking down, fingering through a stack of mail. As he used his foot to push the door closed behind him, she raised the solid item and slammed it down on the back of his head. The location was strategic—not enough to kill him, but enough to put him out for a while. She'd learned the difference from an old friend several years ago. A quick "umph" sound escaped his lips, and he crumpled to the ground. She dragged his body away from the door, shut it, and flipped the lock back in place. Now she had to act quickly.

Sonya returned to the desk area, setting the statue where she'd found it along the way. She removed the back of the picture frame, and, sure enough, he'd taped a small key in the corner. After removing it, she set the picture down and turned to face the file cabinets. The first two drawers had labels with handwritten letters, one from A to Q, the next from R to Z. Probably client files or invoices. She unlocked the third and pulled it out. Inside were several unlabeled files, along with various office supplies haphazardly thrown into the back of the drawer. She'd expected more paperwork, but this would do. Glancing toward the front door to make sure Luke's body remained still, she decided it was best to take the documents with her and look through them later. She didn't want to risk him regaining consciousness before she left. Sonya removed the papers from the unlabeled files, fumbling as a result of her gloves. She folded them in half and placed them in her interior coat pocket. Glancing around, her eyes were drawn to a nearby printer. Sonya grabbed a bundle of fresh paper about as thick as what she'd removed from the folder, and placed the sheets inside. She quietly closed and locked the drawer. After returning the key to its original hiding place, she tiptoed to the back door. A few minutes later Sonya was again the happy tourist returning on her walk. She drove straight back to Luke's house, anxious to read the files. She'd just sat on her bed to review them when her phone vibrated, and she realized she'd forgotten to turn the ringer back on after her little excursion. The caller ID included only a phone number, but she knew who it was.

"Yes, Carlton?" She didn't care that she sounded annoyed.

"Any luck?" he asked.

"I'm still working on it. Some patience would help."

"Just a heads-up. Some local women have been nosing around down at UNR, asking questions about Scottsfield. We're keeping watch on—"

"What?" she cut in abruptly. "How could this happen?"

"Apparently they are friends with one of the kids involved in the research. They are trying to find out why his position was unfunded," he said. Sonya stood, not sure where to direct her frustration. They had planned so carefully. Things were going well. The last thing they needed now were two more people to deal with.

"Shit, and shit again!" Sonya cursed. "What are you doing about it?"

"I'm watching one of them now. My partner has located the passenger and is tracking her."

"Who are these women?"

"It looks like they both do some kind of environmental work. That's how they knew the student. We're trying to learn more about Ms. Smith and Ms. Winters now." Sonya froze.

"Winters?" she snapped into the phone, a sick feeling forming in the pit of her stomach.

"Uh, yes." Carlton sounded surprised by her question. "Kristina Smith and Rachel Winters. What—"

"Son of a bitch," Sonya yelled. Sometimes this world was far too small. "Tell your guy he can take the afternoon off. I'll deal with Ms. Winters—personally." Sonya hung up and slipped the papers between her mattresses, anxious to look them over but knowing she had to take care of this new situation with Rachel quickly before it could escalate. Frankly, she was looking forward to it.

~

At the alert of a text, Ted glanced at his phone, careful not to look too long, as he drove north on Highway 395. It was his partner, Nolan Ramos, informing him that Mr. Luke Reed had been by earlier asking for Ted. He made a mental note to call Luke the next time he stopped. His first call, however, would be to Jill. Carson Valley had just come into view when he finally had full cell service. Although he hated the speaker, he didn't want to stop, so he relied on his vehicle's voice-activated dialing system to call Jill. She answered on the fourth ring, just as he was debating whether or not to leave a voice mail. For the next few miles Ted told her about Rachel's requests along with his small "side mission" to try to locate the missing professor.

"Ted, are you ever going to take a day or two off just to relax?" She laughed.

"What's that mean? I'm unfamiliar with that word." Ted played along.

"Good question," she replied. "Well, if anything, you've given me a short break from dealing with my current case, and for that, I thank you," she sighed.

"Which one?" Ted knew Jill often worked numerous cases at once, sometimes performing multiple autopsies in one day.

"Edward Nunez. You know—from when I was in Reno. I never told you the full story, but let's just say I was training a new hire for a friend," she said.

"I thought you had completed that one?"

"Yep. I sent my findings in, and now they want to get a second opinion. I think someone is pushing for this to be an accident, clean and simple."

"Which suggests it's probably anything but," Ted inferred.

"Not necessarily. Sometimes people just want to get the paperwork done or help loved ones get closure. Who knows why?" He heard her shuffle papers around.

"Are they giving you a hard time?" he asked.

"Not anymore. After quizzing me with the same questions for a good hour, I think they gave up. Figured out I wasn't going to change my results. My boss just told me about their request for a second opinion. I don't like it. Not that I have any concerns with someone double-checking my results—if that person is objective. But I get the sense they will handpick the next medical examiner and this may be declared an accident. I just don't think it's that simple."

"Well, I'm about done with this favor for Rachel, so when I get back to town, I'll follow up with Luke. I guess he's looking for me anyway." Ted fiddled with the knob to turn down the temperature of air blowing from his fan system.

"That couldn't hurt. I suspect that whoever wants this wrapped up may also be edging for an end to the search for Luke's sister, too."

They continued speaking until he was about ten miles southwest of Minden on Highway 88 when the signal dropped. As the small general store in Woodfords passed on his right, Ted thought about the two odd situations he'd somehow become involved in. How his friends got themselves tangled up in these things was beyond him. Luke's interest was obvious. However, Ted suspected that Rachel's effort to help her friend might be, in part, to distract herself from recent problems with Luke. They hadn't mentioned anything to him directly, but he could sense things weren't perfect in paradise.

As Ted descended into the Tahoe Basin from Luther Pass, the view of the recovering forest on Angora Ridge appeared in his forefront. The fire in 2007 left a notable scar, with most trees on the ridge gone, or remaining as tall, needle-free reminders of how devastating a hot forest fire can be. He also noticed the sun was starting to hang lower in the sky. This time of year there should be at least some snow up on the peaks, but Lake Tahoe was likely looking at another year of drought. It took a few more miles until he had a signal again. He dialed Luke's home number—no answer. Same with his cell. Ted decided to stop by his office first, thinking perhaps Luke had decided to distract himself with work. It's something Ted would do in the same situation.

When he saw Luke's car parked in front of his small office, Ted was relieved. If Luke was working, it meant he was dealing with the situation, at least on some level. He knocked on the door, but there was no answer. Ted banged louder, waiting. He finally leaned into the front window, framing his hands around the sides of his eyes to block out the glare. He peered inside. As his vision adjusted, Ted was shocked to observe Luke's body on the floor, spread out as if he'd just fallen in place. Ted slammed his fist against the window, but Luke didn't move or open his eyes. He ran around to the back door and kicked at the lock. It burst open, and he rushed inside.

"Luke?" he called out. No reply. He kneeled beside his friend's still body. He'd been inadvertently holding his breath. It escaped when he saw the up-and-down movement of Luke's chest. Ted looked for any signs of physical injury. He found no bullet wounds—his initial fear—although when he reached behind Luke's head, something wet covered his hand. Ted retrieved his fingers, now smeared with a thin layer of blood. "Damn it!" he said, reaching for his phone to call 9-1-1. As he tapped the first number, Luke's body shifted. Ted set the phone down, looking at Luke's face. "Luke, hey, man, you with me?" he asked.

"What . . . oh, holy . . . crap, my head hurts," he mumbled, trying to sit up.

"Don't move. I'm calling an ambulance."

Luke touched Ted's arm. "No, wait. Just . . . give me a moment first." Ted waited as Luke reached behind his head and winced. "I opened the door and came inside. That's all I remember. That . . . and a shifting sound or something."

"Do you think you interrupted a robbery?"

"Who would do that?" Luke uttered, blinking a few times as he rolled onto his knees and struggled to get to his feet.

"Dude, I don't think you should move."

"I just want to get into this chair." Luke slowly crawled up until he could sink back into an overstuffed high-backed chair. He waved toward the small kitchen area and whispered, "Would you grab me a glass of water?"

Ted nodded, standing. He noticed Luke staring intently at the shelf behind the desk. "Did you remember something else?" Ted asked.

"No, but I think that someone moved one of the pictures," Luke said, using the arm of the chair to push himself up. After rising a couple of inches, he crashed back down in the seat. Ted knew it would do no good to suggest he stay put and was pleasantly surprised when Luke remained seated rather than trying to stand again. He handed him the glass, and Luke stayed quiet for several minutes, slowly drinking.

"You should at least put ice on that," Ted said, reaching into the freezer in the kitchen for ice packs. He located a hand towel and wrapped it around the chilled item as he walked over to Luke.

"Thanks." Luke placed it on the back of his head.

"Sure," Ted said as he patiently sat in a chair across from Luke.

A few more minutes passed before Luke tried to stand up again, this time succeeding. Luke slowly walked to the back of his desk.

Ted joined him and watched as Luke picked up a picture of one of Tahoe's famous sunsets and turned it over. "The pictures were moved. Someone found my spare key. Well, kind of." He turned toward a tall wooden cabinet.

Ted noticed Luke flinch and place a hand on the shelf nearby. "You need to see a doctor, my man. Seriously."

"I'm fine. Just moved too fast," Luke replied, intently focused on the picture.

Ted sighed. He had to admit, if the situation were reversed, he'd probably do the same thing. "What do you mean?"

"I don't expect stuff like this—break-ins—around here, but I still plan for it. I placed a false key here. In case anyone ever went looking, they'd find old dummy files. It was a trick I'd read about years ago in an old novel."

"You mean all of these files are fake?" Ted glanced around.

"Well, I do have important documents in two of the drawers.

Just not my active client files."

"Like your past clients, then? Or your personal files?" Ted inquired.

"A few older clients, but more like the manuals that come with appliances, extended warranties, documents like that. I've searched enough offices to realize that it's pretty dumb to make it that easy to find stuff, and now that we can save everything electronically . . ."

Ted chuckled. "That's pretty smart. And witty. I should try that," he said. "Although seems like a lot of unnecessary space and paper. Why not just use an alarm or something?"

"Because that would interfere with *the setup*." Luke paused and then partially grinned. "Okay, I tried. I kept setting the damn thing off. I gave up and opted for plan B."

"So, did they take anything?" Ted asked as Luke opened each drawer, pausing when he examined files in the third.

"Yes. They got away with a bunch of environmental reports from Rachel's recycle bin and the instructions for my new TV." They both laughed, then Luke stopped as he half-collapsed into his desk chair. "Look, I'd rather not report this for now."

"Why not?"

"Just a feeling I get. Maybe the less attention, the better. But if you'd like to run your print kit through here, it wouldn't hurt." Ted always carried supplies ready to dust for prints and search for other evidence. He also had a knack for finding details other detectives might overlook until scenes were processed by expert crime scene investigators. Ted made a point to spend a lot of time continuously learning from technical people.

"One more time, then I'll shut up. But I think it would be good to have a doctor look you over," Ted commented as he glanced around the room in search of anything else that seemed off.

"No thanks," Luke said.

Ted knew it was best not to argue. Luke accused Rachel of being stubborn—which she was—but he also failed to see he had his own streak as well. Something on one of the desks caught Ted's eye. He stepped over to it and examined it closer.

"There's a drop of blood here, next to this statue thingy." Ted circled the wolf statue, looking at it carefully without reaching for it.

"I think this is what someone knocked you out with."

"I guess that means they weren't planning to attack me," Luke concluded as he leaned back in his chair. "Why would anyone break into the office in broad daylight? On a Thursday, no less? I'm usually around," Luke said.

"Opportunity?" Ted wondered, looking back at Luke. "Okay, I'll agree not to report this, for now. But you owe me. I'll go get my kit," he declared as he walked through the busted back door so he wouldn't accidently ruin potential prints on the front door. As Ted walked to his SUV, he considered the situation. The only new element in Luke's life—and a questionable one at that—was Sonya.

Chapter Nineteen

The caller ID read "unknown number." Rachel usually let them go to voice mail. However, she thought it might be the staff person from Susanville with whom she'd left a message.

"Hello?"

"Rachel, it's Sonya. I hope you don't mind; I looked up your number on Luke's phone list." Her full sentence came out in a rush. Rachel was disappointed it wasn't Mr. Holden but tried not to let it show. That and the fact that something about this woman irked her.

"Um, sure. Everything okay?"

"Well, they haven't found Kimmy. Luke went to talk with his cop friend. I'm feeling a bit cooped up and restless. He mentioned you did a lot of hiking. I thought maybe you could help a girl out, show me around one of the local trails?" This was surprising. To Rachel, Sonya didn't appear to be a large hiking enthusiast, especially on a cold late afternoon. But she was stuck. Saying no to a good friend of Luke's sister—that didn't seem right. Especially when they were still trying to figure out their relationship. Glancing at a stack of papers she needed to review for one of her clients by tomorrow, Rachel resigned herself to a late night. She was a big girl, after all, and she had made the decision to delay the work in order to go to Reno. Now, she'd pay for it.

"I'm sorry to hear it—about having no news. I suppose I can break away for a bit. Were you thinking a stroll or more of a climb?"

"I could use a good workout. I heard about an old wagon trail that went up out of Christmas Valley. That might be nice."

"Hawley Grade?" Rachel wondered how this woman had heard about a relatively unused trail in just a few days' time. The path, which began along the Upper Truckee River a few miles south of Meyers, gently ascended about two miles to Echo Summit. Locals primarily used it for short after-work or weekend hikes. But since Luke seemed intent on helping Sonya, Rachel felt obligated.

"I think that's it. Goes up to the summit?"

"Yep," Rachel confirmed. They agreed to meet Sonya in the Lira's parking lot in Meyers; Sonya would follow her in her rental to the trailhead from there.

An hour later they were walking up the path while Bella excitedly ran her usual "radius" around them; except here, she'd learned to stay on the trail in certain sections. It had taken a few squirrel chases downslope for the pup to decide climbing back up wasn't worth the chase. While it was a wide path, it dropped off steeply below. Rachel kept the conversation light, revealing the history of the trail and pointing out unique vistas. She assumed Sonya would talk about Kim, or Kimmy, as Luke called her, if and when she wanted. They crossed a large swath of boulders and rocks configured as steps that normally boasted a beautiful waterfall.

"When this freezes over in the winter, it's absolutely breathtaking," Rachel commented as they crossed the now-dry rock-laden path. Finally, they reached a spot where a narrow, distant view of Lake Tahoe could be spotted from the trail.

"Mind if we take a short break?" Sonya asked, bending over and placing her hands on her knees.

"Sure. In fact, Bella's probably thirsty." Rachel reached in her small pack for Bella's portable water dish.

"Thank you. You may have noticed I'm not a huge hiker," Sonya said, standing back up and placing her hands on her hips. Rachel poured water into the dish and bent over to set it on the ground. As Bella walked to her and tipped her head to drink, Rachel noticed a fast movement in her peripheral vision; something slammed into her shoulder and pushed her toward the downhill edge of the path.

Instinctively she placed her right foot out to catch her balance. There was nothing but air, and Rachel helplessly tumbled down the slope.

Prickly bushes and fallen branches swiped at her legs as she rolled. Finally, her fast descent came to an end. Eyes still closed, she lay for a moment, dazed and uncertain about what had just happened. She could feel the rough edges of dry woody bushes against her side. That must be what stopped her fall. Her memory kicked into high gear—not everything in between, but at least what caused her tumble. *Sonya!*

In the distance she could hear the chiming sound of the bear bell attached to Bella's harness. It grew louder; the dog was approaching her. She wanted to move, to sit up. Make sure she *could* do both. But something inside told her to remain still. Keep her eyes closed. So she stayed frozen in place, even as Bella's wet nose nudged at her cheek. After a few more pushes and licks went unheeded, Bella stopped, lay down next to her side, and whimpered. Rachel remained completely motionless for what felt like an hour. At every small sound around her, she imagined it was Sonya, coming down to finish her off. *Did Sonya mean to kill her?*

When she finally risked opening her eyes, she realized she was too far down to see the trail—at least without rising up. She remained in place, concentrating on ignoring the pain that radiated throughout her body and instead on assessing the damage. Fingers worked. Toes and legs functioned. Everything hurt, but she could move. Tomorrow would bring new aches, but for today she needed to warn Luke—well before tomorrow. She also couldn't stay here forever. At some point, she had to move and hope Sonya was gone.

"Bella, sweet girl," she whispered, in part to reassure the canine, in part to make sure she could speak. Bella raised her head and pushed against Rachel's arm. Her left shoulder was too painful, but her right arm worked; she reached around and quickly rubbed the dog's ears. Rachel moved to access the cargo pocket on her hiking shorts and retrieved her cell phone. The display read "no signal."

"Go figure," she mumbled. She'd have to get back up to the trail, somehow, and then move along the path until she could get a signal. Rachel mentally braced herself to feel more pain before sitting up. After a small wave of dizziness passed, she examined the cuts and scrapes on her legs and arms. Blood was slowly oozing from a large cut on her lower left leg. *That bitch*, she thought. That part of her shin is right where her ski boots chafe, and the forecast suggested they finally might see several feet of snow next week. Kirkwood had just enough man-made snow to provide a base; now it needed a good, natural covering to open.

"Yes, as if that's my biggest concern right now," she said aloud. To Bella, of course. Rachel managed to remove her handkerchief from her pocket. Using her right foot to hold one side of the cloth against her leg, she managed a loose but secure wrap. Rachel began crawling her way back up, stopping frequently to take deep breaths, check her cell phone for a signal, and scan the area above her to make sure Sonya wasn't peering down over the edge. If she found herself losing strength before she reached the top, she would try to dial E-9-1-1. She had used the "boosted" emergency signal to call in drunk drivers in the past; she just needed the faintest scrap of a signal. Chances were better the higher she got. But if she could manage it on her own, she'd rather not raise that kind of attention——or be stuck with excessive emergency room bills.

~

Sonya had waited over ten minutes. Rachel hadn't stirred. She couldn't see her fully, but raised on her toes, Sonya managed a distilled view through various bushes. Rachel's limp form rested about fifty feet down. She'd hoped to take care of the dog, too, but the mutt jumped off the path before she could grab at her. Sonya whistled and called out, but the dog didn't respond. She considered going down to check the woman's body on her own, but it was a steep and rutted slope. It would take some time, and as people began to get off work, other hikers were bound to start showing up. She wanted to be off the trail before that happened.

Sonya considered waiting a while longer for any signs of movement but then heard voices in the distance. There had been no other vehicles at the trailhead, so she assumed there would be no other hikers——at least, coming down the trail. But now, someone was uphill and heading in her direction. Sonya tossed the dog's water dish over the edge and quickly walked down the path. She moved swiftly but periodically stopped to carefully check around each corner in front of her. She didn't need any witnesses to her being here. She made it all the way back to her car without encountering anyone.

"Piece of cake." She swiftly unlocked the car door.

Her plan was to return to Luke's and be there sulking when he arrived home. He was likely still crumpled on the floor in his office at this point. Although if he had regained consciousness and returned home sooner, she could easily claim a grocery run. Always careful to have a fallback plan, on the way to meet Rachel, Sonya had stopped and purchased two full bags of grocery items.

~

With obvious concern, Ted watched while Luke settled into his Subaru. Luke had remained in his office chair for over an hour, periodically pressing ice against his head and watching Ted look around for prints or other evidence. By now, Luke figured if he was going to black out again, it would have already happened.

"I promise I'm going straight home. I need to take a warm shower and start thinking this through." Luke pulled the seat belt across his body.

"Just don't pass out on the way home. It would be a shame to see this sweet car get crushed." Ted slapped the top of the door frame. "I'll keep looking around here, but so far, it looks like the perpetrator wore gloves." Luke nodded, abruptly stopping when pain rammed through his skull. He must have visibly winced.

"More ice?" Ted interjected.

"Sure thing."

"Are you going to mention this to Sonya?"

"I suppose, if she's there." Luke had noticed the odd tone in Ted's suggestion. "You still think she's hiding something, don't you?" Ted nodded. "Look, she confessed something to me earlier. I'm still not sure how to feel about it, but maybe it's why everyone seems to get these odd vibes from her." Luke looked up at Ted, who nudged his chin forward. Luke knew this meant that he should continue. "She told me she felt guilty because she'd had an affair

115

with Kimmy's husband a while back. She was going to tell Kimmy everything, but hadn't found the right time."

"Slept with her best friend's husband? Wow, that's harsh."

"Yeah. So . . . that could be why she seems a bit emotionally . . . reserved, maybe?"

"Could be. Or not," Ted acknowledged, shifting his gaze toward Luke's office and then glancing back at Luke. "Look, you head on home. I'll wrap up here and be in touch." He stepped back. Luke nodded, pulled the door shut, and put his car into reverse. On his way home he tried to call Rachel, but it went straight to voice mail. His clock read 4:28 p.m. Chances were good she was out hiking, out of range. He left a short message and hung up just as he pulled into his driveway and parked next to Sonya's car. As he closed his door and stood, a brief wave of nausea swept over him. He placed his hand on the hood of her car to steady himself. It felt warm, but he was too anxious to get inside and lie down to give it much thought. He opened the front door, announcing himself.

"I'm back," he called and then chastised himself when head ache increased. He heard the shower on in the guest bathroom. Luke walked to his own bathroom, swallowed a pain pill, and then grabbed a beer from the refrigerator and an ice pack from the freezer. He'd intended to shower right away but changed his mind. It could wait. A folded blanket against the back of his sofa provided a soft headrest. Luke sat and leaned back. Once the shooting pain in his head began to subside, he was able to concentrate. And ponder.

Although it could really have been someone taking advantage of the vacancy of his office and the nearby homes, the timing of the break-in was odd. A lot had been happening these past few days, and, although Rachel's quest was an unrelated matter, it was certainly strange that so much was going on around the same time. He also wondered how there could be literally no sign of his sister. Even one shred from her belongings or clothes scattered somewhere beyond the car. It wasn't adding up. Luke's reverie was broken when the guest bathroom door opened and Sonya emerged, dressed in a pair of sweatpants and a tight-fitting T-shirt. He was about to say something when he saw her bloodshot eyes. He felt an immediate sinking feeling in his gut.

"Did they . . . ?" he asked. She nodded and then wiped at her eyes.

"Yes, they found a f . . . female body about half a mile down the river," she stuttered. Luke's heart sank. So it was what he'd expected. He'd lost the chance to reunite with his sister.

"Have they confirmed it's her yet?" Luke asked, unsure of what else to say.

"No, but I think it's pretty obvious, given the circumstances."

"Crap," he said, looking down. Luke began peeling the Sierra Nevada Brewing Company label from his beer, something he hadn't done since his teens. He heard Sonya begin to cry as she rushed into the guest room. Luke sat there on the couch, staring at the bottle. Tears began to run down his cheeks. It wasn't long until the calming effects of the Vicodin kicked in, his headache decreased to a dull ache. For once, he welcomed the mildly foggy feeling that could be a side effect of the narcotic.

Chapter Twenty

Jill was asked to return to Reno to perform the autopsy on the woman everyone believed to be Kim Reed, aka Kim Nunez. When contacted, the new medical examiner happened to be at a dinner function, and slightly intoxicated. After driving the forty-five-minute commute to Reno, Jill found the woman's body already waiting for her as she entered the lab. While throwing on her lab coat, Jill's mind wandered. Everyone should be allowed to enjoy their off-time however they choose, but at the same time some jobs could require people to act quickly and be sober, even when off the clock. Jill's scheduling problem wasn't alcohol, though. It was her kids and how to juggle them. Especially as a single mom. *No thanks to her cheating ex-husband*, she thought.

Jill checked the body for injuries and features that could help confirm identification—unique markings like tattoos, scars, and birthmarks. The problem was the body had been partially submerged in water for days, and that was presumably after it had been washed down the river. There were many scrapes and postmortem bruises, which could easily have been the result of water thrashing the body against rocks. In the end, she found nothing that could easily identify the woman. There were no potentially fatal wounds on the body, and all organs appeared normal. The evidence indicated drowning was the cause of death. Although it would take time to compare, Jill knew Luke would readily provide DNA for comparison.

As Jill finished typing up her report, she felt the vibration of her cell phone in her lab coat. She reached in her pocket and tipped it just enough to see the screen. It was Ted. She'd barely said hello when he jumped into the story about what happened to Luke. It was something he often did when he got excited with a case. Finally, he stopped for breath.

"I'm sorry, Jill. I just dove into that one, didn't I? How are you doing?"

"Actually, your timing might be perfect. I can't confirm this until we run DNA samples, but they appear to have located the body of Kim Reed. I was just finishing up my findings now." Jill glanced at her computer screen.

"Oh, man. Poor Luke. Are you sure it's her?"

"Well, it's all circumstantial so far. I'll do my best to obtain her medical records. I also assumed that worst-case scenario Luke could provide a DNA sample. Did he ever talk about anything notable that could help? Like a birthmark or something?"

"He didn't even mention his sister until recently, so, unfortunately, no. I suppose her friend Sonya might know if she had a tattoo or anything distinctive. But . . . I'm not sure how reliable she'd be." Ted's tone revealed obvious distrust of the woman.

"You still think she's not on the level?" Jill asked.

"I don't know. She gave Luke a story about how she felt guilty over having slept with Kimmy's husband some time ago."

"Seriously? That's a pretty pathetic thing to do to your friend."

"Yes, doesn't quite suggest the best character, does it? But . . . I just don't think that, alone, explains the strange vibes I get from her. Rachel agreed that something didn't seem right."

"Think Luke knows about the body yet?" Jill asked, looking across the office toward the exam room.

"I'd expect the Truckee PD would have informed him by now. But I'll check in with him, too."

"Just remind him that we haven't confirmed anything."

"Got it. And thanks." Ted hung up. Jill sat for a moment, considering her next move. She decided that after she finished recording her findings, she'd spend some time trying to locate medical files for Mrs. Nunez.

~

Sonya couldn't believe her luck. She'd barely been back at Luke's house when he had arrived. She had just received a call from the officer in Truckee, informing her that a body had been discovered that could be Kimmy's.

"About time," she muttered. Sonya had been getting nervous as the hours passed and yet the body hadn't been located. It had to be for this plan to work. She glanced at her clothes, realizing they might give away her recent outdoor activities. She quickly grabbed her suitcase and walked into the bathroom, pausing to collect the papers she'd stuffed between her mattresses. A shower could easily be seen as a soothing action when someone learns bad news about a loved one. It would also give her cover to look through the papers uninterrupted and wash away any evidence of her excursion with Rachel.

That was another situation that had worked out well. There could be no suspicious circumstances. However she handled Rachel, Sonya had to make it appear as an accident. Luke had mentioned Rachel's regular forays into the forest; actually, he'd complained about them. Either way, someone hiking alone could easily lose balance and fall. Unlike the professor's body that was likely rotting in Agnew Lake, she expected Rachel's would be found soon. She had been lucky, she thought. They had passed no one on the trail going up, which she'd anticipated after reading several local hiking blogs. Sonya had even been prepared to suggest another desolate path mentioned in the blogger's comments had there been cars parked at the trailhead, but it was conveniently empty. All in all, the evidence would suggest a short hike had turned into an unfortunate fatal accident. Taking care of Rachel was like killing two birds with one stone. She knew the woman was suspicious of her; when Carlton had told Sonya about her meddling at UNR, it was an easy decision to simply remove her from the picture.

She turned the faucet on and then opened the files she'd taken from Luke's office. The first page was blank. The second page was covered in what appeared to be legal language. She felt excited until she realized it was related to some kind of building project. As she flipped through, Sonya became more agitated. There was nothing in the file but a bunch of unrelated paperwork. Had Luke suspected her? She didn't think so, nor could she recall a time he might have slipped over to his office to set this up. There must be some kind of mistake or filing error. Damn, she thought. Now she'd have to figure out another way to get his files. What she needed was access to his laptop. Although frustrated by the wasted trip to his office, and annoyed by the amount of time spent dealing with his little tramp, Sonya quickly calmed as the hot water seeped down her body. She would improvise. It was a skill she'd had as long as she could remember.

Before shutting off the water, she purposefully washed soap into her eyes so they would appear red and irritated—from crying, of course.

~

Kristina looked over the files that Everett's friend had obtained. Although this was more Rachel's bailiwick, she too had spent a good deal of time pouring through environmental documents and scientific studies. Perhaps she could get a sense of something. She skimmed through the multiple pages, pausing upon reading a comment that said, "Compare to CASF-DSM results: 2012." Rachel didn't answer her phone, so she decided to keep plugging away. Searching the Internet turned up nothing. She looked at the fish tank next to her desk, hoping for inspiration. Sometimes the gentle movements of the fish helped her relax and concentrate. She was rewarded when something Everett had mentioned came to mind. She plugged in the search term "Superfund DSM." The results referred to locations in Iowa. After changing her search to "Superfund California," a long list of sites popped up on her screen. She selected the first link. It was amazing how many contaminated areas there were in California alone, Kristina thought. After feeling Nemo brush his soft fur against her leg, she picked him up and placed him on her lap.

"Hey, buddy. So, think the CASF stands for a California Superfund site?" She waited, but as usual Nemo didn't respond. He did, however, begin to purr as he kneaded the tops of her legs before lying down. She was thankful she didn't have shorts on.

Kristina continued, searching the list for anything that resembled the letters DSM and year 2012. A file for Desmond Shute Mining was the only project listed for Lassen County.

"Susanville is in Lassen County. I think we're on to something, Nemo," she said, stroking the cat's back. The reason listed in the table for the project was: "Surface water, sediment, soil, fish and wildlife contamination by mercury from historical gold and silver mining operation." She clicked on the link, which was designated "complete as of 2012," and began to read.

~

Rachel felt something cold and wet touch her face. As she struggled through the fog in her mind, she realized it was Bella's nose. The memory of the afternoon, and the fall, returned. She looked down at her leg. The handkerchief was completely soaked, blood still freshly seeping around it.

"Oh, shit," she gasped, panicked, although it came out as no more than a whisper. This was serious; she'd passed out. Forget avoiding hospital bills—medical debt was nothing compared to bleeding to death. Rachel reached into her pocket for her cell phone, planning to dial the emergency number. It was blank. She pushed the power button. Nothing. Her battery had died.

"I am officially an idiot!" She'd been stupid, letting the fear of medical debt delay her call for help, and now she may pay for that mistake with her life. She started to call out, hoping someone would be up on the trail. Dusk was approaching, but many locals took their dogs for a walk after work. The problem was her voice—it was no louder than the sound of fluttering hummingbirds. She looked at Bella. She was losing her strength, fast. The adrenaline must have worn off.

"Okay, let's try something else." There were several broken branches nearby. Rachel grasped one and tossed it up the slope as best she could with her right arm. It appeared to have gone only ten feet. "Bella, get the stick!" she commanded. The dog immediately obeyed, heading up to retrieve her newest toy. Rachel hoped that Bella's excitement over the branch and her typical desire to run around on the trail and show it off to others could help her get attention if anyone was remotely nearby. It was a long shot, but it's all she had. Bella brought the stick back just as Rachel managed to sit up. She threw the stick up again, gaining slightly more distance this time. As Bella retrieved it, Rachel glanced down at her leg. It was still bleeding, barely. She needed a tighter bandage. It took some time to unwrap the light sweater around her waist. With one arm, she tried using her teeth to tear a segment off. It was too thick to rip. Bella again returned with the stick.

"Go get it, girl!" she said in the most enthusiastic voice she could manage as she tossed it again. She looked back down at the sweater as Bella took off. Then her eyes moved to a pile of nearby sticks. A few had sharp edges. She placed the sweater across her knees. Doing her best to ignore the pain, Rachel slammed down the sharp edge of a branch on the cloth. It moved with the stick but didn't puncture as she'd hoped. She'd have to hold it with her left hand, which was, unfortunately, attached to a rather immobile shoulder. Grunting, she stepped on it with her "good" leg to hold it in place. Again, she attacked the sweater with the natural tool. This time, it tore, and she found she could use her teeth to rip apart the rest. After one more intermittent fling of the branch for Bella, she had separated enough of the material to tie around her leg. As she'd expected, Bella's excitement over the stick game had increased. After each retrieval, the dog would run a bit farther uphill in her victory circle, searching for someone to impress. Another throw, then Rachel used her right arm and uninjured leg to try scooting herself up the slope. Bella took the stick all the way up to the path this time. Rachel managed another six inches upward before Bella returned. She threw the object again and continued to slowly scramble her way up the slope. Finally, Rachel heard a sound that filled her with hope. A new set of dog tags. She paused and looked up. She couldn't see the dogs above her, but she could hear them playing.

"Help," she called but couldn't manage anything more than a whisper. The sound of a man's voice broke through the puppy play. She tried again; her words still too quiet. Now a female voice talked to Bella, asking where her "human" was. Bella then tumbled down toward Rachel, stopped a few feet away, and climbed back up the slope. Rachel didn't hear any responses. Bella repeated her effort. It occurred to her that she was probably just low enough to be out of a hiker's line of site. She located the longest branch she could find, wrapped the remnants of her sweater on top of it, and swung it back and forth above her head. Rachel was thankful she'd chosen a bright-red sweater today. Bella came down to her again but didn't immediately run back up. Rachel heard a man call out.

"Hello? Is someone down there?" She waved the sweater again, trying to hold the makeshift flag up higher. The sound of snapping branches indicated someone was coming down the slope. Rachel almost burst into tears when she heard him. "I see you. I'm coming." She continued to wave her makeshift flag until a figure emerged into her line of sight. "Oh my God. Are you okay?" The man wore a ball cap with a thin layer of grey hair sticking out underneath. He had dark sunglasses on, which he pulled off upon seeing her. A golden retriever came to his side while he kneeled next to her.

"I could use some help," she said, attempting to smile. She looked down at her leg. His gaze followed.

"Um, sure." He looked up and called out, "Tracy, can you get down here?" Focusing back on Rachel, he said, "I'm not sure if we should move you."

"I've already moved myself, and all body parts seem to be working. I'd really love to get up on the trail, for starters." He nodded and looked back up the hill.

"Once my wife gets down here, I think if we can prop you in between us, we can manage," he said. She heard the two dogs bouncing around nearby.

"By the way, my name is Rachel. That wonderful dog who alerted you on my behalf is Bella."

"I'm Davis." He nodded. "That's Pike." He waved toward his dog. A moment passed, and Rachel saw a woman carefully stepping toward them. "And that's my wife, Tracy." Ten minutes later Rachel was back on the trail, sitting on a nearby boulder.

"Did you trip?" Davis asked as his wife set a dish down for both dogs to drink.

"Not exactly." Rachel wasn't sure if she should tell them what really happened, but in the end, the couple seemed sincere enough. "I was shoved off the trail. That's one reason I don't want to call for an ambulance, if you can help me down." The silence hung in the air for just a moment, broken only by the sound of tousling dogs nearby. The canines were happily playing tug with Bella's special stick.

~

Carlton received word of the discovery of the woman's body. *Good.* He had been watching Miss Smith's residence, but she had not left. After Sonya's call, he'd contacted his partner to come meet him and take over so Carlton could tend to other matters. He saw the car pull up behind him. The headlights flashed once. He dialed.

"Just stay here. Don't make contact. Call me if she has any visitors or goes somewhere. I'll continue tracking her phone calls, but I need to get back to Reno," Carlton said, looking at the shaded outline of his partner through his rearview mirror.

"Got it boss."

Carlton ended the call and drove away. During his drive back to Reno, he was informed that Miss Smith had contaced a number for Rachel Winters, but the call had been less than ten seconds. Clearly, they had not spoken. This did not surprise him; Sonya was good at what she did and always followed through on her promises. If she had a plan to deal with the other girl, then the other girl would be dealt with. He had been curious why she seemed familiar with the woman's name, but he didn't need to know. Sonya had never been an open book; he'd accepted that.

As he drove on the newest segment of Highway 395, or 580— why they couldn't just keep the same name was beyond him—from Carson City to Reno, he used his verbal command system to dial Sylvester's line. He pictured the man enjoying the cooler air in Virginia City, sitting in his favorite chair at the Bucket of Blood Saloon. In fact, it seemed the bar was more of an office than Sylvester's actual office in Reno.

"Silver, it's me. Just checking in," he stated when the call was answered. "How are things?"

"We're drafting the papers now. The deal should close in the next day or two, and then we're home free. However, your female companion is going to need to finish up her loose ends soon to make this work."

"She will. If anything, Sonya always does what she says she will."

"How's my boy doing?" Sylvester asked, and Carlton struggled not to sigh or otherwise reveal his annoyance.

"A few mistakes, but he seems to be learning." That was an understatement, indeed, Carlton thought.

"Good." He paused and then said, "Sonya's been the stronger one. It's best we continue to have her lead."

"Agreed," Carlton quickly replied. The call went silent for a moment.

"I did get word that the first ME's report on the male victim in that car noted something suspicious," Sylvester finally interjected. "Can you imagine why?"

"No," Carlton replied, truly perplexed.

"I made some calls, and they are going to obtain a second opinion. But I thought you should know."

"All right, I'll inform Sonya." He heard a gulping sound come through the line before Sylvester spoke again.

"I'll be in VC tonight, waiting to hear back on the counteroffer we sent. Call me if anything develops. Otherwise, I will be in touch." Sylvester hung up. Carlton had, at first, wondered why the man spent so much time in Virginia City at that damn saloon. Eventually, he figured out that it's where he met his connections and, more recently, his buyers. With the recent Comstock Lode mine operations, a lot of new people in the industry were in town. Carlton didn't doubt his boss—who wanted everyone to use that ridiculous self-appointed nickname, Silver—had other lucrative deals in the works. The plans for the land in Susanville were probably just a dent compared to what else the man had in the works. In fact, he had no idea why they were storing the box in an old mine shaft. It was apt to cave in when the next round of blasts came from the nearby mining operations. But it wasn't his job to ask.

Chapter Twenty-One

There had been no prints or other signs of a break-in to the office. Ted wondered who would have the skills, and tools, to pick the back door's lock—and to do so without leaving any scratch marks. That seemed odd, especially if this had been a crime of opportunity; although he had suspected from the get-go it wasn't, but he didn't share that with Luke.

There were likely two other keys to Luke's office. Rachel would have one. The other would be a spare, probably at Luke's house—where a stranger has been in residence for days, often alone. It was time to do some official digging into Sonya Blake. He bypassed his new partner, knowing he'd be useless, and dialed his captain directly.

"Cap, it's Ted," he announced when Captain Ron Taylor answered the phone.

"Can't you take time off and actually *take time off?*" Ron criticized in jest. Ted wasn't known for being very good at using his vacation time.

"I try. I really do. But something has come up, and I could use a little help."

"Which case?" Ron asked.

"So far, it's not official. At least, it's not ours. But there's a woman I could use some background information on." Ted waited. This was not a normal request.

"I can't just go digging around without a reason, *officer,*" he said.

Ted understood the implication; he was an officer of the law and couldn't do background checks at his leisure.

"If you can swing it, let's meet up at Sprouts, and I'll give you a rundown. Then, well, I know you'll tell me what you think." A large sigh was followed by the distinct sound of a creaking chair.

"Okay. When can you be there?"

"Ten minutes?"

"I'll see you then." Ron hung up, and Ted took a moment to strategize regarding exactly how much he'd share. He trusted his captain, but Ron also did everything by the book. Ted had generally been the same way and mostly still was. But he'd learned sometimes exceptions had to be made. Ron may very well shoot Ted's request down, but Ted knew he wouldn't have the ability to use the department's resources to look into the woman on his own.

Ted was sitting down at a small table with a fresh mug of hot honey-infused tea when his phone rang. It was a local number, one he didn't recognize, so he answered tentatively. The voice that responded sounded like Rachel, although he could barely hear her.

"Where are you? Whose phone is—"

"Ted, listen. I'm on my way to the ER. I can explain more later, but—"

"What? Are you okay?" Ted couldn't help but cut her off. Sometimes she could take too long to get to the point.

"I'll be okay. Probably need some stitches. Look—Sonya tried to kill me. You need to warn Luke; he's not answering his phone."

"She what? How?"

"I was naïve enough to agree to go on a hike with her. She pushed me off Hawley Grade." Ted could hear the signal on her end was going in and out.

"Did she say why?" Ted asked, keeping himself calm.

"No, it was just out of the blue." Ted could hear her voice losing steam. However, he couldn't help but to ask for more details.

"How did you get—"

"I'll explain it all later. We're about here. Just—warn Luke. Please."

"Of course," he said, briefly staring at his phone before hearing

Captain Taylor's voice from nearby.

"Ted, you look like you just saw a ghost," the man said as he sat in the chair opposite him.

"Could have been possible, apparently. That was my friend Rachel." He looked up at Ron. "Yes, the same one who was involved in those trail murders last summer." Ron nodded, probably wondering how this had anything to do with Ted's hasty request. "The woman I hoped you could run a background check on . . . well, she just tried to kill her." Ron sat up in his seat and stared at Ted.

"What?"

"I guess we'll be opening a local case after all. For attempted murder," Ted stated. "I need to try to call Luke Reed—can you hang for a moment?" Ted scrolled to Luke's number on his phone.

"I'll go order," Ron said. Ted tried Luke's cell and landlines to no avail. He left urgent messages and also sent a 9-1-1 text.

Ron returned, asking, "So, where's Miss Winters now? Is she ready to file a statement?" All lightheartedness had left the conversation.

"She's heading to the ER. I don't know the details. Something about a hike and the woman pushing her off the edge."

"And let me guess, there's only Rachel's word on this?" At this, Ted looked astonished.

"Yes, and that matters why? Everything she said last summer was proven true, correct?" he inserted defensively. Rachel's reports the previous summer had, at first, been doubted, but eventually the evidence emerged to support her statements. She had simply become involved in the wrong end of a bad situation.

"Of course. But, as you know, it's always easier if there are witnesses. And unless someone saw her with this woman, well, people trip and fall while hiking all of the time. Is there any reason someone might suspect Rachel had any feelings against this woman?" At Ted's look, Ron held up his hands. "Again, I'm thinking like a defense attorney. We can open this case, arrest the woman, but these questions will come up. So, how do these two women know each other?"

"The woman is staying with Luke Reed, Rachel's boyfriend." As

Ron gestured a type of "there-you-go" wave, Ted continued. "Apparently she's a good friend of his sister's. There was a car accident up off I-80, and his sister's husband drowned. It looks like his sister was also killed, but they hadn't located her body until today. Just . . . let me start from the beginning," he requested.

Ron sat back, scooted his chair out, and whispered under his breath. "I need some coffee." He walked over to a nearby table, poured thick black liquid into a mug, and returned. After retrieving his notepad and pen from his coat pocket, Ron looked at Ted. "All right, catch me up."

~

"Miss Smith just received a call from a local number. It traces back to an emergency room," Carlton said the moment the call was answered.

"And that means what?" his partner asked.

"I don't know yet, but is Miss Smith leaving?" Carlton didn't care about the impatience in his tone.

"Not yet . . . oh, wait, there she is. She just came out of her house. She's locking the front door now."

"Follow her. Then call me when you know more." He clicked off. Carlton had considered contacting the emergency room directly, but chances were they weren't going to list off all of today's patients to an anonymous stranger on the phone. He sat at his desk, looking out toward Peavine Peak. Towering to the north of the otherwise flat basin of Reno, it now grabbed one's attention after a recent storm dusted the top with white. As he waited, he tried to locate movement on the mountain. There were trails for hiking, biking, off-roading, and who knew what else up there. The people often looked like ants crawling around an anthill. Just as he saw a red dot moving about halfway down, his phone rang.

"Yes?"

"Her friend—the one I was watching—was just admitted to the urgent care. It's about a block from the ER and—"

"Son of a bitch!" he shouted. It wasn't like Sonya to make mistakes. Ever. But apparently she had.

"Has she said anything?"

"I don't know. She tried the ER first, but they sent her to the

Urgent Care. That's where I overheard some guy on the phone talking about the injured hiker he and his wife had helped save." Carlton could hear the sounds of distant traffic in the background as his partner spoke. He needed to find out more from Sonya, but in the meantime there was one thing that could be done.

"Get to her, and make sure she doesn't talk to anyone," Carlton commanded.

"But what if she already—"

"Just do it, Nathaniel."

~

He didn't know what to do at first. How would he even get to the woman? Nathaniel thought of TV shows he'd seen. Could he really steal someone's scrubs and just walk through the facility? People did it all the time on TV, right? He sat in his car out in front of the waiting room and looked around. It was a relatively small building. Although there were several pine trees nearby, it was well lit by the sun; no place to easily sneak in. A man in a set of bright purple-and-pink scrubs emerged from a door on the side. A moment later he lit up a cigarette. There weren't very many cars, and Nathaniel wondered how many people worked here. Would it be better to have more or fewer employees around?

He exited his car and walked back into the front room. The woman behind the glass at the registration counter was on the phone. Her eyes appeared focused on something on her desk; he doubted she even noticed his presence. However, he still made an obvious point of looking around and appearing pleased when he saw the restroom down a side hall. Walking toward it, his eyes scanned to the sides and in front of him. There were several other doors down the hall. A few more steps and he was out of view from the woman at the check-in desk. The hallway remained empty. The first unmarked door he saw was locked. He tried the next one, and it opened to what looked like a blood-drawing area. The third door opened into a room with two chairs and a raised table typical of individual patient rooms in family practice offices. In the corner there were two bins: one for trash, the other labeled "used gowns." He smiled.

A few minutes later Nathaniel peeked out of the room, his

paper gown tied closed behind him. Considering the exterior layout of the facility, he suspected there would be more rooms if he headed down the hall in the opposite direction from where he'd come. He'd have to slip by the reception area and hope there were no new arrivals in the waiting room. Walking slowly, he carefully listened for any new sounds or voices. The woman was still chatting on the phone. Nathaniel glimpsed around the larger waiting area and saw two older people now sitting against the opposite wall. The man stared anxiously at the receptionist while the woman sat in one of the chairs, her head resting back behind her. He walked on, unnoticed.

Once again hidden from view of the reception area, he tried the first door. It opened to a small closet filled with medical supplies. A voice came from around the corner, so he quickly jumped inside, pulling the door closed behind him. He could see through the slight crack he'd left open that it was the woman he'd been watching for Carlton, Kristina Smith. She breezed past and opened the door to the women's restroom. The hallway again empty, he walked in the direction from which she had approached.

Just around the corner was another door. He opened it. There she was. The woman who'd slammed the car door against his arm. He rubbed the bruise on his wrist as he approached her bed. Her eyes were closed, her body relaxed on the tall table. An IV dangled from her arm with multiple wraps circling the lower half of one of her legs. Bloody cloths rested on a table nearby. He glanced at the IV line and noticed one of the bags was labeled with a type of morphine. Numbers were displayed on a screen, along with very clear up or down selections. It was as if the room were set up specifically for him to make his move. As he approached the bed, she stirred, groggily opening her eyes.

"Kris? Back already?" Their eyes met, and although her gaze was fogged over, it was clear she recognized him. She tried to scream, but he quickly placed his hand over her mouth while repeatedly tapping the up button on the IV monitor with his free hand. She clawed at him for a moment, but the additional medication streaming into her veins quickly took hold; her hand dropped limply as her eyes closed. He carefully retraced his steps, exited her room, and began walking down the hall. The smoker in the pink-and-purple outfit had returned and stopped him.

"Sir, can I help you?"

"No, uh, I was just waiting so long in my room that I wanted to come find out how much longer," he said.

"I can check with the front desk if you'd like. What's your name?" the man asked, smiling.

"It's okay. I know someone will get to me when they can. Probably a bigger emergency than mine came in." He scooted past the man and headed toward the first patient room where he'd tucked his clothes into a small cabinet.

"ER can't plan worth a damn, and now they're sending people to us," the man grumbled before continuing down the hall.

Deciding it best not to exit through the front room, Nathaniel considered the door the smoker had used earlier. Once dressed, if he could get to that exit without incident, he'd be free. No one would use an emergency exit, armed with various alarm systems, to take a smoke break, so it had to be a safe means for his departure. He put his clothes back on and walked in the direction of the door. It lay just beyond the restrooms. He wasn't sure whether Kristina Smith was still in the women's bathroom or not. Nor had he planned what he'd do if she opened the door as he walked by. He had to take that chance and improvise if need be. Nathaniel was just reaching for the handle when he heard the restroom door click open behind him. He didn't turn around. The exit opened, and he stepped outside and quickly walked back to his car. Once inside, his adrenaline rush began to subside, and he sagged, suddenly very exhausted. He left and drove to a vacant parking lot next to Lake Tahoe, then dialed Carlton.

"She won't be talking to anyone," he said, hearing his pleasure with himself reflected in his tone.

"For how long? Or . . . forever?"

"Not sure. Depends on her tolerance to certain medications. It was all I could manage." He paused, waiting to see if this would please or further upset his boss.

"Fine. You've at least bought us some time. Stay put, keep an eye on both of them, and report to me hourly," Carlton instructed. It was perhaps the first time Nathaniel had not heard judgment and anger in the man's tone. It felt good. It was ironic, though. Nineteen years and he hadn't once heard anything but criticism and disapproval from his own father.

~

"I guess she's asleep," Kristina said when a nurse entered the room a few minutes after she had returned from the bathroom.

"That's odd. We didn't anesthetize her . . . ," the woman said, approaching Rachel's bed and examining the IV equipment nearby. She suddenly looked alarmed and quickly reached up, pushing frantically at one of the buttons. "Did you touch this?" she demanded. Concerned by the woman's reaction, Kristina jumped out of her chair.

"No! What's wrong?" she asked nervously.

"I need to get the doctor. You—go wait in the front room." She sensed the woman didn't believe her.

"Is she okay? What's happening?" she cried.

"She's had a potentially lethal dose of morphine—that's what's wrong!" the nurse yelled, pushing Kristina out the door and calling out for the doctor. A man in a white lab coat accompanied by another male in bright-colored scrubs burst around the corner. Kristina barely managed to get out of their way as they flew past her, the nurse shouting, "Get the naloxone!"

Kristina walked on unsteady feet toward the waiting room and dropped into a chair across from an older couple. Both sat quietly, the woman's head leaning back against the wall behind her. They didn't pay her any attention. Kristina removed her cell phone and typed what she guessed was the correct spelling of "naloxone" into her search engine. It was an antidote for morphine overdose. She was relieved that Rachel was receiving immediate care, but what had happened? How did the dosage get turned up? And why? She hadn't seen anyone near Rachel's room. Then she recalled the tall figure exiting the building as she'd emerged from the restroom. Kristina hadn't paid much attention at the time. She stood up and ran out front, dialing Ted as she scanned the parking lot and adjacent streets for anyone that might fit the image she recalled.

Chapter Twenty-Two

Sonya knew time was short. She had business to deal with in Reno that could not be done by phone. But she had not yet found what she needed from Luke, either. It was time to prioritize. It pained her, but she acknowledged her business in Reno demanded the more immediate attention. She also suspected the body they'd found would be hauled to Reno. Not because it was closer, but because it's where Eddie had been taken. A quick call to Truckee confirmed her assumption. She asked the officer—someone she didn't recall having met—where she could view her friend's body. After attempting to discourage her, the officer finally provided the number of the ME's office. Sonya didn't want to actually view the female figure, but it might be the best story for explaining a sudden trip to Reno. She made a decision, changing into jeans and a T-shirt.

"I'm going to Reno to see the body. I can't stop wondering if it's really her," she announced to Luke as she left the guest room, her leather purse slung over one shoulder, suitcase rolling behind her. He looked up at her, a bit surprised and a little dazed, she thought. Sonya also noticed he was holding an ice pack against the back of his head. She paused.

"What happened?"

Luke hesitated and then replied, "I fell, hit a rock." *He was actually a fairly good liar*, she thought. Before she could respond, he continued. "Reno . . . will they let you do that?"

"I won't give them the option to turn me down," she asserted, chin raised in defiance. Internally she was pleased he'd lied about his head wound. It made it easier for her to justifiably leave.

"Maybe I should go with you, then," he commented, although his voice lacked enthusiasm. This was the last thing Sonya wanted. She paused, letting go of the handle on the suitcase.

"I'm not sure that's a good idea. You haven't seen her in how many years? I don't see how you could help." She made herself appear to relax and sit in the chair across from him, speaking quietly as if comforting a friend while setting her purse on the end table nearby. "Look, I need to do this. For Kimmy. If it's her, then you can always decide to come and view her, although I'd recommend against it. You don't want that to be the only image you'll have of her as an adult." She waited for him to respond. He finally nodded.

"Okay, you make a good point. Can you call me when you know?"

"Of course." She stood up and reached for her purse. "I appreciate all you've done, Luke. Really." Sonya took hold of the suitcase handle and walked toward the front door.

"Thanks, Sonya," he replied softly. She reached for the knob after turning to go. As she backed out of his driveway, her phone beeped. That's when she noticed she had a voice mail. The missed call was Carlton's number. Although 90 percent of the time she would return his call immediately, the urge to get to Reno and resolve her business tugged at her. She decided to wait and check it once she was at the ME's office. She despised using the hands-free Bluetooth device anyway—her car speaker was worthless. The last thing she needed was to be pulled over for holding her cell phone to her ear.

~

As he placed the ice pack back into the freezer, Luke noticed it was almost six o'clock. He must have dozed off for a good half hour. But at least now he could move without his head exploding in pain. He walked into the guest room and switched on the light, noticing Sonya had taken everything she'd arrived with. He wasn't sure what to think of that. It seemed innocent enough. It was late; she'd likely find a room in Reno and be in touch. However, her departure had been rather abrupt. Returning to the kitchen, he tried calling Rachel's number, anxious to simply hear her voice. Yet again, it went straight to voice mail. *Was she ducking his calls after their argument last night? No,* he thought. *She's not like that.* She'd more likely call him back and flat out say she wasn't in the mood to talk than to play the silence game. In the meantime he needed to clean up, wash the blood from his hair, and refresh his brain cells.

After a nice long hot shower, Luke wrapped a towel around his waist and walked back into the kitchen. He had to admit it was nice to be alone, to roam freely again without having to get fully dressed. His cell phone rang. Hoping it would be Rachel, his hopes were dashed when he noticed Ted's number on the screen.

"Luke, are you alone?" Ted asked with a sense of edginess in his voice.

"Yes. Why?"

"I need to speak to you about Sonya," he said.

"She's on her way to Reno. To look at . . . the body."

"Shoot. She's getting away!" Ted's anxiety was obvious.

"What do you mean?" Luke questioned. It wasn't like Ted to be so curt.

"Sonya attacked Rachel this afternoon, and—"

Luke felt his stomach drop. "What? Is Rachel okay?"

"They think so. She's at the urgent care now."

"What the hell is going on?" Luke asked, rushing into his room to get dressed while keeping the phone pressed to his ear.

"I'm not sure, but I'll see you when you get here." The call ended. Luke threw on a T-shirt and pair of jeans, all the while picturing the last time he'd seen Rachel, lying in her bed, her lips moist and cheeks flushed.

~

Ted turned to Kristina. "Luke's on his way."

"I just don't understand all of this," she murmured.

"I'm wondering if Sonya is just a very unstable person. Or perhaps she developed some kind of possessive attitude toward Luke and felt Rachel was a threat?" he brainstormed and then asked, "Where's Bella, by the way?"

"The hikers who brought Rachel in said she asked them to stop on the way and leave Bella with her neighbor," Kristina replied. Ted let out a small laugh.

"Why does that not surprise me? She's bleeding profusely, suffering a possible head wound and Lord knows what else, but that dog comes first."

"Always." Kristina chuckled. The doctor had indicated Rachel may be asleep for a couple of hours or more; they had administered the antidote and felt confident she would be fine. Ted hadn't yet been able to question staff regarding the man Kristina had seen leaving but saw his opportunity as one of the nurses approached him. The man wore surprisingly outlandish purple-and-pink scrubs.

"I was told you have some questions for me?" the man asked, no pretense, no smile.

"Yes, thank you. I know you're busy, but I wanted to ask if you noticed any other people in the hallway, or maybe a stranger in one of the rooms, about an hour ago?"

"It's urgent care. Most of our patients are strangers," the man responded, obviously annoyed. "Now the ER is sending patients over to us—our waiting room may not be full, but our patient rooms sure are. I can't keep track of—"

"I get that. But . . . do patients usually wander the halls? Did you encounter anyone who seemed alone or out of place?" Ted waited and watched the man's expression. At least he appeared to give it some thought.

"No. Oh, wait. There was this one patient. He seemed lost. I offered to help him out, but he opted to go wait in his room."

"Can you describe him?"

"A few inches shorter than me. Clipped hair under a ball cap." The man squinted. "I think he was wearing a pair of yellow Vans. I recall noticing that and thinking how ridiculous they looked with the patient gown." Ted wrote in his notepad and then prompted him to continue.

"Anything else? Something abnormal in his voice or posture?"

"He sounded young. Maybe had a slight redneck accent." He paused. "You know, Southern. Look, I need to get back to work. Anything else?" Clearly his patience had worn thin.

"You've been a big help. Here's my card. Please call me if you recall any other details. Even if they seem benign." Ted handed him a business card. The man stuck it in the front pocket of his shirt, nodded, and quickly left the room. Ted stepped outside, called Captain Taylor with an update, and then sat next to Kristina, waiting for word on Rachel and for Luke to arrive. He also hoped Jill would return his call soon. He had contacted the Reno PD to report on Sonya, suggesting she might stop by to ID the victim. It would be an opportunity to arrest her for the assault on Rachel. Captain Taylor was now busy trying to organize a cooperative effort between their two departments.

"You okay?" he asked Kristina, noticing the nervous tap of her foot against her chair.

"Yes, just freaked out by all of this, I guess." She laid her hands on the wooden armrests and stretched her legs out. Ted reached over and placed his hand on hers.

"She'll be fine, and we'll figure this out."

Kristina nodded but didn't look at him.

Chapter Twenty-Three

It had taken Sonya less than two hours to drive to the ME's office in Reno. She had decided it would be best to perform the ID first, giving her the rest of the evening to take care of her other errand. She'd almost forgotten about the voice message from Carlton. She should hear what he had to say before she went inside the building.

Incredulous, she listened to him explain Rachel Winters had been found alive. He indicated the woman wasn't going to be able to talk to the police for some time, but that she'd likely told at least one person what happened.

Sonya slammed her fist into the dashboard. How could she have been so sloppy? The girl hadn't moved for over fifteen minutes. Not to comfort her whimpering dog, nor to try to save herself. Blood had streaked several of the boulders on the hillside. Everything indicated she'd died in the fall. *Yet how could I have been so stupid?* Sonya thought.

Putting the car into reverse, she hastily retreated from the parking lot and drove ten blocks before pulling to the side and dialing Carlton's number.

"I'm in Reno. I just got your message. I . . . screwed up. I have no excuse," she spoke quickly and then waited.

"Yes, you did," he sighed. "You at least get the files you needed?"

She hesitated. "No, I thought I had them, but—"

"Did you accomplish *anything* worthwhile?" He snapped. She looked around, noticing the bright lights of the casinos in the distance, wishing she were anywhere but here.

"I'm going to Fred's now. *Irena* needs to get that signature from her grandpa this time. I'll figure out a way to fix this." Sonya despised the pleading tone of her voice. She always came through. That Carlton would so rudely doubt her now, after just one mistake, was irritating.

"You better," he instructed. Sonya tossed the phone onto the seat next to her and put the car back into gear. She was so annoyed she almost sideswiped a parked Jeep as she pulled back onto the street.

~

Old Red Fred slowly walked back to his worn leather chair. Although he hated this nickname, the "old" part was sure spot on. Every movement took longer, and he often ached in the process. Now some dimwit had told him he was losing his memory. Losing time. But there were two things that had been passed down through generations to the men in his family. One was the annoyingly strategic thinning of hair from just the top of their heads. The other—sharp and fully aware minds until they day they died. These traits had never once skipped a generation, so far as he knew. He dropped himself in the chair and picked up the papers resting nearby. He felt a sense of déjà vu, as if he were repeating motions he'd already performed in the past. His thought process was interrupted when the short man who'd chastised him moments before for trying to take a walk out front entered the room, followed by a woman.

"Miss Irena, sir," the man said and then stepped to the side.

"Grandpa!" she exclaimed. He focused his gaze behind the man, his heart lifting at the thankfully familiar voice.

"Irena, my dear. Oh, I've missed you," he said, reaching out. His granddaughter approached. Her long brown hair was pulled back in what his wife used to call a ponytail. The scent of lavender reached him moments before she did, and his smile widened. After the loss of his wife, son, and brother over the previous few years, he held on to his two remaining blood relatives as tightly as they allowed. Fred's no-good stepson, Sylvester, however, could go to hell.

Fred reached for the TV remote with his free hand and hit the power button to silence the noise. "So, tell me what you've been up to lately, my dear girl," he inquired. The small obtrusive man who'd guided her in left the room, and Fred watched her expression grow serious.

"Grandpa, I'm so sorry. I didn't want to say this in front of Sam, but don't you remember? I was just here yesterday." Her voice was full of sympathy; her eyes briefly looked away.

"Yester . . . yesterday?" he stuttered. This couldn't be. He hadn't seen her in weeks.

"Yes, and the day before that. Honestly . . . we've had this conversation several times. I'm so sorry," she said, reaching up to pat his shoulder. "Nathaniel stopped by, too—a few days ago." Fred looked at the empty TV screen, trying to pull the image of his grandson to mind. He gazed down at the papers he'd set aside when she'd entered the room.

"I don't understand. What's going on?"

"The doctors aren't sure why, but you're having memory problems. It's been getting worse. Much worse, I'm afraid." She leaned back and sighed.

"How long has this been happening?"

"It started maybe six months ago. I have to admit, I never know if you're going to be lucid when I show up. Sometimes you've even forgotten I'm here and you greet me all over again. But I really need to talk to you about something while you're aware."

Fred felt a fear he'd never known gnawing at him. He couldn't imagine not remembering his own life, his own family. "Okay," he softly complied.

"Your . . . affairs. You can't oversee them anymore. We've managed to cover for you with your utility bills and the like, but it's getting worse. Our family's attorney—remember Josh, Grandpa?" She waited as he grudgingly shook his head.

"No."

"Well, he suggested that we have you sign over the power of attorney so we can help you take care of yourself." He stiffened and she continued. "This isn't the first time we've asked. I know you want to remain independent, but I think it's past time to face the fact that you need our help." She waited. The silence in the room was unbearable. Had he really talked to her about this before? Why couldn't he remember it? Maybe she was right.

"What would it take to do this?" He heard mild resignation creeping into his voice.

"I have the papers. You just need to sign. Sam can bear witness to your current . . . awareness." She pulled a document from a large purse and handed it to him. As he took it, she called out Sam's name, and the short man returned. Fred read through each page but could feel his mind wanting to drift away to a more serene place. Maybe that was a signal that he'd soon lose his ability to think at all.

"All right, I will sign this, but only because it's you. I am sorry you are taking on this extra responsibility." His voice cracked, but he held back tears at the thought of becoming a burden to his grandchildren. Especially Irena. They'd always shared a special bond. Nathaniel, with Fred's blood only partially flowing through his veins thanks to his daughter taking up with that criminal, had always been a distant creature to him. Irena handed him a pen.

"It's fine. We love you and want to help." She removed her hand as he flipped through the papers to the last page, looking for a signature line. Using his armrest to provide support, he signed his name and handed the sheets back to her. He noticed how they shook in his hand. She was kind enough not to say anything, instead taking them and handing them to Sam. After he also signed as a witness, Irena quietly tucked them into her purse. Sam nodded and left the room.

Fred looked over at the dark TV screen, wondering why he'd turned it off. Movement to his side surprised him, causing him to jump in his seat. When he turned, he saw a young woman smiling at him. She had dark-brown hair pulled back in what his wife used to call a ponytail. She looked familiar. It took him a moment to place her.

"Irena! You've come to visit me," he said, reaching out.

"Grandpa Fred, I'm so happy to be here."

~

Sylvester looked across the small table at his visitor. By his guess, the woman was probably in her late fifties, her shoulder-length dark-brown hair speckled with grey. In previous meetings, she consistently wore a classy pantsuit, heavy necklaces made of pearls or large stones, and earrings that stretched her earlobes well beyond what nature intended. It was far from attractive, but it didn't matter. She wasn't here as his date, nor did she need to physically impress him. She was the realtor who represented the buyers, and that's all that mattered to him. So what if he played it up a bit, bought her an extra drink, gave her an occasional wink?

"My clients have accepted your counteroffer," she said, sipping champagne.

"I'm glad to hear it," he responded, raising his glass. "Shall we celebrate?" He waited. A half smile formed on her lips, and she clinked her glass to his.

"Now, Silver, I must say you're a charming man, really. But don't think I fall for that act for a minute." Now it was his turn to smile.

"I never assumed you would, Joan. But it makes for pleasant meetings, wouldn't you say?" She nodded, taking another sip before scooting her chair back.

"That, I will concede, is true." She stood up. "I will be in touch." She turned to go, and Sylvester smiled as she walked away, leaving the half-full glass of bubbly liquid on the table. Now that was the most appealing conversation he'd ever had with her.

~

Nathaniel's phone rang. Since they frequently used disposable phones, he'd come to simply answer all "unknown callers."

"Where are you?" Carlton demanded.

"I'm parked in front of Kristina Smith's house. I figured it wasn't safe to stick around the urgent care," Nathaniel responded.

"You figured right. The cop is likely there by now, and I suspect others will be on their way. Now, did you learn whether these girls tracked down anything we should be concerned about?" Carlton interrogated, his voice strained as usual. It had always annoyed Nathaniel.

"No," he replied curtly.

"I suggest you take advantage of Miss Smith's absence and do some digging." The line went silent. Nathaniel swore as he got out of his car. He'd been doing a lot of petty jobs for Carlton lately, and frankly, it was getting old. The man was a bully, and Nathaniel was about to become very rich. As far as he saw it, Carlton should show *him* more respect. Nathaniel looked forward to the near future when he never had to take orders from people like that—including his father—again.

Kristina's front door was locked as expected. He'd watched her turn a key in the deadbolt before she left. The neighborhood was fairly quiet. There were some people walking down the street and others watching kids play in the yard. No one seemed to be paying any attention to him. He walked to the side of the small house and peered over a four-foot-high wooden fence. No dogs roamed the backyard. He tugged the string hanging down from the side of the gate, and it opened inward. No locks, although by the squeaking sound that rang out, and the thick pile of dry pine needles scraped to the side as the gate pushed open, it didn't appear to be used very often. After stepping into the backyard, Nathaniel noticed a solid wood door above a small cement step. The handle was locked, but it was old and easy enough to pick open. Although there were homes nearby, the surrounding pine trees screened him from most neighborhood windows. He entered the house swiftly and shut the door. He was standing in a small laundry area. At the end of a short hall, a toy—the flashy material attached to a long pole, obviously for a cat—lay on the floor. A few more steps and he stood in a compact living room. To his side he saw an old computer tower on the floor next to a chair. He clicked the power button, and it resumed from hibernation mode. He sat down, moving the mouse to open the Internet browser. She'd closed it, but he expected to easily access her most recent searches.

Suddenly a sharp pain ripped across his right leg, accompanied by a low growling sound. He jerked back and looked under the desk. An overweight orange-and-white cat hissed at him. He kicked at the feline, feeling one more swipe of his shin before it bolted into another room.

"Damn cat," he said and shifted his gaze back at the monitor. It hadn't been that many years since he last captured and skinned a cat, just to see how it looked inside. He'd always been curious about that kind of thing. First, he performed small investigations on frogs, then squirrels and chipmunks, and eventually the stray cat that bunked in their barn. Of course, that's the one that Irena had found and immediately told their father, Sylvester, about. He was shipped off that night, spending the next year of his life in an enclosed facility for crazy people. He'd since learned how to be more discreet with his hobbies. A beep from the computer broke him from his stroll down memory lane.

The screen gave no indication of why it had alerted him, yet he heard the sound again. He finally realized it wasn't the computer but a nearby printer. An LCD icon indicated "low ink." But it was the printout resting below the small display that really caught his attention. Although the text was extremely light colored, he could make out most of what was on the paper. He tensed as he read through each line. It was a copy of the EPA's website for Superfund sites with a summary of the DSM project—the very same DSM project *he* was counting on. He looked around but saw no other printouts. After checking her browser and finding nothing more, he tucked the paper in his pocket and quietly left her house, retracing his steps through the backyard. Once he was safely seated in his car, he called Carlton back.

"She's got a printout of EPA's summary for the DSM site," he relayed as soon as the call was answered. There was a moment of silence before Carlton replied.

"Anything else?"

"Not that I found." Nathaniel glanced at the paper on the seat next to him.

"Okay, stay near your phone. And don't leave town. Get a motel room or something."

Nathaniel leaned back in the driver's seat. He started his ignition and drove toward Highway 50, where he was sure to easily locate a nondescript small motel room for the night.

Chapter Twenty-Four

"I've got it," Sonya said when Silver answered his phone.

"Why if that's not one of the top two news items I've heard today!" he replied, and she could hear the mild slur in his voice. Obviously he'd already had a "business meeting" or two at the saloon.

"What's the other item?" she asked, removing the itchy brunette wig and tossing it in the backseat. Luckily she looked enough like Irena that combined with his neurological confusion, it didn't take much more than the wig to fool Fred.

"The buyers accepted the counteroffer. The timing couldn't be better."

Sonya was relieved. But at the same time, one part of her plan hadn't succeeded. Yet. This deal wouldn't be enough on its own. She couldn't let her plan for Luke Reed go unfulfilled. "Great news. How quickly can we close it?"

"I'm waiting for the signed acceptance from their attorney. After that, it should go fairly quickly. It's a cash transaction, of course." Sonya rolled her eyes when she heard him take another loud sip of what she assumed was his usual straight-up whiskey.

"As long as it happens before the next batch of students goes poking around," she replied. "Look, I need to take care of one more thing in Tahoe. I'll check in tomorrow." She ended the call, determined to get the files she needed from Mr. Reed no matter what it took. She'd just have to be more discreet about her presence.

She recalled Carlton's statement that Nathaniel was in South Lake Tahoe. Perhaps her infamous little brother could keep watch for her this time. If Luke rushed off to visit that little tramp after her unfortunate accident, maybe he left his computer behind. This time, there was no reason not to just take the whole damn thing and figure out the password later when she was far enough away. Sure, the timing might be suspicious to them, but so long as she was careful, and if she took some other items, who could say it wasn't just a random burglary? Sonya smiled, her foot pushing on the accelerator. Once she was on the highway, she dialed Nathaniel.

~

Rachel watched helplessly as the Camry sped up behind them, bashing into the back end of her pickup. Although light, the impact still caused a noticeable jerk. Luke sat next to her in the passenger seat, rummaging through a bag for something. No, not something. He was looking for the gun. Bella nudged her shoulder from the cab's backseat. She looked in front of her again, struggling to drive straight ahead without succumbing to the taunts of the driver chasing them. Suddenly, as if by magic, Luke was sitting on the edge of the open passenger side window. The top half of his body was outside of the truck. Rachel's adrenaline surged from fear. The Camry rammed into the truck again. But now, it wasn't a Camry. It was a semi tractor-trailer. How could that happen? She held the wheel tight. The semi backed off. Rachel saw a shiny object emerge from the driver's window. There was a loud popping noise. Popcorn rained down, covering her front windshield. As she reached to turn on her wiper, Rachel felt the steering wheel immediately pull sharply to the left. At over eighty miles per hour, the grab of the blown tire pulled her vehicle sideways. Inertia took over as the pickup flipped over on its side and began to roll. She looked at the passenger side. Luke was gone. Bella wasn't behind her seat in the cab anymore, either. The truck kept turning over and over again, sending her head slamming back into the headrest with each full turn. She yelled but couldn't hear her own voice over the crunching metal and breaking glass. She closed her eyes, tight. The sounds began to drop away.

"Rachel?" A voice penetrated the the distant sounds of her Tacoma bashing into the asphalt. She tried to listen closer, but the throbbing in her head dulled her senses.

"Rachel, it's Luke," the voice interrupted again. It was a struggle, but she managed to open her eyes just enough to see bright lights outlining a dark blurred image. It moved. "You never were good at waking up," he joked. She realized her left hand felt warm. Luke's fingers were wrapped around it.

"What happened?" she asked groggily. "I feel kind of weird."

"Do you remember anything after the fall on the trail?" he asked gently. Rachel could picture herself lying in dirt, rocks, and woody bushes. Bella was next to her. Memories flooded in, and she remembered Sonya's push, the feeling of falling, unable to stop, pain with each tumble as the earth tried to grab a hold of her. The man—Davis—and his wife. And a dog, Pike.

"Hiking. Sonya. Then . . ." She looked around, her vision clearing as she focused on the room and then down at the IV drip in her arm. That glimpse spurred the image of the man who put his hand over her mouth and did something to the controls. "Someone messed with my IV. Quick, call the nurse!" she said, panicked at what he might have put in her tube. As she reached with her right hand to pull the IV out, Luke's fingers lightly touched her arm, stopping it in midair.

"It's okay. They caught it. You're going to be good as new," he assured her. Rachel paused, still feeling scared, but the sincerity in his expression convinced her not to worry. She relaxed her arm.

"Did they catch him?"

"Not yet," he replied. "But they have a description. Ted's got several officers on it now."

"What about Sonya?" Rachel paused, not sure whether Luke knew the full story. "Did they tell you what she did? To me?"

"Yes. I . . . I don't understand it. I know Ted suspects she was imbalanced or had some irrational fantasy about me, but that just doesn't sit right with me. We can't figure out, though, why she'd do this to you. Maybe she's just crazy?" Luke reached up and scratched the stubble on his chin. "She didn't say anything that might explain her motive toward you?"

"Nothing obvious," Rachel sighed. "On the trail, she was very much into idle chitchat. She kept asking me about different mountains in the distance. What were their names? Were there official hiking trails to the peaks? That sort of thing. It felt forced the entire time, but I was trying to be nice and give her the benefit of the doubt. Not that I could ever have imagined she'd be so extreme as to try to kill me."

"I'm sorry. I'm the one who brought her into our lives, and—"

"You have nothing to be sorry about; you didn't ask her to push me . . . right?" She grinned. This time, he relaxed. Their eyes met, and a familiar warmth flooded through her. It wasn't the instinctual sexual attraction she had for him but more like an unspoken understanding. The moment was broken when a nurse entered the room.

"I see you're finally awake. How is our little druggie here?" The woman's voice was pleasant, although it seemed too high pitched to be coming from the older woman Rachel saw in front of them.

"Okay, I suppose," Rachel responded and then asked, "How bad was it?"

"If not for the quick work of our doctor, you might have drifted away on a cloud of opiate overdose to the stars above," the woman said. Rachel was, at first, surprised at how casually the nurse was joking about her second near-death experience of the day but then thought she'd rather have them make fun of it than be serious and mournful.

"Was that guy trying to . . . ?" Rachel let the last part remain unspoken.

"Likely," Luke responded.

She paused briefly, her mind needing a moment to comprehend this new information. "Well, I'm attempting to think of a witty response to that, something involving being high and loopy and all, but I'm coming up short," she said. "Then again, I can tell there's still something in my system. Oh, I was having this horrible dream about the Camry and I-80 last summer . . ."

"Did I miss the shot this time?" Luke played along.

"No, my tire blew before you could get that far."

"Ouch," Luke winced. "But I have a suspicion . . . didn't you recently blow out a tire after the not-so-intelligent decision to drive your bare wheels across an OHV road out by Forestdale?" Rachel smiled. It was true. "The drugs probably just blended it all together," he said, grinning.

"I would have appreciated a good sex dream much more," she blurted and then looked embarrassingly at the nurse, who smiled as she finished logging the readings from various machines. "Sorry."

"Girl, no apologies needed. I'm completely with you on that one." She patted Rachel's arm. "The doctor will be in shortly to check those stitches." She glanced toward Rachel's leg; it was covered by a thin sheet. Rachel nodded.

"I almost forgot about that. Guess there's still some morphine somewhere," she said as the nurse walked out. She turned her attention back to Luke. "Seriously? I've just beat death, what, twice, and you go and throw one of my more embarrassing moments out like that? You have no shame!" She tried to keep a straight face but burst out laughing. Luke joined her as he stood up and bent over to touch his lips to hers.

"Anything to see that smile," he said, gently kissing her. "As for a good sex dream, I'm happy to make that a reality."

"Not again, you two!" Ted called from behind as he walked into the room. Rachel felt Luke linger just a moment longer before he ended the kiss and sat back in the chair.

"Do you mind?" Luke feigned annoyance.

"Just warn me next time," Ted said, pulling an empty chair up next to the other side of her bed. "I hate to ruin the moment here, but I'm hoping you can remember exactly what happened?"

Rachel talked about the man in the patient gown with as much detail as she could recall. When Ted seemed to exhaust all of his questions, she looked back at Luke. "Any word on your sister?" Luke and Ted exchange solemn glances.

"They may have found her body," Ted responded. "I'm playing phone tag with Jill to learn more."

"Given the new light that's been shed on Sonya, plus what Jill discovered on the man's wrists, do you think she had something to do with the accident?" Rachel inquired. An odd expression came over Luke's face.

"What about his wrists?" he asked, looking at Ted.

"Oh man. Sorry, I thought you knew by now. Jill found unusual bruising; the pattern suggests he may have been handcuffed."

"No, I guess the Truckee cops didn't tell me. Or . . . come to think of it, Sonya made a couple of calls to check in. Maybe she didn't relay that particular finding." Luke stood and began walking anxiously around the small room. "Then again, why would she, if she had something to do with it in the first place? I can't believe I didn't see this."

"Stop beating yourself up. We've all been duped. Add to that the emotional toll from the connection to your sister and no one can blame you," Ted reassured him. "Plus, someone is trying to keep it under wraps by ordering a second autopsy." Luke paced a few more times and then sat back down. Ted looked at Rachel. "I have been so busy trying to find the guy who did this to you that I haven't had the chance to consider the alternatives to the car accident theory. But what you said . . . that could make sense. About Sonya. I'm going to try Jill again, or see if anyone up there has looked at the female's body yet." He stood, put the chair back against the wall, and glanced at Rachel. "By the way, Kristina is anxious to talk to you. She said something about Everett's project." Rachel nodded as Ted left the room. She turned to see Luke's questioning gaze.

"It's a follow-up to our Reno visit," she answered quickly.

"Ah yes, the *visit* where someone also tried to kill you?" The sarcasm in his tone suggested this was still a sore subject. Rather than engage, Rachel took the easy way out—to the extent her pride would let her.

"Yes, the visit where Kris and I happened to be in the wrong place at the wrong time," she corrected. He appeared to consider saying more but decided against it.

"On that note, I need to tell you something as well . . ." He trailed off. Rachel looked at him encouragingly. "I don't know if Ted told you, but someone broke into my office earlier. I guess I also had the wrong-place, wrong-time syndrome."

"What do you mean?" Rachel asked, scanning him up and down for injuries.

"I walked in the front door, and someone coldcocked me. Next thing I know, Ted's yelling out my name."

"You're okay?" she asked, rising up in the bed.

"Yes, fine. And—I get it. The not telling me right away part."

Rachel reached her hand up and caressed the side of Luke's face.

"It's all right. We're good. Now let's kiss and seal this deal before anyone else shows up," she said with a smile. He complied.

~

Jill listened to the second message from Ted. It would be best to return his call before he left a third one. She began speaking as soon as he answered. "No, I have not been able to obtain any medical files for Luke's sister—*yet.*" She emphasized the last word.

"Sorry for being so pushy. With everything that's gone on here, and the attacks on Rachel, I just—"

"Attacks? As in multiple?" she gasped. He'd told her about Sonya's attack earlier, in the same message where he'd warned her the woman may attempt to come identify the body—presuming she was unaware Rachel had survived to tell her story. Ted explained about the IV incident.

"Okay, Teddy, so I'm surmising we aren't just dealing with one crazy woman here."

"Apparently not," Ted confirmed.

"And I'm going to guess that you suspect this new victim, if it's Kim Nunez, may be a homicide?"

"You got it."

"All right, I'm going to put in another call to see about those records. I'll let you know when I've completed the autopsy," she said, her mind already thinking about whom else she could contact that might be able to track down the woman's medical files. There's no guarantee of *if, or where,* files from her adult life existed, but she knew where Kim Nunez had grown up. In a wealthy family, she no doubt didn't lack medical care. Those records could help to identify the woman—that is, if the woman was Kim Nunez.

Chapter Twenty-Five

After Luke left the room to confer more with Ted, Kristina bounced in and provided Rachel with the short version of her search for the Superfund site. Rachel then shared her findings in the files from earlier that day. After swapping stories, they both paused for a moment, deep in thought.

"The file listed the project as completed?" Rachel asked.

"Yep. I printed it out but then got the call about you, and, well, it's probably sitting on my desk at home."

Rachel thought about that for a minute. "Mercury contamination. That's no easy fix." She knew it was a toxic metal historically used to assist in recovering mined gold and silver. Contaminated mine tailings were a problem in the Sierra Nevada and in the Virginia Range, where the Comstock Lode was found in the 1850s. Mercury caused harm locally and globally, and it was especially troublesome in bodies of water where it would accumulate up the food chain. High mercury levels in fish, and other wildlife like birds, remained a problem in many contaminated areas.

"But if it's marked completed—as in cleaned up—that doesn't make much sense," she said. "I know various methods have been investigated for removing mercury contamination, but none that I have heard of work that quickly and thoroughly."

"How about for now let's set that mystery aside until we can look it up again? I'm wondering what the big deal is about this project? It seems to be the key connection between Everett's situation, the missing professor, and other odd coincidences, don't you think?" Kristina looked up at the small window for a moment. The room grew silent once again.

Rachel briefly debated about whether to vocalize her idea because it sounded so far-fetched—even to her, and she'd seen a lot of twisted things in the past few years. She opted to go ahead and speak. "Here's what I'm thinking. If my theory is too far out there, blame the meds," she said, smiling before she continued. "It seems that someone, or some entity, doesn't want anyone looking at the data from the samples collected as part of, or maybe just nearby, this DSM Superfund site. And they are going to a lot of trouble to make sure that no one's looking. Or left to ask questions."

"That's horrible. I mean, wow . . . I suppose it's possible." Kristina gazed at Rachel and then glanced at the IV bag hanging next to her. "Um, so here's a thought. That guy down by the campus with the gun . . . do you think?" She pointed.

"I certainly wouldn't dismiss the idea," Rachel said. After the unexpected "adventure" last summer involving murderous intentions, as she and Luke had come to call it, she could believe that stuff like this actually happened.

"What should we do now?"

"Here's my thought: let's write out what we've found so far, get a copy to Ted, and look up that project. Ted's busy with Sonya Blake, but if we lay out what we know, perhaps he can follow up on it sometime soon." Rachel noticed Kristina began rubbing her hands together. After watching her prepare for public speaking many times, Rachel knew it was a subconscious action that revealed her coworker and friend was nervous.

"I'm kind of freaked out about all of this," Kristina admitted.

"Me too," Rachel said. "But I've also learned that if we really have stirred something up to the point where someone comes after us with a gun . . . or who knows? Maybe that same someone is the guy who gave me the morphine buzz . . ." She paused, the connection making more sense as she lingered on the idea. "Where I was going with this is that whoever is behind this is probably not going to quit. Even if we did." Kristina's head bobbed slightly, as if accepting what Rachel said but unsure of how to respond. Her hands continued rubbing. "Can you ask Ted to come in here? I think we should tell him all of this right away—and, well, Luke, too."

"Agreed." As Kristina jumped up, her phone dropped from her pocket. She bent over to pick it up. "Oh, looks like Everett called. I'll listen to it after we talk to the guys," she mumbled on her way out of the room.

~

Nathaniel considered Sonya's request. "Carlton told me to stay put, find a room for the night," he replied.

"I don't see why you can't just slip away for a bit. I need you to be a scout for me. Give me a heads-up if Luke Reed is coming. Last time I did this alone, he showed up. I had to improvise, but it caused problems."

"Look, *dear sister*, if Carlton tells me to stay in this motel room, I should stay in this motel room." He could hear the sound of highway noise radiating in the background. Sonya had said she was on the lakeside of Spooner Pass, so she couldn't be too far away. Maybe he could leave. Just briefly. She was certainly pulling her weight on this deal.

"Carlton's not up here. He wouldn't realize how quick of a trip it will be for you," she replied, filling the silence. He relented.

"I'll give you twenty minutes. Then I'm heading back to this room. Tell me where to meet." He looked around for stationary paper but saw none. He pulled a wadded-up receipt from his pocket and spread it out, writing instructions on the back.

"I'm about twenty-five minutes away now. When you get there, drive past the house, then turn left on the first street and come back around. Park on that corner so that you can't miss any cars that drive toward the house. Text me when you're there." Nathaniel looked at his watch, noting the time. He'd have to leave in about ten minutes to match her arrival. He just hoped Carlton wouldn't call in the interim.

~

Sonya parked several blocks down the street behind Luke's house. Considering it was still daylight and that she may have been seen before—a red-headed visitor out for a stroll not long ago—she placed her brunette wig back in place and boasted her Prada sunglasses. She knew their large size covered much of her face, and the fashion would be expected on an out-of-town tourist. As she neared the back of his home, she received a text from Nathaniel. He was in place. Sonya dropped her cell back in her pocket and walked across an empty forested lot until she was on the street in front of Luke's house. She strolled up to his porch as if she belonged and used the spare key she'd located the day before to let herself in. Once inside, she locked the door behind her and walked straight to Luke's bedroom. She was still hopeful he left his laptop there after learning of Rachel's condition. Sonya was surprised to discover his bedroom door was locked. Perhaps word of Rachel's accident had been accompanied by information about who caused it. No problem, it was a fairly cheap lock. She could probably pick it with a bobby pin if she wanted. But that seemed unnecessary at this point. Instead, she grabbed one of the kitchen stools nearby and slammed it into the door, hitting the locked handle with the seat of the stool. The door jerked inward. Tossing the broken furniture aside, Sonya looked around. No laptop.

"Son of a bitch!" she yelled. She searched through his bathroom, around his bed, and in his dresser drawers. There was no sign of his laptop or any papers that might represent backup copies of what she was looking for. She paused and looked around the room again. Those documents had to be somewhere. She'd assumed that when she didn't locate hard copies in his office, he must have scanned copies on his computer. However, many people also kept spare paper copies at home. Who didn't back up their paperwork that way? But perhaps she just hadn't located the files yet. *Okay, Luke, you couldn't have had time to move anything after getting a call about your ill-fated girlfriend and my involvement, and you were too trusting of me from the get-go to have moved anything beforehand, so where would you normally keep those papers?*

Sonya looked between the mattresses, on the bottom of the

dresser, in the back of the bathroom cabinet, and even in the fuse box she'd noticed in his bedroom. She found nothing. As she moved around the items on his closet shelf, she knocked over an old bicycle helmet, causing it to fall to the floor. When she looked down to kick it out of her way, something inside caught her attention. The scraped-up dirty black helmet contained a thick white envelope. She reached for the helmet and pulled the paper from inside. It wasn't the paperwork she'd been searching for. But it contained fourteen $500 bills and a small key. Probably a safety deposit box. She took both, uncertain of how she might deal with the box but acknowledging that she may never find the papers she searched for at this point. Money was money, and seven thousand in fresh green bills would help cushion the blow of losing a much larger amount.

Her phone buzzed in her pocket. Nathaniel texted to warn her that a cop car had just passed by him, driving in her general direction. Sonya pocketed the bills along with her cell phone, ran out of the room, and left the house through the back door. Luke's yard was partially fenced by solid wood panels. The remaining areas were bordered by the typical flimsy stacked-log fences the forest service put around the urban parcels they managed. She jumped over the wooden fence and walked once again across the adjacent forest lot. She looked back toward his house. Reflected in the tall, wide figures of two large cedars in his front yard were the red-and-blue lights of a patrol car. She'd made it out just in time.

~

"Next time I'm hurt, no morphine drips," Rachel said.

"Let's not plan on a next time, please?" Luke responded.

"I've sent patrols to watch all three of your houses," Ted interrupted, standing in the open doorway. He was looking at his phone while speaking. "I can't believe this is all happening at once. You two had better buy everyone you know tickets to the next department fundraiser."

"Sorry," Kristina said. Rachel saw that she was standing nearby, hugging herself. But at least she wasn't rubbing her hands together. *That was a positive sign.*

"How soon until you are released?" Luke asked. "Have they said anything?"

"I was told so long as I wasn't alone for the next twenty-four hours"—she looked at him and winked—"that I can probably leave in about an hour. I'll need to take some care of these stitches, though, and keep ice on my shoulder."

"I think I can assist in that regard," he responded.

"It will certainly make me feel better if you're with each other," Ted said. "Just leave out the details, please." He turned toward Kristina. "Same for you. Is there someone you can go stay with until we figure this out?" Kristina looked uncertain. Rachel knew her family was on the East Coast. She had friends around town, but most were married with kids. She could understand why Kristina wouldn't want to impose on any of them.

"She can stay with us, too. I'm assuming we'll be at my house . . ." She turned to Luke, waiting for disagreement. It was certainly easier at her place. For one, it was set up to withstand the "Bella bomb." But he still had his "male ego" moments. She was relieved when Luke nodded. Rachel continued, "I have a spare room."

"I appreciate that. But . . . what about Nemo?"

"Bella will be happy to play with him, too. If he's okay with dogs." She laughed. A quick image from a recent hike flashed through her mind. When Bella saw fish swimming in the deep section of a stream, she'd reacted as if they were initiating a game of chase with her. Rachel always said the pup would play with anything; fish, however, had been a surprise.

"Nemo may not agree. He's not too friendly toward the canine species. What if Everett came to stay with me?"

"That couldn't hurt. We'll keep a unit on your place as well," Ted replied. He then turned to Luke. "I'll call if I hear any word related to your . . . the body from the river." Luke nodded solemnly.

It took two more hours before Rachel was finally released. She could walk, albeit slowly and carefully.

"Mind if I run by my place and grab some items first?" Luke asked as he helped her into his Subaru.

"No problem," Rachel agreed. The extra morphine had worn off, and the regular dose waned. The pain in her shoulder, neck, and leg had become excruciating. She'd promised, with some reservation, to continue a regular dose of prescription painkillers for the night. Now her head was growing slightly foggy again from the medicine. She let it fall back against the headrest. Luke slid in the driver's seat.

"Meds kick in again?" he asked, softly laughing.

"Maybe. Just . . . keep your comments short and simple," she said.

"Don't worry. I can say a lot without saying a word." He smiled, placed his hand on her leg, and reached for the ignition.

"I look forward to it," she returned, noticing how quickly her skin had gone from warm to cold after his hand was removed.

~

As they pulled into Luke's driveway and parked next to a police car, a uniformed patrol officer emerged from his front door. Luke didn't know what to think, but this wasn't a good sign. The man approached as Luke stood up from his car.

"Luke Reed?"

"Yes, that's me." He glanced toward the front door. "Did something happen?"

"You had a break-in. Officer Benson asked us to check around, and we noticed a few things that looked suspicious when we looked through your window." Luke quickly thought of Sonya. He couldn't figure why she'd risk coming back to his house once she'd gotten away. She could easily go to Reno or Sacramento and get on a plane, or take I-80 and be on her way to just about anywhere. Luke nodded and bent down to confer with Rachel in the passenger seat. He smiled when she looked at him with her glossed-over blue eyes.

"Did you hear that?" Luke asked.

"Most of it. I'll just stay here while you go check it out," she said. He chuckled; a sober Rachel would have wanted nothing more than to join him and be part of the action.

Luke followed the officer through his front door and into his living area. He immediately noticed the broken stool and the splintered door frame.

"There's quite a mess in there, but if you can determine whether anything's missing, that would help," the man said, waving toward the bedroom. Luke walked in and saw several drawers half-open, the items they once contained now scattered on the floor. His bed was mussed, as if the burglar—Sonya, he assumed—had lifted the top mattress to check underneath. He couldn't imagine what she'd be looking for. She couldn't have known about the spare cash he'd started keeping around after they'd had to flee so quickly last summer. He looked at his closet. Half of the items from the shelf were now on the floor, including the helmet. He picked it up. Sure enough—his envelope was gone, along with the cash and the key to his safety deposit box, where he kept his most important paperwork.

"I had some money stored in here. It's gone," he said to the officer, who had remained in the doorway, watching.

"How much, sir?"

"Seven thousand." The room went silent. Luke suspected the officer was probably wondering why he would keep such a large sum in his closet. Or how Luke had obtained such a significant amount of money in the first place. "I like to keep it around for emergencies," he explained, deciding that getting angry—seven thousand wasn't chump change—or providing the officer with a detailed explanation about why he kept such cash around would needlessly take up time. "I have a feeling the woman who was here, and who attacked my girlfriend, is the one who stole it," he said, assuming Ted had at least provided general information about why the cops were watching Luke's house.

"Yes, Officer Benson gave us a rundown." He paused, looked at the helmet, and asked, "Did she know you had this money here?"

"I don't see how she could have."

"So, you're saying that she returned from Reno, after escaping apprehension, to the town where numerous cops are looking at her for attempted murder, to obtain cash she didn't know you had?" Although his skepticism was frustrating, Luke had asked himself the same questions.

"Makes no sense, I agree. Unless she was looking for something else and found this instead. But what that could be, I don't know."

"Okay, let me contact Officer Benson. I'll get a CSI team out here and see what evidence they can find. Will you be staying here?

Or where can I reach you?"

Luke provided his contact information and packed a few clothes and toiletries for staying at Rachel's. His headache had returned with full force, so he quickly took a Vicodin and then tossed the pill bottle into his shaving kit. After putting his bags in the car, he went back inside and retrieved his bicycle. As he walked it toward his car, he heard Rachel's slurred voice call out.

"Going for a ride tonight?"

"Just a quick one to get your truck from the trailhead," he said as he loaded his bike onto the rack.

"Oh, that's right . . ." He saw her head tilt and her eyes close. Before heading out, Luke took one last look around his thrashed bedroom. He'd tell Rachel about the mess and the theft of the money once she was more lucid.

Chapter Twenty-Six

Sonya heard Carlton shift in his chair after she broke the news. "I'm sorry to hear that," he said. "How do you expect to come up with the rest of the money?"

"Well, I'm sure once we close the deal in Susanville I can use some of the profit to make up for it. Find a worthwhile investment, so to speak?" she said, once again driving north toward Reno.

"But it's still less than we'd planned. Then what?"

"Ask Silver. He always has something up his sleeve. Perhaps we can help him with another job?" Sonya heard the desperation in her tone and hated it. They had it all worked out. They'd get the money through Luke and pay off her debt to that damn loan shark. She'd known better than to borrow money at such a high interest rate, but her credit score was too low for any reputable institutions to give her a loan. And, of course, the whole identity theft thing could get tricky. Now when the property deal closed, they'd be set for life and long gone before anyone noticed the problems with the land. Or before Fred's real granddaughter, Irena, returned for another visit.

"I'm not sure he'd want to work with us again after these screwups."

"We'll figure it out. We always do," she said, ending the call before he could respond.

~

Kristina knew she'd left the printout on her computer. But she couldn't find it anywhere. She was on her knees, checking to see if it could have fallen behind the tower. Nemo sometimes jumped around and wreaked havoc on her piled paperwork. Head tucked under her desk, she barely heard the knock on her front door.

"It's me," Everett's voice chimed from outside.

"One minute," she called out, feeling inside the small space. No paper. She rose and walked over to open the door. "Thanks for being willing to bunk here. I just didn't feel safe alone."

"Sure. I noticed a police car down the street. Is that for you?" he said as he walked inside and dropped his small bag on the floor. She nodded. "I see this is quite serious," he said apprehensively.

"Yes, it seems so. And on that note, Rachel and I are trying to figure out what's going on with the project you were involved in. It may be the reason this is happening. Well, minus the jealous, crazy friend of Luke's long-lost sister, that is."

"Oh, I do believe you need to catch me up." He sat down in a nearby chair. Kristina told the story about what they'd learned, what had transpired in Reno, and then what happened at the urgent care, all the while watching him nod and clearly struggling not to interrupt her.

"Will the police be looking into these events?" he finally asked.

"Yes, but they don't have the understanding of the science like we do. I was hoping you'd be willing to assist?"

"I suppose," he stuttered nervously. She excitedly sat in front of her computer while he pulled the chair next to her.

"Something about this Superfund project is not right. Here, let me show you what we've located," she said, accessing the website she'd printed out earlier.

~

Sylvester took another sip from his glass while glancing at his phone to read a new e-mail. The attorney had just sent the signed documents. The accompanying request to meet at the property tomorrow was unexpected. A nuisance, but he had no choice. He replied with a curt e-mail, stating the time he would be there. Next, he informed Carlton.

"I need you and Sonya to join me for a trip to Susanville tomorrow."

"For what?" Carlton sounded rattled. That was not like him.

"The buyers want to view the property one last time before we finalize the deal."

"Should we be concerned?"

"No, I've seen this before. I think it's more sentimental than anything," Sylvester said as he traced a line of condensation on his glass. "Why do you sound nervous? Has something gone wrong?"

"Sonya wasn't able to get what she needed from the brother." It poured out of Carlton in one long breath. Sylvester was only mildly concerned.

"I'm sorry to hear that. Yes, it puts a damper on your plans, but I don't see what the big concern is. We're all about to make a lot of money."

"It's not enough for her. She has some debts to pay."

"That's her problem." From Sylvester's perspective, Carlton seemed far too concerned about Sonya's poor spending habits. It wasn't the first time he had wondered whether something more was going on between Sonya and Carlton. "For now, we need to ensure this deal goes smoothly tomorrow. Then Sonya, and anyone she may choose to work with, can figure out how to resolve her own *personal* problems." He hung up, irritated. Given a moment to consider, he decided some concern was warranted. When people get too greedy, well-laid plans could fall apart. Sylvester had to make sure Sonya didn't make another more egregious mistake.

Chapter Twenty-Seven

The smell of vanilla was the first thing he noticed. The second was the feeling of Rachel's soft skin next to his. Luke opened his eyes and saw sunlight pouring in around the sides of the window curtains. Although his brain wasn't yet awake, his body quickly reacted. He gently caressed her bare shoulder. Bella began to stir at the foot of the bed.

"Be careful of your mom's leg," he told the dog, observing where Bella's paws were placed and examining the outline of Rachel's leg under the covers. The night before he'd suggested Bella sleep in her own bed on the floor, but Rachel had said she'd be fine. She was a good sleeper, which Luke knew was true. But he questioned whether Rachel had considered the excited morning greetings.

"Bella, let's get you off the bed." He gestured toward the floor with one hand and rubbed her ear with the other. The dog complied after a hesitatant glance at her owner. Just as Rachel had once confessed her own suspicions, Luke too wondered if there was a human trapped inside that dog.

"Morning," Rachel said, her voice groggy. He turned and kissed her shoulder.

"Good morning."

"I'm sorry. I guess those meds put me out last night." She turned to look at him.

"That's okay. I'm glad you got some rest. How do you feel now?"

"It hurts, but not as bad as yesterday. I think I'll try ibuprofen first and see if that's enough. That Vicodin turns me into an airhead."

"A very entertaining one though. You were on quite a streak last night, busting out knee-slappers left and right," he grinned. She rolled her eyes.

"My apologies."

"So," he said while propping himself up. The covers fell to his waist. "I need a shower. You?"

Rachel smiled coyly. "Yes, and I think I'll need assistance. You know, to keep my leg dry where these stitches are."

"I think I can help with that." Luke reached under the covers and lightly brushed his fingers across her upper thigh.

"And my shoulder still hurts a bit," she said.

"Hmm, you may need some help washing yourself as well. I strongly suggest you let me assist." He reached for her hand. "I'll let Bella outside and then come join you. How's that sound?"

"Like an excellent plan."

Five minutes later he stepped into the shower next to Rachel. The hot water beat down on them as steam fogged up the small window above. Her leg, the lower half wrapped in plastic, was propped up on the side of the tub.

"Oh boy," Luke said, making a show of looking her up and down. She smiled, leaning her head back as the water soaked down her hair. "Okay, I guess I'm supposed to, er, get the soap . . . or something like that." He leaned against her, one hand bracing the wall behind her, the other reaching for the bar of soap in the corner. At the first touch of their bodies, he heard a small moan escape her lips. He smiled, quickly kissed the crook of her neck, and began washing her. He enjoyed watching the lather from the soap drip down her body. Luke traced an imaginary line down her leg and then back up again, pausing when he reached her inner thigh. Another moan.

"Don't forget I'm balanced on one leg here," she reminded, her voice barely more than a whisper. Luke noticed she held onto the top of the shower door. Luke stood up tall, setting the soap aside.

"Of course. Let me help keep you upright." He moved in closer, propping her between the shower wall and his own body. He felt her form mold to his. Her lips began to softly skim across his collarbone. This time, the moan he heard was his own.

~

Rachel was ever thankful for her large water heater. She'd never had so much fun in the shower. As Luke bent over to dry off her leg, she felt his wet lips against her thigh.

"Keep doing that and we won't make it out of this room," she warned.

"And the problem with that would be?" He laughed. She didn't have a response. She didn't see the urgent need to leave anyway. But, at the same time, resolving the mystery behind the Superfund project, which may be the reason their lives were threatened, tugged at her.

"Good point," she said. "But I suppose we have to be responsible adults—at least sometimes."

Luke stood back and began toweling himself off. She studied the small beads of moisture glimmering on his skin. She ached to trace her lips from his shoulder down to the small scar on his chest where he'd been shot last summer. "Rachel, you're gawking again." He grinned. She paused, a deer in the headlights.

"Yes, right . . . responsible adults." She sighed and reached for her clothes.

"I must say I'm feeling more awake than I'd be after three cups of coffee. Perhaps this should be a morning routine," he suggested.

"Good idea. But are you still going to have your coffee?"

"Of course."

Rachel rolled her eyes.

Luke quietly laughed as he helped her dress, being careful not to aggravate her sore shoulder. He kissed her once more and then went to brew coffee. Rachel entered her kitchen a few minutes later.

"I guess I'll check in with Kristina. Oh, do you have your laptop with you? Mine's in the other room, but yours is faster."

"It's in the car. I'll go get it," he said. The dripping sound of percolating coffee filled the room.

"No worries. I'll just get mine booted up, then give her a ring."

When Kristina answered the phone, she sounded both tired and excited. She explained how she'd stayed up with Everett, finding what they could about the Superfund site. "Supposedly they tried a new technique for mercury remediation up there, and they claim it was successful."

"Hmm, can you send me the links to what you found?" Rachel's computer was on, her browser now ready. Kristina agreed. A minute later, a new message appeared in Rachel's in-box. Several links were listed in the e-mail. She clicked on the first one just as she felt Luke's breath next to her ear.

"What have you girls found?"

"Do you mind not doing that right now? You're turning me on, and it's breaking my concentration." She pretended to be annoyed.

"Oh, you mean this?" His lips touched her earlobe. "Or this?" Her neck.

"Seriously. You're killing me here," she whispered as goose bumps flushed across her skin.

"Okay, got it." He rose up, his hands in the air. "So, what's the scoop?" He sat next to her as she read through the first web page.

"They claim a small company—now defunct, of course—performed a successful remediation on an old mine site up by Susanville. In other words, that the mercury contamination was effectively removed from the area."

"That sounds like a good thing."

"It would be—if it were true." She pointed to the screen. "But there hasn't been any follow-up monitoring that I can find. Plus, the files from UNR show high levels of mercury in the sediment, water, and the tissues of the bugs they tested. According to the files, those were collected less than six months ago."

"I know you mentioned before that sometimes government agencies are a bit, shall we say, lax on doing the right kind of monitoring? Wouldn't someone be checking that area? Doing some kind of measuring or something?"

"Well . . ." Rachel clicked on the fourth link. "According to this, it looks like the local fish and wildlife office was 'following up.'

Whatever that means," she murmured before she perked up. "Want to take a drive?"

"To that mine? Isn't Susanville a bit far for a day drive?"

"Maybe about three hours or so. I haven't been up there in years, but with the new bypass south of Reno, it doesn't seem so bad." The sounds of a squeaker suddenly emanated throughout the room. It was Bella's way of requesting attention, usually when Rachel was on a phone call for too long. Their conversation was obviously too long by the canine's standards.

"I guess so. I'll drive, for obvious reasons. And I assume Bella's going with us?" he said.

"I think she'd like to." Rachel laughed.

After a quick call to Kristina and a voice message left for Ted, they were on the road.

~

Ted glanced at his watch as he listened to Rachel's recorded voice. They hadn't found the man who attempted to kill her with the morphine overdose, nor had Reno PD or any other department been able to locate Sonya. Worse yet, he hadn't figured out the connection between the women's questions at UNR, a potential carjacking in Reno, or the attack on Rachel at the urgent care facility. Or even whether they were connected at all. Now Rachel and her friend had apparently uncovered a can of worms involving this special project in Northern California. Meanwhile his department was focused on the crimes they could prove at the moment—the attack on Rachel and the theft at Luke's. He'd taken a drive over to the police station and discussed the bigger picture with Captain Taylor, who agreed to make some calls outside jurisdictions. But it wasn't enough.

"I've got a feeling. You know how it is. I'm happy to take the day off, but I think I should join them up at that old mine site."

"Ted, I realize they are your friends, but you've given how much of your recent personal time off to this?" Captain Taylor looked down at his desk and then back up at Ted. "My take? They're adults; if they want to go up to see the property, knowing the dangers, that's their decision."

"But consider this, captain. According to Rachel's message,

there's evidence that this remediation project at the old mine didn't work. The consulting firm paid to do the work is off the radar. The UNR professor and his students who may have stumbled upon the pollution are missing, dead, transferred out, or mysteriously disconnected from the project. Rachel and Kris go nosing around, and now they're in some kind of danger. Something is going on here." He paused and added, "And I have to say something like this project, which was funded by the Environmental Protection Agency, well, there should be more information after the project was completed. That no one seems to be looking, I just have to wonder who might have interfered." He watched as the captain leaned back in his chair and rubbed at his forehead as if a sudden headache had come on.

"You mean politically, don't you?" He let out a long sigh. Ted nodded. The captain dropped his hand back down to his desk. "Maybe we should call someone else in. Someone with direct jurisdiction."

"I agree. But in the meantime, Rachel and Luke are heading into a potential hornet's nest with no backup."

"All right, for now, this is on your own time. I know nothing about it."

"Got it," Ted replied, standing up from the chair.

"*But*," the captain said with so much emphasis that Ted stopped and looked at him, "if you need anything, call me directly. I'll do what I can."

Ted quickly grabbed his wallet and keys from his desk and took off at the fastest pace he could get away with in the office, short of running. He heard his partner, Nolan, asking where he was going. Ted ignored him and walked out the front door. Seated in his SUV, he decided to check in with Jill as he drove out of the parking lot.

"I've got nothing," she answered abruptly. She then summarized the requests she'd made for Kim Nunez's records to several Southern California hospitals the day before. She hadn't received anything in return. Then to his surprise, she asked if he could pick her up on his way north.

"I'd like to go along. The kids are with their father until tomorrow. Until I hear back on any medical records, there's not much to do." Ted relented, knowing that if push came to shove, one thing Jill knew very well was how to aim and shoot. She had done two tours with the army.

~

Nathaniel was still seething with anger from the night before when Sonya had told him to get back to Reno. After being her lookout at Luke's house, he'd driven straight to his motel room, waiting for the next move. Usually his instructions came from Carlton. God forbid his own father would speak to him directly. But then again, he had to admit, his dad—or rather Silver, as he'd instructed Nathaniel to refer to him for the last few years—had taken him into his confidence, trusting him to be a part of this job. Nathaniel was still sometimes torn between telling the man to go screw himself and wanting to earn his praise. As for Sonya, he felt an odd indifference. It was much like the way he felt when he looked at the blood dripping from Danielle's skull out on the hiking trail. Curiosity about whether she felt anything. Wondering about her last thoughts. But all in all, not caring. Not that Nathaniel wanted to kill Sonya. Or he hadn't thought of it before. In fact, in the beginning, he was sympathetic toward her. He had also been charmed by her when his father and Sonya had told him about their plan, assuring him his real sister, Irena, would be safe and kept from harm. *When did his feelings toward Sonya change?* He couldn't recall. Well, now she was working with Carlton, and he had to follow Carlton's orders. That included taking her orders as well.

But when she had instructed him to leave Rachel Winters alone and immediately drive home, he'd wanted to wrap his hands around her throat and squeeze. If she'd been next to him, instead of on the phone, he probably would have. He longed for the chance to get back at the two women who had bested him at the university. Yet in addition to berating him for what she referred to as a 'ridiculous obsession' with the women, Sonya had told him to leave them be. So now he was back in Reno, sitting in the small apartment his father rented for him, waiting for news. Carlton had called earlier in the morning, telling him to "sit tight and stay out of trouble" until he heard back from one of them. Nathaniel leaned back against his sofa and grabbed the bottom of one of the cushions. The seam was torn, and he began ripping the threads, one by one, as he stared blankly at the muted television in front of him.

Chapter Twenty-Eight

The chirp of a text message alert awoke Rachel from the fitful sleep she'd fallen into as they drove through Reno. The lull of the tires on the highway combined with the pill she'd conceded to take when her leg began throbbing twenty minutes into the drive worked together to make her doze off. At the start of the drive, she'd managed to continue searching online, but their signal broke off in Washoe Valley, and she'd given in to the call of the sandman. Her search had mainly resulted in more articles about mercury, mines, and remediation techniques—nothing specific about the location where they were heading.

Rachel opened her eyes and reached for the phone in her pocket, uncertain where they were. Luke must have noticed her stir.

"Good timing. We're a few miles out, and I need to know exactly where we're going," he said. The light weight of Bella's muzzle pressed down on her right shoulder. Bella had a tendency to rest her head like this on passengers. It usually caused said passenger to reach back and pet the dog. Rachel was sure Bella was simply training the humans to her liking. She glanced at her cell phone display. It was a text from Ted.

"I planned to wake up at just the right time. Seriously." She smiled, looking his way, and then glanced back at her phone. "Ted said he's driving up here with Jill and that we should be careful." The phone beeped again. A new shorter message also from Ted.

"Jill wants you to know she hasn't located Kim's records yet. The autopsy showed the victim was a healthy female with a good heart, lungs, generally good health all around. Likely in her late twenties or early thirties. Cause of death is drowning." The car went silent for a moment as Luke presumably digested the news.

Finally, he nodded and then spoke. "I can help Jill with that. I didn't even think of it until just now." He paused. "And Ted worries too much. But maybe he has a point. Just keep your eyes open."

"I'll try," she said and then looked toward Luke. "On that note, sorry to nod off."

"It's okay. It meant I didn't have to listen to those atrocious sounds you call music." She smiled.

"Ouch," she said.

"Your leg?" He tensed.

"No, your opinion of my tunes." She chuckled. She liked country western, from the '70s on up, along with modern pop. He was all about the classic rock. Period. They often bartered over various items or exchanged massages or foot rubs to decide what to listen to. "I printed up a map of the roads around the mine before we left, just in case the GPS didn't work." Rachel opened up the paper she'd tucked into her purse. "It looks like we'll want to take a left a few miles after Highway 395 branches northeast."

"We just passed that intersection so give me fair warning before the road."

Rachel nodded and looked around; the area was beautiful. It was rimmed on three sides by the Sierra Nevada. The white top of Mount Lassen provided an almost surreal backdrop to the valley. Another minute passed before she saw the side road they were supposed to turn on.

"Up here," she pointed. Luke nodded, switching on the turn signal. As they began down the narrow road, she noticed a large open field that stretched up toward the mountains. Just as she began thinking how great it was the land had been preserved and kept open, she saw a large "For Sale" sign. Hanging on the bottom by two small chains was a smaller sign that read "Pending."

"Figures," she mumbled.

"What? Did I miss a turnoff?" he asked. She turned her head

toward him. He, too, was surveying the area.

"No, sorry. Just thinking it's sad that such a beautiful area will probably be covered by another subdivision of homes in the near future."

"What makes you say that?"

"That 'For Sale' sign." She waved. "It advertises the potential to subdivide this into quarter-acre lots." The car went silent for a few moments, and then Luke pointed toward a dirt road up to their right.

"Is that the one we want?"

"I, uh, think so. Let me check . . ." Rachel skimmed over the printed map. It appeared to match their general location. "What the heck? Let's give it a try." They had traveled about two miles before she observed the first remnants of old mining equipment on the uphill side of the road. Another few hundred feet and they drove around a small corner. Once the road straightened, Rachel looked up the mountainside, seeing the light-colored edge of what appeared to be a common pile of mine tailings. They stopped moving. Just as she was about to ask why, she looked forward and noticed the stream crossing the road in front of them. It was more than a trickle—not something they'd want to drive through. At least, not in Luke's Subaru.

"Well, good a place as any to stretch a bit," he said, turning the ignition off. Bella bounced around in the backseat. Rachel slowly opened her door. When Luke appeared in front of her, she was surprised. She hadn't realized he'd walked around the car.

"How's the leg?" he asked, reaching a hand out. She took it, and he helped pull her out of the seat.

"Minor throbbing, but much better than three hours back." She propped herself against the car as Luke let go of her, reaching to open the door for Bella. The pup jumped out of the car and ran toward the stream. "Bella, no," Rachel commanded. She didn't want Bella to drink anything downslope of those old mine tailings. The dog returned and sped past them, bolting in the other direction.

"What was that about?" Luke asked. Rachel pointed up to the tailings. "Ah, I see," he said, nodding. Rachel looked behind him, her gaze following the path of the stream as it drained into a large pond several hundred feet below them. A number of small areas of standing water were noticeable in the distance. The flow of the water eventually led into the valley that lay spread out between the mountains and the highway. Rachel guessed the wide expanse of land had to be several hundred acres, at least. The chime of Bella's identification tags indicated the dog had returned.

"Mind setting her dish out with some water?" she asked.

"Sure," Luke responded, reaching into the backseat for Rachel's backpack.

"I think that's all up for sale," she sighed. "Those ponds could be where the samples were taken by the UNR folks. That's the only place I see that could have the kind of bugs that were being tested." She paused a moment, trying to open her mind to a thought tugging on the periphery. Finally, it came to her. "Whoever owns that land down there stands to make a fortune if it's sold and subdivided. But if it turned out that there was contamination spread throughout that valley . . ." Her words trailed off. She heard the sound of Bella slurping. Luke looked at her and then back out into the distance.

"Son of a bitch, Rachel," Luke uttered, leaning against the car next to her and looking out over the broad expanse of land. They stood there in silence. "You said Ted is on his way?"

She nodded solemnly.

"That could be a good thing. A really good thing," he sighed. Rachel noticed a vehicle coming up the main road from the highway. It was still far in the distance, and all she could tell was the color—white.

"That could be him now." She motioned. Before they could discern the details, the view of the vehicle was blocked by small hills situated between them and the main road.

"Or not." Rachel watched Luke walk around to the driver's side of his Subaru, open the door, and reach below his seat. She glimpsed the black image of his gun before he put it in his pocket. She hoped they wouldn't need it. "It might not be a bad idea to find some cover."

"You don't think you can maneuver your car through that stream?"

"It's too wide and muddy. Subaru's kick ass in the snow, but we'd probably get stuck in that," he said, looking around and then up. "Not much in the way of trees here. Think you can make it up that slope if I help?"

"Sure," she said as she immediately took a few steps without waiting for his full support. She tripped, just a minor stumble-on-a-rock kind of misstep, but the correction in her footing must have pulled her skin just right. The flash of pain from her stitched leg took her breath away. Luke quickly rushed toward her. "Oops. Okay, so, yes, I could use some help, please." She gave her best impression of a smile, although she was a bundle of nerves on the inside.

"Always Miss Independent." He chuckled as he reached for her right arm, helping her limp along and relieving some of the pressure on her left leg. She looked to her side as she whistled. Bella appeared a moment later. Rachel retrieved the thin six-foot leash she had in her pocket and attached it. "Sorry, girl, but need you to stay close," she whispered.

"If we can get around this one corner, we can look down from that ledge toward the car," he said, pointing up another fifteen feet.

She groaned and mumbled as they continued. "I so hope this is Ted."

"And here I thought my mountaingirl would be all over this new adventure."

"Normally, yes. But today, cowboy, I'd sure love for this adventure to be on horseback." As they moved, Rachel's anxiety ebbed. That familiar sense of calmness began to settle over her instead—the same feeling she'd get on her recent climbs. And when Sonya had pushed her off the slope. *What the heck is wrong with me?* she wondered. Before she could ponder the question for long, Luke helped her up the last few feet of the small overlook. They lay flat on the top so they could see who was about to arrive—hopefully, before that person considered the idea of looking up.

~

Sonya and Carlton had met up in Reno, making the rest of the drive to Susanville in his pickup. Sylvester shouldn't be too far behind them based on when he left. No more than half an hour, she mused. The man always drove his two-seater sports car. Sonya had suspected he not only loved the car, but also loved the excuse to ride solo. There was no backseat.

"I don't understand why we need to be there. Silver can handle this from here on out," she complained. Not only was the time involved in this field tour a nuisance, but having to don her itchy disguise added to her frustration with the trip.

"He has his reasons, I'm sure," Carlton sighed.

"Don't miss the turnoff." She gestured to the jutting road on their left. He slammed on the brakes and skidded around the corner. "Glad no one was behind us," she quipped. He grunted. They drove in further. Sonya glanced at the "For Sale" sign. "It's all about to work out."

"Yes, it sure is," he said and then turned to her. "I wasn't sure that mercury-mixed-into-scented-oil deal would work with Fred," he mentioned. She smiled. It had come up in one of her science classes in junior college—how exposure to mercury was to blame for the Mad Hatter character in Lewis Carroll's *Alice's Adventures in Wonderland*. The process used to make European and American hats in the 1800s required mercury, and hatmakers, known as hatters, were constantly exposed to its harmful vapors. It made them go crazy.

"I had to think of some way to render him unstable and do it in a way that no one would figure out, least of all Fred. Then it came to me. Finding old thermometers and other electronics with mercury inside isn't as difficult as one would expect."

"Putting it in the scented oil was brilliant. Perfect way to ensure it would be heated up to volatilize into the air." Carlton placed a hand on her leg. She shrugged. He waited a moment before asking, "Are you over the Luke Reed situation?"

"Of course not. But I can't go back, not now." Sonya looked up toward the mountains and noticed a glare coming from the old mining road up the hill. "Carlton, do you see that up there?" She pointed.

"What? Oh, yes, I see something catching the sunlight."

"I haven't seen that before, and old rusty equipment wouldn't do that. Probably some kids getting their kicks off-roading, but I think we should check it out." She looked at her watch. "We have a good twenty minutes before the meeting." Sonya didn't think it was anything to worry about; people wandered out here all of the time. But she was anxious and upset over her failure to get what she needed from Luke. Checking to see what caused the bright reflection would also help pass the time. They continued up the road as the shining object was temporarily hidden behind a sage-covered hill. They reached the dirt road that bordered the property and turned right, heading up the old rutty path. When they came around a corner, Sonya gasped.

"How the . . . ? That's Luke Reed's car!"

"Are you serious? I mean, are you sure?" he interrogated, and she noticed him pat his right hip, likely checking for his gun.

"There's a small round faded bumper sticker on the corner. I can't read it from here, but I recognize the Tahoe Rim Trail sticker. And a long scratch over to the right." She hadn't expected anyone, much less Luke, to come up here. Although Rachel and some friend of hers were nosing around the UNR project, she never imagined this.

"Think he's alone?" he asked, scanning the surrounding area. Sonya, too, did a visual sweep. She couldn't look up because the roof of the truck blocked the view from the passenger seat. She noticed a small bundle of some sort next to the car. It took her a moment to realize what it was—a portable water dish for dogs.

"No, he's not alone. *She's* with him."

"They've got to be up there, unless they walked through that water and around the bend. But I don't see any tracks in the mud." He gestured forward where a stream had washed out the dirt road about thirty feet in front of Luke's car.

"I agree, but the roof is blocking my view. Are they up there somewhere?"

"I don't see anyone, but they could be hiding on any number of the ledges up that way. Let's go." He reached for his door handle.

"Wait, I have an idea. If I can't see them from my seat here, they can't see me. They would have no reason to expect me to be here. Why don't you head up, and I'll duck out and come around the other side. If they are up there somewhere, we'll have them."

"Good idea." Carlton opened the truck door and stepped out. Sonya noticed he didn't say anything or look back her way. *Smart guy.* Although she had also figured that if Luke decided to shoot first and ask questions later, Carlton would take the hit, not her. She watched Carlton as he looked to both sides and then back uphill again. He took a few steps up, careful to avoid stirring the bushes intermittently covering areas of the hillside. She'd wait and let him get farther up first—enough so that if someone were watching his ascent, they weren't likely to catch her movements in their peripheral vision.

~

Sylvester was just a few miles away from the property. Finally, this day had arrived. When Sonya had approached him with a slightly different plan, he'd been intrigued. It was almost four years ago that he first met her, the woman dating his stepdaughter.

He despised gays. It wasn't right. Marriage should be between a man and a woman. That's how he was raised, end of story. Apparently Irena hadn't intended to share information about her choice of a partner, nor the actual partner, with him. She'd brought Sonya to Nathaniel's on the same day he happened to check in on his son. He recalled the shocked looks on all three faces when he walked in the door, unannounced, finding his stepdaughter casually leaning against another woman on the couch, her arm wrapped around her. It was clear they were more than just friends, although to any stranger on the street they looked similar enough to be mistaken as sisters.

At first he yelled, blaming Irena's biological father, who'd passed away the year before. The man must have had dysfunctional DNA. After all, *his* son, Nathaniel—albeit created with her sleeze of a mother—was just fine. Next, he blamed the newer generation, which, he believed, made it "cool" to be gay, disregarding the Lord's word. Although Irena had just celebrated her twenty-ninth birthday—far beyond her experimental teenage years. She was old enough to make responsible choices, but this wasn't one of them. Nathaniel tried to intervene, but he was in high school then, still a lanky teenager. Sylvester stomped away, ignoring their pleas to talk.

About a week later, he had been surprised when his office manager announced a visitor. A young woman had come to speak to him about his stepdaughter. Curious, he'd agreed to see her in his office. The door opened, and there stood the other woman. She seemed taller than he recalled, although it may have been the high-heeled shoes she wore. It was quite a different, and far more appropriate, look for a woman of means. Especially compared to what she'd been wearing when he'd first seen her.

"What do you want?" he snapped, expecting this to be one of those Hallmark Channel visits where she tried to convince him to "see the light."

"I think we may have some things besides Irena in common. Frankly, I've done some research on you," the woman said, sitting in his visitor's chair without waiting for an invitation. She remained there, her posture stiff and a gaudy purse resting on her lap.

"I have nothing in common with you," he spat, looking back at the papers in front of him, hoping she'd take the hint.

"I wouldn't be so quick to judge, Sylvester. Or should I call you Silver?" At this, he jumped from his seat.

"How dare you be so presumptuous!"

"How dare *you* be so rude to someone who is coming to you with an offer that I doubt you'll want to refuse." She remained calm, her tone and stature exuding confidence. He paused, noting her neatly folded hands resting on the top of her delicate bag. A large, rather shiny ring was on the middle finger of her right hand. Next to it was a smaller band. At a glance, it appeared to be lined with diamonds. He sat back down.

"Fine, just make it quick. I've got a lot of work to do." He waved, trying to exhibit disinterest.

"It's my understanding that you like to make deals. Big deals. And your father has been getting in the way of a rather large opportunity." This, he had to admit, got his attention.

"Fred is not my father," he asserted.

"He married your mother. Fine. Your *stepfather*." The room went silent.

"I see you have been doing some digging, Miss . . . ?" He waited.

"Blake. Sonya, please." She smiled.

"What opportunity do you *think* you've discovered?"

"The ranchlands, of course."

He stared, uncertain he'd heard her right. She continued. "Irena has complained about the pressure you've put on her grandpa to subdivide it and sell it off. She said her 'sweet Grandpa Fred' agreed with her choice to keep it as one large parcel and build a ranch house. She blathers on and on about having horses and cows, and maybe even running a small dude ranch or something else just as ridiculous. Personally, I don't see her being able to handle even half of the work that would require."

"Aren't you dating her, or whatever you queers call it these days? Why are you telling me this, Ms. Blake?" He spread his hands out on the desk in front of him, preparing to push himself up out of his chair.

"Sir, call me whatever you want, but I know a good opportunity when I see one. Same as you." She waited, a knowing smile pasted on her face.

Sylvester relaxed. "Okay, I'm listening. But, now, one of the problems with that little idea is the old mine above the property. Any chance you stumbled upon that little fact in your 'research' into my business?" He leaned back in his chair and crossed his arms.

"Of course. I'm always thorough." She winked. He didn't respond. "I know a few people who are familiar with such situations. There's a lot of interest in old mine operations around Reno, you know."

"Exactly how would you propose to get around the Superfund classification on that particular old mine?" He placed his hands behind his head, still not sure what to make of this woman.

"Meet me for lunch in one hour and I'll tell you," she said as she edged forward and wrote the name of a restaurant on his desk calendar. She stood up, purse in hand, and walked out. He looked at the handwritten location and then at the clock above his office door. If this woman was putting him on, she was going to pay. But if not, well, he was certainly intrigued. Fred was a strong, stubborn man. He paid attention to details, so Sylvester knew he couldn't pull the wool over the man's eyes. Fred also loved his grandchildren—both of them, although there was obviously a soft spot for Irena. If

Sylvester's stepdaughter agreed with Fred, there was little anyone could do to sway the man. This made Ms. Blake's suggestion even more intriguing.

A rut in the road pulled Sylvester out of his reverie, and he became aware that he was nearing the turnoff. A white SUV in front of him also switched on its blinker to turn left. He slowed, wondering if the vehicle held the buyers. A few moments later Sylvester glimpsed the "For Sale" sign and smiled, again recalling how they'd set this all up. It had taken years, but that had been fine. He had multiple deals in the works on any given day, and they rarely fell through. He was a patient man.

Back then, forecasts by various realtors had suggested land values would increase in that area. Sonya had even learned, in advance, about a new well-known company that was planning to construct a facility nearby. The demand for housing would rise, the town would grow, and the property would be well situated for new homes. All that, and someone else—the government, no less— would be paying for the supposed cleanup of the mine site. His family wouldn't have to worry about ever being tasked with paying toward the remediation. Even better, a good portion of that government money had been extremely helpful in gaining the support of select local people in the right positions. It had taken some encouragement for them to see beyond the mine's contamination. After all, it wasn't like it was a popular area for sports fishing. No one was going to start stuffing his or her dinner plate with mercury-laden fish. It had been just a few months later when Sonya had fully developed her plan to help remove Fred and Sylvester's stepdaughter, Irena, from the picture.

Chapter Twenty-Nine

Luke waited until the sound of the motor stopped before daring a peak down. His heart sank. It wasn't Ted. Rather, a white Ford pickup had stopped behind his car. He moved back and whispered to Rachel.

"It's a white truck. No one's getting out." He looked down and saw she was tightly gripping Bella's leash. He sought out her gaze. Her face appeared rather calm. Luke heard the click of a door opening and slowly inched forward to peer down again. A tall, well-kept man in khakis and a light coat emerged. His head began to angle upward. Luke slouched down. He held his gun firmly, still hopeful this was nothing more than an innocuous, unrelated situation. A few moments passed, and they heard the sound of someone brushing against the bushes. Luke stole another quick glance downward.

"Gun. And he's coming up this way," he mouthed to Rachel before looking around for ways to escape unseen. The ledge they were situated on was roughly fifty feet wide and protruded about twenty feet into the mountain. There appeared to be a small hole, more likely the remnants of a now deserted mine shaft at the innermost junction with the mountain. The opening wasn't big enough for an adult.

Luke concluded their best option was try to climb down the other side of the ledge before the man reached them. He pointed.

Rachel understood and began carefully scrambling across the discolored mine tailings. If not for the tense situation, Luke would have laughed at Bella's behavior next to Rachel. The dog scooted along on her belly, literally crawling next to Rachel's side. Luke began to move across on his knees, forming a shield between Rachel and where he thought the man would approach from. They were about ten feet from the edge when Rachel bolted upright, doing her best to half run, half hop the remaining distance. Luke jumped to his feet, facing the direction of the ledge they'd moved away from. His attention was so heavily focused on where he expected to see the armed man emerge that he barely heard Rachel's loud intake of breath behind him.

"Luke," she said, her tone serious—and loud. He wondered why she'd give away their position. The man's head was just beginning to show from behind the ledge when Rachel called out again. "Luke, stop." Before her words could fully register, he took one more step back and felt his body bump against hers. She was thrown off balance but regained her footing after grasping his shoulder. They stood back to back.

"What?" Luke said as he watched the man's face come into view and tightened the grip on his weapon.

"It's not what, but whom." A woman's voice—not Rachel's—came from somewhere beyond her. It took a moment for him to place it. Finally, it clicked. *Sonya. But what would she be doing here?* Luke wasn't sure what to do. The man now stood nearby, gun aimed at Luke's chest.

"She's got a gun," Rachel said. Luke turned in her direction, noticing Rachel's glare was fixed on Sonya. He manuevered back around.

"Put it down," the man said. "We won't hurt you. We just need you to keep quiet for a good day or so, and then you two can forget all about this." Luke watched the man wipe sweat from his forehead.

"Why should we believe you?" Rachel called out behind him.

"Because we really don't want to have to deal with your bodies. Today's a big day for us. Your timing is really, really inconvenient,"

Sonya interjected. "And frankly, we've both got guns on you. You might get a shot off, but one of you will go down."

Luke considered his options, but Sonya was right. There was no scenario where he could save them all. Even if the man was shot first, whoever was left standing could take out one of them. Begrudgingly, he slowly bent down and placed his weapon on the dirt and then raised his hands above his head. He glanced sideways. Rachel had done the same, although her left arm was only held halfway up. Bella had moved, her body now rubbing against his leg. His attention shifted between Sonya and the man.

Finally, Luke asked, "Now what?" The strange man began to walk toward them.

"Over there," he said, his hand motioning toward the small gap Luke assumed to be an old cave. Luke held Rachel's arm, helping support her weight as they walked backward. His mind raced, weighing their options. If they had any. Rachel suddenly tripped, and her body slammed into his. She reached an arm around him, presumably steadying herself from a fall.

He heard her faint whisper before she stood back up. "Ted's SUV."

"Knock it off," the man ordered.

Luke briefly glanced at Rachel, acknowledging he'd understood.

~

Rachel had almost fallen over backward when the tall, thin figure of Sonya Blake suddenly appeared in front of her. It had taken a moment to recognize the woman. She now had shoulder-length brown hair. Clearly a wig. Her face was partially obscured by a dark pair of sunglasses. But Rachel immediately recognized that smile.

As she gazed in the direction of the weapon, Rachel noticed another white vehicle approaching in the distance. Her brain quickly determined it was Ted. She'd forgotten about the sports rack on top of his SUV; the vehicle clearly held two parallel black racks. As they'd been forced back, Rachel tried to surmise a way to let Luke know. She imagined he was, like her, silently running through their options. She wasn't sure if he'd seen Ted's vehicle. Rachel decided to pretend to stumble. It gave her the chance to alert him to Ted's proximity. When Luke's eyes met hers, she knew he'd understood.

They closed the final few feet and ended up against the dirt wall, facing Sonya and the man.

"What's with the disguise?" Luke prodded Sonya. Rachel felt Bella squirming next to her and looked down. *Poor thing, she has no idea what's going on.* She had draped her right arm through the end of the leash, although the idea of disconnecting it so Bella could run away crossed Rachel's mind. But she suspected Bella would either stick with them or run up to one of the two criminals and be shot. The scene had grown eerily silent. Rachel looked back at Sonya. She watched carefully as the woman placed the large sunglasses on top of her head.

"Oh, Luke, you really shouldn't have come up here today," Sonya said, shaking her head. She was still breathing hard, apparently from climbing up the hill.

With her face now fully uncovered, Rachel observed details she hadn't noticed before. With the sunglasses pulling her hair back from her face, the width of her forehead was more pronounced. There was also an odd linear shape to the angles around her hairline that weren't straight enough to be from the wig. And there was something familiar about the way she stood. Rachel had only seen the woman wearing either slippers or hiking boots. She seemed taller, and Rachel noticed her cowboy boots raised on full-soled heals. A gust of wind blew, molding the woman's loose outfit to her body. She was much thinner than Rachel had realized.

"Like we said, we're out of here after today," the man responded. Rachel saw him look toward Sonya and ask, "Well, what now?"

Rachel didn't know why, but her mind suddenly focused on something Luke had said on their drive up. He'd been talking about how Kimmy began to wear high heels in her early teens and frequently bragged that she was an inch taller than her brother. That was well before their relationship went sour.

Suddenly the knowledge struck like a large bucket of ice-cold water being poured over Rachel's head. The information in Ted's text that had been nagging at her—the body in the morgue. A *healthy* female around thirty years old. No heart damage. And the way the woman in front of her now stood assertively in the heeled boots. The notable posture.

"Let's tie these two up. Maybe we can stash them in their car somewhere," Sonya sighed. "Or maybe we should just shoot them. I'm sure there are places to hide them for a good day or two." Her tone was completely relaxed, as if discussing something no more important than what to prepare for breakfast.

"Sonya, just let us go. We'll be on our way," Luke interjected. "You're far more likely to get away. Right now, you're only charged with attempted murder. Add murder to that and you'll be on everyone's watch list, well beyond this area."

Rachel knew Luke was stalling to give Ted and Jill time to arrive. As she listened, another memory flashed through her mind. A few months ago, she'd convinced Luke to go to a Garth Brooks concert with her. When he drove up to her house in cowboy boots and a black Stetson hat, the gesture had made her start crying. He'd looked sexy as hell but also moved awkwardly as he attempted to walk in the tall boots. She remembered a certain bend in his posture that day. That same nuance was now clear in Sonya's stance.

"Sure, we'll just let you go and trust you won't say anything, right?" Sonya scoffed.

Rachel's mind was turning at full speed. Rachel knew who Sonya really was. "No way . . . ," she whispered.

"What?" Luke asked as his eyes darted between the man and Sonya.

"Shut up!" Sonya demanded.

Rachel looked directly at her and spoke. "Are you really prepared to kill your own brother, Kimmy?" Thankfully her voice had more strength than she felt. Clearly this woman had no qualms about harming anyone. Sonya's expression immediately confirmed Rachel's suspicion. She felt Luke tense up next to her.

"Huh?" he grunted, glancing in Rachel's direction before turning his intent stare toward Sonya. The woman paused, looked back at Rachel, and then began laughing. At this, Rachel sensed a twinge of nervous energy in the woman. A moment passed, and Sonya quieted. Silence hung in the air. Rachel heard only the sounds of wind blowing through nearby trees.

Finally, Sonya spoke. "All right, you got me. So, what gave it away?" Her tone was now so casual that they could have been two friends chatting over a glass of wine.

"Cosmetic surgery can't change your posture. Or cure your eating disorder. Or repair your heart."

"Excuse me, my heart?" She appeared curious, if not slightly amused.

"The woman you set up to supposedly be Kimmy—the one who they found down the river—she had a healthy heart. Kim Reed, or Kim Nunez—whatever the hell your name is—has a damaged heart. Those eating disorders can sure wreak havoc on your internal organs." As Luke continued to stare next to her, Rachel was working hard to exude a confidence she didn't feel. Inside, she was a mess, just waiting for the bullet to tear a hole through her own heart any minute. She also no longer thought they'd have time to wait for Ted to arrive, let alone for him to figure out where they were. Her only thought was to keep Sonya, or Kimmy, talking. If Luke could get beyond his shock, she trusted him to come up with some kind of move. Silence hung in the air.

Luke finally spoke and, at the same time, edged a bit more in front of her. "Kimmy? . . . Why?" As Luke posed this question, Rachel felt him grab her hand.

"Money, dear brother. What else?" She smirked.

"Mom and Dad's fortune wasn't enough for you?"

"I wouldn't call what they left us a fortune. I blew through that in a year. I mean, really, do you know what it costs to live in Beverly Hills these days?" She waited and then tilted her head before continuing. "You have no idea what happened to them? Really?" She gaped at Luke. More silence. Again, Rachel heard only the wrestling sound of the wind weaving through pine needles. She hoped the breeze was enough to cover the sounds of Ted's approach. Sonya stood up straight and shrugged her shoulders. "Figures. Well, it doesn't matter now. All you had to do was stay out of it." A brief pause. Rachel noticed Luke hesitating.

"What were you searching for in my house?" he finally demanded. Of all the things one might ask in this situation, Rachel thought Luke's question was odd. However, as Luke spoke, she felt him press three fingers deeply into her palm. Although clearly a signal, she couldn't imagine what for. But it was some kind of a countdown. She focused on not reacting. *Three.*

"A copy of your will, of course. Mom felt remorseful about what Dad did—mind you, it was after he was locked away and she went off to rehab—so she had papers drawn to give us each half of their fortune. You probably didn't even know that, did you?" Again, he took his time responding. Rachel felt another stroke of pressure. *Two.*

"It was you at my office," he acknowledged. She nodded. Luke continued. "Yes, I got some calls about a year back from the family attorney. I assumed they were trying to pull me back in. Presumably make amends. I never called back. Same with a letter or two." Luke paused and then added, "Just like you never returned five years' worth of my calls." *One.* Rachel tried to be ready for anything.

Just as Sonya smirked and opened her mouth to reply, Luke ripped off the sunglasses he'd been wearing and tossed them over the ledge. "Bella, go get it!" he shouted.

The leash burned Rachel's skin as the dog quickly took off to chase the artificial "stick." It had surprised all of them, which may be why Bella made it to the ledge and jumped over without any shots ringing out. There was no time to celebrate.

Rachel turned her attention back to Luke. He moved fast. A roundhouse kick at Sonya's gun-wielding hand and the weapon was airborne. Luke swiftly turned and threw his body against the man, and both of them crashed to the ground.

Chapter Thirty

Luke had reacted purely on instinct. He was still grappling with the idea that this woman, *this killer*, was his sister. But now was not the time for emotion. It was time for action. And Bella tumbling down the hill was not only a distraction, but also a way to alert Ted.

It was risky—jumping on someone with a gun. But for a split second, the man's gaze hadn't been focused on either of them. Luke took advantage, propelling himself into the air and slamming his fist into the man's face with the full momentum of his body's weight behind it. He felt the resistance in the man's arm slightly weakening. Luke shifted to his side and rolled off of him. The gun now wavered over the man's stomach. Luke grabbed at it. The man's fist tightened, and a shot rang out. Luke registered no pain. He hadn't been shot.

Luke managed another knuckle to the man's kidneys. This time, the man's grip on the weapon relaxed. He heard struggling nearby, but Luke had to incapacitate this man. Rachel could think on her feet. The man grunted. Luke pried his hands open.

Just as Luke secured his fingers around the handle, the man's other hand came around and slammed into his cheek. It was more than a tight fist—apparently the man had found a palm-sized rock to add to the effect. The impact heaved Luke backward. The weapon dropped. Seeing the guy was solely focused on retrieving the gun, Luke swung his foot up with all of the strength he could find. His boot caught the man in the chin, snapping his head backward. He landed with a loud thud, arms flailing. The gun flew into a clump of nearby bushes. One more solid blow from the side and the man's eyes shut. Luke turned to face Rachel and Sonya—*his sister.*

Chapter Thirty-One

As Luke sprang into action, Rachel reacted. Sonya had turned away, eyes searching the ground nearby. Instinctively, Rachel lunged and slammed all of her weight against Sonya's side. It worked. They both fell, landing on the soft dirt. Rachel blinked as the light dust of mine tailings drifted into her eyes. She couldn't do much to keep the woman down, especially with her injured shoulder. Sonya pushed back, applying pressure to the worst spot possible. Breath escaped Rachel. She rolled off the woman. It took a moment to realize something sharp poked into her back—the pistol. A shot rang out nearby, and Rachel flinched.

Luke, no! She screamed inside, instantly recalling the terror when he was shot last summer. Before she could raise her head to look in the direction of the two men, Sonya kicked her hard and then frantically began sweeping her hands through the dirt. Rachel moaned, lifting her shoulder and managing to scoot a few inches to her side. She bent her right arm behind her to retrieve the weapon. Just as her fingers brushed the handle, Luke appeared in her line of sight, looking around frantically. Relief swept over Rachel—he bore no bullet holes. Movement to her side quickly refocused her attention.

Sonya edged toward Rachel. She must have figured out Rachel was lying on the gun. Sonya didn't yet seem aware of Luke's approach. Rachel's hand finally clasped what it sought just as Luke reached down and firmly grabbed Sonya's ankle. He yanked hard, dragging Sonya a good foot away from Rachel. Getting a moment to look directly at Luke, Rachel observed a few drops of blood dripping below a cut on his cheek. One eye was going to swell shut. Rachel shook off the thought and raised the gun, finger on the trigger. Luke remained standing, although weaving as if fighting to keep his balance.

"Sonya!" Rachel yelled a second too late. Sonya's foot slammed into Luke's stomach. He fell backward. Sonya turned her attention on Rachel. She was grinning. Her skin was flushed. Sonya's eyes widened when she saw Rachel's hand.

"You wouldn't," she scoffed.

"Oh, I would," Rachel replied, careful to keep her hand steady. Although deep down she wasn't *100 percent sure* she could pull the trigger.

"Then why haven't you already?" Sonya said, launching herself toward Rachel. Her arm knocked Rachel's hand to the side, and they rolled across the ground. Somehow Rachel managed to hold on, although she could feel the woman's fingers trying to claw the weapon from her grasp. With the barrel aimed toward the mountain, Rachel pulled the trigger. Sonya paused and looked up. Rachel struggled to push the woman off of her. A good kick and Sonya fell back but not down. Ted's authoritative voice erupted from nearby.

"Give it up, Sonya, or I'll shoot."

Sonya didn't respond, nor did she make any moves to disengage from Rachel. A glance in the direction of Sonya's male counterpart confirmed Sonya had no backup.

"She's not Sonya," Luke's rough voice croaked from behind Ted. He was attempting to get to his feet. Luke's gaze was focused solely on the woman, an expression of absolute disgust. "Ted, meet my sister, Kimmy." He wiped his cheek, smearing the crimson blood into two long streaks.

"Whoever she is, she's two seconds shy of an easily justifiable bullet hole," Ted responded, his department-issued weapon held steady in his hand. Another second passed before Sonya dropped back away from Rachel and placed her hands in the air.

Bella was safe. They had survived. Rachel turned to see Luke stumbling toward her. He fell to his knees in front of her, eyes watering, and enveloped her in a tight embrace. Rachel gladly leaned against him. A moment passed, and then she looked around the scene for Bella.

Nearby, Sonya lay on her stomach while Ted placed handcuffs on her wrists. The woman coughed, and a cloud of dust swirled around her. Ted stood and walked over to the man as he spoke to Rachel.

"I'm going to take care of this guy, and then you have some explaining to do," he said, retrieving a second pair of handcuffs.

"Is he alive?" Rachel heard Jill's voice a moment before she saw her peering from the other side of the ledge. Bella followed behind her. Rachel smiled.

"Yes," Ted responded. The clink of metal on metal echoed. "Looks like someone beat the crap out of him. Nice job, Luke."

"How did you find us so quickly?" Rachel asked as Luke relaxed his hold.

"The Bella bomb," Jill said, walking toward them. Rachel could almost see Jill's mind turning as she assessed their injuries and decided where to go first. "We had just driven up behind that white truck, and over the hill came this black blur of fur." As if on cue, Bella bounced up in front of Jill and then ran over to Rachel and dropped her front legs down, her butt remaining in the air.

While Rachel scratched just above the pup's tail, she whispered to Luke, "Thank you." Tears filled her eyes. He reached up and caressed her cheek. "You're not hurt?" she asked. He shook his head, leaned in, and placed a soft kiss on her lips. They were immediately interrupted by a wagging tail beating against their faces. Pulling apart, Rachel laughed and glanced at Bella's enthusiastic posture. When she turned back to Luke, she noticed a strain in his expression. She couldn't imagine the betrayal he must be feeling. Or, frankly, any emotion he might be dealing with from this. He turned his head for a moment and quietly glimpsed his sister as she lay, cursing, face down in the dirt. Rachel brushed his cheek and then dropped her hand. She was losing steam quickly. The adrenaline rush was dying off. Her leg throbbed, and blood was slowly running from the torn bandage. She reached to assess the damage. The quick drop of her hand must have caught Luke's attention. He looked at her and then down at her leg.

"Jill, need your help here!" he called out, alarm in his tone.

"No narcotics," Rachel mumbled, feeling dizzy. "I need to lie down." Luke quickly pulled her against him, placing her head on his chest as Jill knelt down next to her.

~

Sylvester had been casually leaning against his car, waiting for the arrival of the buyers and their attorney. He'd pondered how he'd enjoyed sparring with the female representative the previous night when he heard the faint sound of a gunshot in the distance.

"What the . . . ?" He turned to look in the direction of the sound. There were at least two cars on the hill above the property. It was some distance away, but he could make out movement. When the second shot rang out, he got nervous. Sonya and Carlton were usually early, if not at least on time. But they weren't here. Something wasn't right. He debated whether to wait longer or go check it out. There were no other cars coming down the road. The buyers would probably be late—people usually were when they knew someone was willing to wait. He looked back toward the hill again and made his decision.

Sylvester climbed back into his car and began driving in the direction of the gunshots. He steered onto the dirt road that led to the old mine and came around a bend. A tall blond man was walking down the hill above the road next to Carlton, whose face was bloody and his step unstable. His arms were behind his back. The man looked in Sylvester's direction and stopped. Sylvester noticed a white SUV parked behind Carlton's truck. Someone was already inside the backseat. As he pulled up in the space next to it, he saw the passenger's face. It was Sonya, staring wide-eyed in his direction. She appeared to mouth the word "help." She made no move to open the door or wave at him. Movement up the hill caught his attention, and he noticed another man looking down from the ledge of an old tailing pile.

Something was amiss; he had to get out of here. Fast. He threw his car into reverse. It kicked up dust as he backed around in a semicircle and then jerked the wheel to turn back down the road. In his rearview mirror he glimpsed the blond-haired man standing against the backside of the SUV, dragging Carlton with him while peering in Sylvester's direction. As far as he was concerned, there was nothing to be done other than to save himself.

As he sped away, Sylvester wondered if Sonya or Carlton would give him up to the cops. *Of course they would.* Sonya would have no qualms about naming Nathaniel, either. It's not like she was really his sister. The real Irena had moved to Europe for a job opportunity she couldn't pass up. Of course, Silver had made a few calls to help prompt the job offer in the first place. He had simply taken the opportunity presented to him by Sonya Blake when the two women "broke up." *If lesbians did that sort of thing*, he mused as he dialed his son's number.

"Nathaniel, it's me," he said when he heard an annoyed greeting.

"I've been sitting here waiting for instructions all day! Where are Carlton and Sonya? And—"

"Boy, shut up and listen. We need to leave town for a while. Drive to the gas station in Silver Springs immediately. If I'm not there yet, wait for me. This is serious."

"But—"

"Got your passport?" he snapped, not wanting to hear any more gripes. It would take him a few hours to drive to Silver Springs. Nathanial was already in Reno. In fact, his son would have time to drive up to Virginia City. Thank God he'd planned ahead, storing the money in that old mine instead of his home or office. Not that he'd had much choice once his ex-business partner had started having him monitored. Yes, Silver had helped himself to some money that wasn't his, but he wasn't about to either admit it or leave the cash somewhere it could easily be found. At the time, he'd expected his house would be searched. He'd been right. But the angry ex-partner couldn't prove anything. Now, having no need to go home first to get his stash was a bonus. They could get away clean.

"Yes, Father, I have *a* passport," Nathanial said, emphasizing the word "a." *Good.* Silver taught Nathaniel to always have a backup plan. But he had worried the kid might not have listened. It's one reason he tasked Carlton to work with him. He hoped it would help straighten the boy out.

"Good. Actually, on the way, I need you to run up by the Comstock and grab our loot. Don't let anyone see you. After that, head straight to Silver Springs."

"What about Sonya?" the kid asked.

"She was never your actual sister. Get over it," Sylvester shouted and then hung up. He slammed his fist into the steering wheel. He had just lost a lot of money. Upward of thirty million dollars—far more than he had hidden in the mine. There had been no way Irena—Nathaniel's real sister—would let them sell those lots. Although Sonya had been willing to kill her, Sylvester hadn't wanted to go that far. He had done a lot of so-called bad things in his life, but murder—at least premeditated—was not one of them. So they'd helped ensure Irena would remain far away, working in the outskirts of Africa. At the same time, her occasional visits home to Fred didn't create any friction. The old man was so messed up from his regular doses of mercury that he couldn't tell the difference between the real Irena and a disguised Sonya. Sam had been paid very well to stay on as a caretaker, managing visits from both women. Silver had no idea where the corpse they intended to be Eddie's "dead wife" came from. That was another secret Sonya had kept. *Not my problem*, he thought. Now it was time to move on.

Sylvester knew they could get away and regroup. He'd done it before. In fact, he'd already set into motion the electronic manipulations needed to lead the authorities to believe they had left the country.

~

Nathaniel couldn't believe it. His father wanted to run away. *And let those damn women win!* The ones who made a fool of him in Reno. *And what happened to Sonya? And his sister? What was his father not telling him?*

"Oh my God. He killed Irena. That has to be it!" he concluded. His mind raced as his eyes darted around his small apartment. "We are not running, Father," he uttered in a voice so calm he didn't recognize it as his own. He was nineteen years old. It was time to stop doing everything his father commanded.

"I'll get your stash in Virginia City all right," he snarled, a new plan forming in his mind. And he wasn't done with those two bitches. Not by a long shot.

Chapter Thirty-Two

"That was pretty sexy back there." Rachel winked at Luke. "That is, you kicking ass and all." He didn't respond right away. He was sitting next to her in the backseat of his Subaru after Jill suggested—or rather demanded—that he was in no shape to drive. Bella was happy to take the front seat, especially when Jill had lured her with treats. Ted was still back at the crime scene, dealing with other officers, although he had first taken time to explain to them what Carlton had confessed about how Kimmy, as Sonya Blake, had pretended to be the granddaughter of the man who owned the land in order to sell it and reap the profits. His two criminals were likely in the back of another officer's car by now.

"You didn't do so bad yourself," he replied. Her leg was propped across his lap, and he gently massaged her knee above the freshly bandaged wound. His head rested against the seat.

"How are you doing? Really?" she asked, waiting for him to meet her gaze. When he finally rolled his head to look at her, she could see the sorrow in his eyes.

"I keep wondering if I set something in motion all of those years ago. For her to turn out like this . . ."

"What else could you have done? Give up your own life in endless pursuit of her?" she asked, taking his hand. He shook his head, as if trying to clear his mind.

"And how could I not have realized it was her? She was in my guest room, for God's sake."

"Not trying to eavesdrop on you two, but the car isn't that big," Jill's voice boomed. "Luke, all I can say is I have autopsied people who look nothing like they used to. The right plastic surgery, speech lessons, and a lot of practice can really change someone."

"You also hadn't seen her in, what, over fifteen years?" Rachel added. He didn't respond. They sat quietly for a few more minutes before he looked up.

"The woman who you examined, Jill, . . . was that the real Irena?" Luke inquired.

"I don't know. Although it sounds like Sonya, or rather Kim, has been involved in this for some time. I didn't catch the full story, but you know Ted. He's going to push until he gets a full report. Also, the body in the morgue hasn't been dead long enough to be Irena—assuming she was murdered back when Sonya took over her identity."

Exhausted and lulled by the sound of the tires on the road, Rachel was quickly growing tired. She let her head fall against Luke's shoulder. Yawning, she looked forward. Staring intently at her from the front seat were two brown eyes. Bella remained still, apparently waiting to see if it was acceptable to wag her tail. Rachel reached up and rubbed behind her ear. The tail began to move. "You, my girl, literally saved our lives," she said.

"That she did," Luke agreed, rubbing Bella's other ear. The dog was in heaven. A few moments later Rachel felt Luke wrap his arm around her, and she closed her eyes.

~

Where is that twit? Silver wondered. He'd arrived at their meeting spot ten minutes ago. The boy should have already been there. His calls went straight to voice mail. Another hour passed, and still no sign of Nathaniel. Sylvester debated whether to drive back to the mine to look for his son or keep waiting.

"Little shit probably tripped," he mumbled. He should go back. Even if Sonya or Carlton had already named him, there would be no reason for the cops to be looking for him there. He could drive up to the mine just to check. Maybe he'd find Nathaniel on the way.

Forty-five minutes later Sylvester stood dumbfounded at the old shaft. The money was gone. In its place was a short note: "*Sorry, Dad, but I've got my own plans.*"

Sylvester grabbed the note and looked around at the empty cave. Frustration and anger started to well up in his gut, but in his heart he was scared for his son. Distracted by his mixed emotions as he walked out, Sylvester almost ran into one of the fake signs he'd posted warning people to stay away from the area due to danger from old, undetonated explosives. Although this place was safe, visitors wouldn't know that, and the sign had served its purpose. He crossed over the rusted barbed-wire fence strung below the cave's entrance and looked in the distance at his car. He wasn't sure he could run and leave his son behind, much as he was disappointed with the kid. He sat behind the wheel and drove south. When he reached Highway 50, east of Carson City, he turned west. *One night. I'll stay one night to track him down.*

Chapter Thirty-Three

"Men!" Rachel opened the passenger door to her pickup. Bella jumped down and walked toward their front porch. Rachel was still stewing over Luke—even after a good few-hour hike out in Charity Valley. It irritated her that her thoughts had continued to dwell on her anger even while out enjoying the beautiful walk, but she couldn't help it. Ever since Luke was released from the hospital two weeks ago—the day after what she had termed their "adventure in Susanville"—he'd been acting strange. Again. Distant. She knew he was having regular headaches. He said the doctors had only prescribed a few days' worth of pain pills, so she'd given him the rest of hers.

But stubborn man that he was, he still refused to consider seeing a new doctor. She'd even suggested he try a chiropractor. Maybe his spine just needed a few adjustments and the misalignment was pulling on his muscles, causing the headaches. He'd certainly been knocked around enough lately. She didn't understand his unwillingness to help himself. Rachel slammed the door shut as she replayed their earlier conversation.

"Even if you want to just take Bella to Kiva Beach, that's fine. We can let her swim in the lake while we relax on the sand." Kiva Beach was one of the few dog-friendly beaches in South Lake Tahoe. It had become one of their favorite locations for after-dinner strolls last fall.

"Should you be going to a sandy beach, with your leg and all?"

"It's healing. I'll just wear a bandage like I have the last few days I've taken walks." Sarcastic, she knew. But his response told her he hadn't been paying much attention lately. She waited.

"You go ahead and do whatever you feel like. I'm going to stay here and do some ice-pack therapy. Maybe tomorrow," he'd finally replied.

"We can carry ice packs to the beach, you know."

"Look, I know you probably want to get some cardio in. So, please, do your thing. Maybe we can plan on Kiva tomorrow, okay?" he'd said.

"All right, but, please, give more thought to the chiropractor. You have nothing to lose by getting checked out." She waited, and he finally sighed.

"I promise to think about it."

That was the most he'd conceded so far, so she had dropped the subject, said good-bye, and taken Bella hiking.

She pulled open the glass door and they entered the small enclosed porch. The door behind them slammed shut, Rachel wincing at the loud sound. She carefully stepped around the canine to unlock the front door. As she pushed it open, Bella looked at her, waiting.

"Good job," Rachel said as she smiled, proud she'd been able to teach Bella to let humans walk through doors first rather than rush through them. Rachel stepped inside and dropped her keys and small backpack on a nearby table before turning back to Bella.

"Okay, girl, come on in." The canine tentatively stepped inside and paused, her snout raised in the air. Her tail stopped wagging, and she took another cautious step forward. The pup focused her attention into the hallway. Rachel's first thought was a chipmunk must have made its way into the house somehow. Her second thought was that she needed to get Bella into the backyard before she inspected further lest a possible dog-versus-rodent chase ensue. "Let's head out back." She motioned for Bella to come with her.

"Nice to see you again," a man spoke loudly from behind her. Rachel froze. She didn't recognize his voice, but it was clearly not a friend. She turned to see a young man in dark jeans, an old black T-shirt, and lime-green shoes. A gun in his right hand pointed straight at her. They made eye contact. She knew this man. He'd ordered Kristina and her out of the car in Reno. And tried to kill her with a morphine overdose. Her gaze settled on the weapon. The ringing chime of the bear bell on Bella's harness was the only sound in the room.

~

Luke had fallen asleep after aiming to simply relax on his sofa. Again. He groggily opened his eyes and looked around his living room. The television was on, but it was muted. The clock read 3:38 p.m. *Was that right?* He looked out the front window but had to close his eyes from the brightness of the sun. His head still hurt with a chronic dull ache. He had not slept well the night before. Frankly, he barely managed more than three or four hours of sleep at a time—about how long the pain pills lasted. He had expected the headaches would go away with time. Rachel had been urging him to see a chiropractor, but he'd had friends who'd been adjusted three times a week for years. He just saw it as a waste of time and money. Plus, the emergency room doctors had warned him he may have some lingering head pain. *Although two weeks without improvement is rather extreme,* he thought.

Maybe it was worth a try. He'd ask Rachel if she had someone to recommend. Usually she checked in by calling or texting when she came back from a hike. If she didn't have as much work to do, she might stay gone longer. She was probably still out and about. Luke sat up, thirsty. Upon moving, the pain got worse. He could barely think. He also noticed his entire body ached, even in places that weren't hurt. That sensation was more uniform and had started—mildly at first—not long before their incident with Sonya and the man. Luke had considered that he may be getting physically addicted to the painkillers. But he needed them right now. Eventually he'd feel better and could easily deal with any temporary withdrawal symptoms.

For now, another Vicodin would take the edge off. By then, Rachel might have returned and maybe he could speak coherently. Ask her who to call. He was desperate; these headaches couldn't continue.

~

After giving some thought to his son's next move, Sylvester's suspicions had been right. The boy was stalking the woman in

South Lake Tahoe. Although he'd promised he'd give it just one day, in the end, he couldn't leave his son behind. Nathaniel had been obsessed with Rachel ever since she'd gotten the upper hand on him in Reno. His son wasn't the most stable person, and his recent behavior had Sylvester even more concerned. So he'd booked himself into an old motel in South Lake Tahoe and kept his head low. When the news reported charges against Sonya and Carlton a few days after their arrests, images of Sylvester and Nathaniel had also been aired. By then, he had colored his hair and grown out a mustache to alter his appearance. He also selected a motel with daily and weekly rentals, where people came and went, mostly not staying for long. During the last week, he'd driven through Rachel's neighborhood. Just a few times each day so as to not draw attention. After more than a week of these regular forays, his intuition finally paid off. A few blocks down the street and around a corner from her home sat his son's car—easily recognizable as the only dark-brown sedan with fuzzy dice hanging on the rearview mirror. Sylvester drove on by, turned around, passed Miss Winters's home again, and then parked his rented car in an empty driveway two houses away. He hoped to get Nathaniel out of there before he called any more attention to himself.

As he walked along the street, Sylvester saw only one other vehicle parked in the area. Otherwise there was no one else around. He stepped around the side of the house and carefully opened the small wooden gate. He looked around the corner. The backyard was empty. There was a small wooden patio protruding out below a large glass sliding door. Keeping his steps light, he made his way over to the deck and glanced through the window. He saw two figures inside.

Chapter Thirty-Four

"Bella!" Rachel cried as the dog lunged toward the man. She watched in horror as he reached out and grabbed the back of her harness. The man—rather Nathaniel Cox, as she'd learned on the news recently—caught hold with his left hand. The gun remained firmly in his right. A sound burst from behind her. Rachel couldn't help but turn and look as her sliding glass door was slammed open.

"Nathaniel!" another voice boomed through the house.

Rachel froze.

"Dad?" She heard the younger man grunt. Then a ringing bell. She turned to look back at Bella just as the dog broke free from Nathaniel's grasp and ran toward the older intruder. She abruptly stopped in front of him, her stance tentative yet defensive. The man looked at Rachel, ignoring the dog. *This must be his father, Sylvester Cox. Not good.*

"Get out of here," Sylvester said. "And take this mutt with you." Rachel's heart was beating so fast she could barely hear his words. The man moved aside, giving them a clear exit.

"Bella, it's okay. Let's go outside," she encouraged, throwing one of the tennis balls she placed by the doorway into the yard. She kept her voice calm. If Bella thought this man was a threat, the canine might not budge. Bella paused but then swept past her and rushed outside after the ball. Rachel was just about a foot from the doorway—and freedom—when she heard the kid's voice.

"Rachel, stop!" he demanded. "Dad, I'm not letting her go!"
She paused, fearing if she didn't, she'd be shot in the back.

"Yes, you are." The man's tone was stern. He wore an unreadable expression on his face.

"Get over here, or I'll—"

"No, you won't, Nate." Sylvester stepped into the kitchen and then turned to Rachel. "Leave. *Now.*" She rushed past him and jumped down the steps, looking around the small yard for Bella.

~

Nathaniel couldn't believe it. His father had just let Rachel walk right out the door. Rather, he'd instructed her to. *How could he?*

"Son, just put the gun down. You've got the money already. We can leave here now, safe and sound." Silver took another step toward him. He began raising his hand. "We can start over."

"I can't just leave her here," Nathaniel spat out. "Do you know what—"

"Yes, you can. Remember what I taught you. Sometimes you need to cut your losses to save yourself. Now it's time to do that here. She was part of a job. It went wrong. It happens." The hand rose up higher. He took another step closer.

"No, it was more than a job. And you . . ." He waved the gun back and forth. "You killed my sister!" Nathaniel watched as Sylvester paused. He appeared completely baffled.

"Irena's just fine. Don't you remember? You even saw her a couple of months ago. At Fred's place." His father's expression changed. Concern had been replaced by pity. For some reason, Nathaniel felt anger rush through him. *He's lying. It's so obvious.*

"I don't believe you, *Dad.*" Drawing out the last word, he pulled the trigger. Nathaniel had never seen such a surprised look on his father's face. The man dropped, his hands clutching his bleeding chest.

"Son, please . . . get h-help," he stuttered as he dropped to the floor. Nathaniel remained where he was, his gaze intent on the prone figure. His father's eyes were closed. Nathaniel continued to stare, mesmerized by the expanding patch of red. It reminded him of the girl on the hiking trail. Only this time he knew what the old man was thinking about before he died. Briefly, a memory of riding on his dad's shoulders through the crowd at a county fair flashed through his mind. Back then, Sylvester had smiled, laughed, and played games with him. But now, Nathaniel couldn't recall the last time he'd heard even the slightest joke from his father. *This isn't Dad,* he told himself. *Just another stranger that was in the way.*

He turned, and his other hand subconsciously rubbed the item he'd inadvertently torn from the dog's harness. *Rachel is getting away. Where is she?* Movement out the front window caught his eye. There she was, standing in the front yard. Nathaniel noticed she held a cell phone to her ear, but she wasn't speaking. Rather, she was bent over, messing with an old manzanita bush. The call must not be going through. No surprise—his cell phone didn't work very well out here, either. A high-pitched sound broke through his reverie. It was coming from his own hand. Nathaniel looked at the object he carried. It was a bell. A smile formed on his lips. He rushed to the front of the house, propped the glass door on the porch open, and then stood back and waited for his chance. *This is going to be fun.* He aimed at the ceiling and pulled the trigger.

~

Bella wasn't in the backyard, so Rachel walked around to the north side of her house. The gate was open—Bella had escaped. *Good girl.* While picking up her pace, Rachel reached for the cell phone in her pocket and dialed 9-1-1. The operator answered.

"9-1-1. What's your emergency?" the voice asked; Rachel almost cried.

"Two men broke into my house. They're armed." She blurted her words as she stepped around the corner, eyes searching for Bella. Rachel darted toward the street so she could run into her neighbor's yard—where she expected Bella had gone. The six-foot wooden fence separating their properties would provide protection in case the kid somehow managed a shot in her direction out the front window. She tripped over a manzanita bush but caught herself before she fell, quickly disconnecting her leg from the offending branch. Her neighbor's yard in view, she panicked. *Where was Bella?* It took several seconds to realize the operator had responded.

"Ma'am? Can you tell me your address?" the female voice repeated.

"I'm at—" A shot rang out from inside the house. Rachel froze. The woman asked for her address again. "I just heard a gunshot," Rachel exclaimed as she began racing into the road, eyes intently searching for Bella. Then she noticed her porch door was open, as was the front door. A sound from inside the house caused her gut to clench. It was Bella's bear bell. *She had gone back inside the house. Oh my God! Did he just shoot her?*

"Bella? Bella!" she screamed.

"Ma'am, have you been injured? What's—" The disembodied voice of the 9-1-1 operator pulled her back for a moment.

"Call Officer Ted Benson," she pleaded. "I'm Rachel Winters. Tell him the carjacker is here!" Without thinking, Rachel ran back into her house, the phone grasped tightly in her hand but otherwise forgotten. Her living room was empty. She had just registered the man lying on the kitchen floor when the front door slammed shut behind her. Rachel whirled around. Nathaniel stood still, grinning. He tossed something at her. It was a small silver bell.

~

Ted hung up the phone and ran out of his house at full speed. He'd just received a call from dispatch about Rachel. When the operator said Rachel's last word was "Bella" before she stopped communicating, he knew something bad had happened. The operator said she had notified his department first, so officers were "on the way." But Ted lived just miles up the highway. He put the red emergency light on top of his SUV and slammed on the accelerator. As he sped toward Rachel's home, he commanded his audio system to dial Luke. It went straight to voice mail. Ted left a message and then tried Luke's house line. The machine picked up after four rings. He repeated his message as he raced through the small community of Meyers with no regard for speed limits.

Chapter Thirty-Five

"I'm kind of surprised you fell for that," Nathaniel said as he slowly approached Rachel. She stared, trying to fully comprehend her situation. She heard her self-defense coach reminding her not to freeze up.

"What . . . what do you want?" she posed, stepping back toward the front door.

"Revenge." He stated matter-of-factly and took another step forward. Rachel tried to get her mind back into gear.

"All this because we got away in Reno? Seriously?" *Think, Rachel.*

"A man has his pride, you know? And, well, you've caused us a lot of trouble." Another step in her direction. Rachel moved back, trying not to look at the gun.

"You killed your own father? Is that what a *man* does?" *Oh, shit,* she thought. *My sarcasm is going to get me killed.*

"He murdered my sister. Turnabout is fair play and all."

"No, he didn't." She paused, waiting a moment for him to understand. He didn't respond, so she continued. "In fact, she's back with your grandpa right now." *Keep him talking, and think!* Rachel held out hope that someone would get here in time. Before he shot her. Nathaniel paused. A look of confusion swept across his face for the briefest moment. Then the smug look returned.

"How would you know that?"

"The news, for starters."

"They lie." He took another step toward her, now only a foot away. He wore an odd expression. He didn't look sane. She recoiled, and her foot caught on something—Sylvester's leg. She stumbled and fell over backward, her fall broken by the still body. As she struggled to move off, Nathaniel closed the gap quickly, grabbed her arm, and wrenched her back up onto her feet. Before she could react, she was slammed against the wall.

"Just look it up! You can see for yourself," she cried out. She felt tears forming and hated that he'd see how scared she was.

"Well, doesn't matter much." He shrugged his shoulders and looked around. He kept the gun aimed at her while he crossed the room and then grabbed a scarf from an old coatrack. Rachel glanced at the back door. It was still open. *Could she run fast enough? And where were the cops?*

"I wouldn't," he said. "Sit down." He waved the gun at one of the kitchen chairs. She hesitated, not sure what to do. "Now!" he yelled. Rachel heard soft whimpers coming from the front porch. Bella must be trying to get to her. She couldn't tell if Nathaniel noticed. She hoped Bella wouldn't attempt to come around to the back door. He'd probably shoot the dog on sight. Rachel looked down at the man on the floor. It might be her eyes playing tricks on her, but she thought his chest was moving up and down. As she sat down, Nathaniel stepped behind her. *Oh my God. He's going to choke me,* she thought. Instead, he roughly grabbed her arms and pulled back. She felt the cloth tighten on her wrists behind the chair.

"What are you going to do?" It was such a clichéd question, but she now understood the nervous energy behind people asking it.

"Not sure yet," he said as he walked back to the coatrack and retrieved another scarf. Rachel looked at the clock through her blurred tears. It was 4:05 p.m. *Where was the cavalry?*

~

Ted debated. Should he drive right up front and announce himself, or should he sneak up quietly? He decided to park down the street and walk in from the side to assess the situation first. As he approached Rachel's house, there was movement by the door. Bella anxiously pawed at the bottom, as if she could make a space to sneak in. He took a few more steps, and she stopped, looked his way, and came running. *Please don't start barking.* He was surprised when she jumped up on him; it was something she'd never done before. He gently set her down and gave her a quick pet before walking toward the side gate. It was closed but not latched. He pulled the top, and it opened. Bella tried to rush in beside him, but he closed it before she could. An anxious dog would not make for a stealthy approach. Ted heard voices as he ducked under a kitchen window. The back door was open. He crouched against the ground and crawled up two small steps, then retrieved a small pocket mirror he'd starting carrying after the reflection from a glass window had saved his life during a recent drug bust. Held correctly, it allowed Ted to peer inside the house without being seen. At least so long as it didn't catch a glare, but that was a risk he had to take. First, he observed the man's body on the floor. Next, he saw Rachel. She was bound to a chair. Her arms were pulled behind her with something he couldn't see, and a scarf had been tied around her ankles. Tears ran down her face. Leaning against a countertop on the other side of the kitchen was a young man. Ted recognized him immediately. Not only were his facial features distinct, but he also wore unique shoes. Acquaintances had noted Nathaniel Cox's strange affinity for bright-colored footwear. The kid had a gun pointed at Rachel. There was no time to wait for backup. Ted quickly glimpsed the yard behind him. He quietly scooted back down the short steps and picked up a fist-sized rock.

~

Luke slowly emerged from the remnants of a dream. With each passing second the small play running in his mind faded, and by the time he opened his eyes, the memory of it was just about gone. His head ached, but it had dulled, thankfully. He lay for a moment, thinking to himself. He couldn't keep doing this. The pain sucked, but the emotional distance, the odd desire to be alone, and lying to Rachel were worse. His thoughts were interrupted by the chirp of his cell phone on the coffee table in front of him. Luke winced as he sat up, but the sharp pain he'd experienced earlier didn't come back. He picked up the phone. Ted had marked his message as urgent. As he listened to it, his stomach dropped. He stood, feeling the mild grogginess of the Vicodin tugging at him to lie back down. But he fought it. He had to get to Rachel. *Now.*

Chapter Thirty-Six

Bella ceased pawing at the door. But Rachel didn't dare turn her head to look. That might raise Nathaniel's attention, and if the dog's actions meant that help had arrived, she didn't want him alerted. Revived by a new sense of hope, she engaged the intruder.

"Please. Your sister is alive and well. Would she want you doing this?"

He laughed. "Of course not. Irena is one of the sweetest, most gullible people I know. I love her. And now she's gone."

"But—"

"Don't talk!" he screamed. He seemed to be shifting from calm, to angry, and then to pensive. Rachel wondered if this was what it was like when people truly went insane. Suddenly something flew across the room several feet in front of her. A loud clanking sound emanated from the front window to her right. Her gaze followed the sound. So did Nathaniel's.

Rachel immediately registered movement to her left. A large figure—Ted, based on the voice—burst through the open back door, yelling, "Police!" Just as Nathaniel turned his way, Ted fired. Nathaniel flinched. He had moved just in time to turn a shoulder shot into a mere scrape of his arm. Nathaniel returned fire, gun aimed where Ted's head had previously been. But Ted had already dropped and rolled in a somersault. Once upright and propped on his knee, Ted shouted, "Drop it!" He held his weapon firmly.

Nathaniel didn't respond. Ted pulled the trigger just as Nathaniel dropped down to the floor on all fours. He leapt toward Rachel, quickly moving to her side. She now served as a barrier between the two men. Nathaniel stood up, gun pressed firmly against her right temple. Rachel could barely breathe.

"Nathaniel, release her. There's nowhere to go," Ted's authoritative voice commanded.

"Go ahead. Shoot me and my finger pulls this trigger. You'll be cleaning her brains off the wall."

At this image, Rachel closed her eyes, the fear sending chills down her spine. Tears leaked from her eyes.

"If you wanted her dead, you would have already done it," Ted stated. Rachel forced her eyes back open. She wasn't so sure she agreed with Ted's assessment. The room went silent. Rachel tried again to loosen the knot around her wrists, but it was a thin scarf and he had pulled it tight.

"That's a dumbass assumption, officer. Please, join us."

Rachel waited. Ted didn't move.

"Put it down. Right there in front of you where I can see it," Nathaniel ordered. Ted slowly complied, setting his gun down near the body of Sylvester. "Now, I get the feeling you're alone. Perhaps off duty. What, exactly, did you hope to accomplish?"

Rachel watched in horror as the gun's aim moved from her to Ted and then back to her.

"Backup is on the way. You won't get out of here," Ted said, both hands raised in the air. Rachel recognized his calculating expression. The gun pointed back to Ted.

"I'll kill you both and be gone before—"

A shot rang out. Rachel flinched. After realizing her own brain remained intact, she expected to see Ted falling to the ground. But he was still standing, his hands apparently feeling his chest for holes. Rachel turned around and looked to her side where Nathaniel still stood. The gun was gone from his hand. Instead, he was frantically grasping at the side of his neck. Blood spurted out, drenching his fingers. Rachel had to fight the urge to throw up. She looked back toward Ted. He was kneeling next to Sylvester. She watched Ted's weapon fall from the man's limp hand. His head was raised, and Rachel thought she saw a tear roll down his cheek. Sylvester's head collapsed back onto the floor and he closed his eyes for the last time. Ted felt the pulse on the man's neck, shaking his head as he glanced up at Rachel. After picking up the gun, he stood up and ran to her. He untied the scarf around her wrists, and she reached to free her legs.

"I thought we were . . . ," she stammered. It was all she could think to say. Ted nodded and then crossed the room to check Nathaniel's pulse. He looked up at her.

"He's gone."

Rachel heard sirens approaching as blue-and-red lights bathed the room.

~

"Ms. Blake," the prison guard called out. Sonya looked up. "You have a visitor." She stood, leaving the blank sheet of paper behind. She hadn't written anything yet, although she'd been staring at it for almost an hour. *What to say?* In the last two weeks, she'd thought a lot about Luke. About growing up. And of course about money. There would be a way out of this. There had to be. Although stuck with a public defender so young she questioned if he even had a driver's license, let alone knew what in the hell he was doing, she remained determined. She would figure a way out of this.

Her first idea involved her brother. He was so gullible; in time, she might be able to convince him she'd changed. That she wanted a relationship with him. He had clearly been affected by the opportunity to have his sister back in his life. Would she really turn her down if she begged for a second chance? It was also clear he had doubts about his decision to stop trying to locate her years ago. Guilt could eat away at a person. Perhaps she could tap into those feelings, just enough to get what she needed. In the meantime, she had to think. They didn't have as much on her as they thought. Sure, Rachel would tell her story. But no one else actually *saw* what happened. Perhaps Miss Winters simply made it up to get attention from her boyfriend who was spending too much time with another female. Her mind buzzed with ideas as she followed the guard into the visitor's room.

She looked up, curious who this person could be. A man, around forty or so by her guess, stood across the table. He was attractive, with dark-brown hair thinning on top and a nice physique. His smile appeared genuine. He nodded and motioned for her to sit—as if she had a choice.

"Who are you?" she asked bluntly as she positioned herself on the cold chair.

"Bob sent me." At this, Sonya jumped up and backed away. Bob was the loan shark she aimed to pay back with Luke's inheritance.

"Guard!" she called. The man remained where he was, his smile never fading. As she was escorted out of the room, he made one last comment.

"We'll talk again soon, Ms. Blake."

Chapter Thirty-Seven

Luke's heart dropped as he arrived at Rachel's house and observed the scene. Several cop cars were parked in the front yard. An ambulance sat nearby. He pulled to the side, jumped out of his vehicle, and ran toward her house, fighting the dizziness that tried to engulf him as each footstep exacerbated his headache. Someone stepped in front of him, blocking his path.

"Sir, I need you to—"

"That's my girlfriend's house! Where is she?" he pleaded, pushing against the man.

"Sir, please."

"It's okay." Luke heard Ted's voice. "Let him through." The officer moved, and Luke stumbled in Ted's direction.

"Where is she?"

Ted pointed as he appeared to study Luke.

Luke sensed Ted noticed something was off. Or was that disappointment he saw? He'd have to deal with that later. He nodded and then turned, his eyes scanning the area for Rachel. Not realizing he'd been holding his breath, Luke exhaled deeply when he saw her. She was sitting on the back of a paramedic's van. Upright. Not dead. Not crippled. She leaned over to rub Bella, who seemed to be on guard at her feet. Rachel looked up and saw him.

"Luke?" she cried. He ran to her, wrapping his arms around her.

"I'm here. I'm here," he repeated, holding her with a strength he didn't feel inside. All he could keep thinking was that he should have been with her. He *would* have been with her on the hike and when she got home if not for this headache. And these damn pills. A guilt so strong that it tore up his insides had started to gnaw away at him the moment he heard Ted's message. He'd had no idea whether she was still alive as he drove to her house.

"I'm so sorry," he whispered. It was like a dam burst when she began to cry. When she quieted, he stood back and dropped to his knees in front of her. Bella immediately licked his cheek. "I should have been here. I need to talk to you about—"

"I'm glad you're here now." Rachel cut him off, smiling. He reached up and gently caressed her cheek. He stared for a moment at her deep blue eyes, noticing the whites were now streaked with red lines.

"Me too," he whispered. He leaned forward and touched his lips to hers. As he gently kissed her, the soft touch of Bella's tail brushed back and forth across his legs.

Epilogue

"How soon until you can go home? You didn't say when you called," Kristina asked Rachel after listening to the detailed rundown of what had happened. Although she'd contacted Kristina while still at the scene, Rachel hadn't told her much. After the medics had released her, Luke offered to drive Bella and her to his home so she could clean up before she made an official statement to the police. But she'd wanted to stop by Kristina's first.

"I have no idea, but I'm not in any hurry. I don't want to go back until it's been cleaned. Like, *seriously cleaned*. Even then it could be debatable." Rachel tried to remain calm, but all she could think about, over and over, was the cold, hard barrel of that gun against her temple. It was like a video clip in her brain set on repeat. She realized Kristina was talking.

"First, I know your aversion to cleaning. So if you can get the department to bring in professionals, please do. Just figure out a reason why they need to clean the *entire* house. That's my suggestion." She laughed and then continued. "And second, if there's anyone who can get past this, it's you." Kristina smiled. "You're too stubborn not to."

"We'll see. Once I have time to let it sink in, I have no idea how I'll feel," Rachel admitted, doing her best to hide her anxiety.

"So, what ever happened to Sonya, I mean, Kimmy? Last I heard, she was still being held without bail?" Kristina's question broke through her silence. Luke stood behind her, squeezing her hand. He remained quiet, just as he'd been on the drive over.

"Yes, I heard she was raising a fit about having to rely on a 'no-good, prepubescent' public defender because she couldn't afford her own," Rachel responded. She spoke without thinking. Kimmy was still a sensitive subject with Luke. At least, he hadn't wanted to talk much about her in the last couple of weeks.

"Serves her right," Kristina said under her breath. "What about the other guy?"

"Carlton? He's also being held without bail, although I hear he's not talking to anyone. I wonder if he thought his dear friend Sylvester was going to hire him a lawyer." Rachel sipped water from the glass Kristina handed her. Her hand shook. She was thankful no one commented on it.

"No honor among thieves, right?" Luke spoke up from his position on the sofa next to Rachel.

"I still find it hard to believe Sylvester would kill his own son to save you," Kristina said pointedly.

"Me too," Rachel agreed as she looked toward the kitchen. "But maybe he realized he was dying himself and decided to take his flesh and blood with him. Who knows? I'm just glad he did." Bella stood on the tile next to the kitchen sink, her tail ferociously wagging as she eyed Nemo's feline form. The cat poised on top of the refrigerator, eyes focused intently on the dog, tail frozen in midair. To an observer, it would appear the cat was either afraid or ready to attack. Although this was the first time they had played together, Rachel suspected this was a friendly game for them both.

"How's Everett?" Rachel asked.

"He's hanging in there. Once word got out about his situation, a local nonprofit group agreed to hire him for a six-month term position, and longer if funding allows. His visa situation has been resolved, too. Although I wouldn't be surprised if he wanted to bolt and go home after all of this."

"He'll be fine. He's strong." Rachel paused, then added, "Just needs a better understanding of dirty politics. And that there is always legal advice to be had."

"And that his friends will do stupid things to try to help him,"

Luke added. Rachel squeezed his hand.

"I prefer to say *brave* things," she replied. Luke smiled. Although it wasn't his usual bright smile, it was something at least. She knew he still suffered from headaches. He'd confided to her on the drive over that he was willing to try a chiropractor. And a massage therapist, she had reminded him. But something else still seemed to be bugging him. Rachel hoped that once they were alone and settled in, he'd open up. She would, too. That included being honest about the weird feelings that drove her to do dangerous things in search of the rush that accompanied them.

After a few more minutes discussing the larger scheme they'd uncovered, Rachel, Luke, and Bella drove away.

"I know I need to shower and get to the police station soon, but I just need to relax first. Even if it's only for a moment," Rachel confessed.

"How about we head over to Kiva Beach?" Luke replied, placing his hand on her knee. She rested hers on over his.

"Sounds perfect," she whispered. A wet nose nudged her ear from behind. Rachel turned to see Bella's tail swishing back and forth, causing her entire body to shake side to side. "I think she agrees." The excited dog placed her chin on Rachel's shoulder. Leaning her head to the side, Rachel let her weight fall against Bella's soft fur, and she closed her eyes as she squeezed Luke's warm hand. And smiled.

Jennifer Quashnick holds a master's degree in environmental science and health and has spent over fifteen years advocating for scientifically supported policy making to protect Lake Tahoe's environment and rural communities. She also makes a point to spend regular time hiking with her dog, Bella, refreshed by the beauty of the Sierra Nevada and the joy of being outdoors.

Jennifer's creative side emerged when she adopted Bella and became inspired by the dog's antics. The *Mountaingirl Mysteries* series is a result of regular time outdoors; years of hard work in environmental science, planning, and politics; and a dog named Bella.

Raised on a small ranch in Northern California, Jennifer's childhood revolved around an outdoor lifestyle with weekends and summers spent in the mountains. Jennifer loves all that the Sierra Nevada has to offer, although she is most fond of hiking, snowshoeing, and downhill skiing, and is typically accompanied by Bella—the true star of her books.